THE LAST RESORT
IN
Lost Haven

ISBN   978-0-9983933-7-7 Paperback

978-0-9983933-6-0 eBook

Dedication

For you, beloved reader.

THE
LAST RESORT
IN
LOST HAVEN

BOOK ONE
OF
THE LOST HAVEN
COZY MYSTERIES

INTRODUCTION

Folks visit Lost Haven year-round for many reasons.

In the springtime they can sail into the protected marina off of Lake Michigan and come ashore for the festive Spring Cleaning Jamboree, annual grand opening of Lilac Park, and friendly (but obsessive) grilling competitions between the town's chefs and any mere civilians willing to try.

During the summer the beaches are warm with fine, soft sand and the restaurants offer fresh, locally-sourced food on breezy decks with live music. Wealthy families from Chicago open their summer homes along the high dunes and rush into the rolling freshwater waves, eager to get that first sunburn out of the way.

The fall color tours are among the nation's very best, and there are dozens of small family farms where you can stop for fresh apple cider, warm donuts, and snow predictions. When the autumn sun sets over the great lake, the seasonal haunted attractions open their creaking doors to send people of all ages screaming and laughing into the night.

Even though the marina is frozen solid during the winter, Lost Haven continues to bustle with a small but internationally acclaimed film festival, art expos, ice sculptures, and a carefully maintained Christmas Village straight out of a child's sugar plum dreams.

The ice mountains created by Lake Michigan's frigid tides bring photographers in from all over the globe to capture them and the infamous Lost Haven Lighthouse, encased in a shell of frozen crystals.

And no matter what time of year it is, people travel to Lost Haven to enjoy local wines, micro-brews, and savory coffee blends while they try to find Sanctuary, the legendary ghost town buried beneath the shifting dunes. They are always welcomed by Lost Haven residents, who tell campfire stories of Sanctuary with a wink and a smile.

Then one Thursday night in early June, murder came to Lost Haven.

It was most unwelcome, and when the truth finally came out—*all* of the truths, really—that murder turned out to be just the beginning.

CHAPTER ONE

Jenna Hooper snapped the last two folding chairs open and scooted them around until they formed something close to a circle with the love seat and other chairs. A small round table in the center held a tray of cookies, brownies, lemon bars, and celery sticks. Steaming carafes of coffee and tea stood near short towers of stackable ceramic mugs.

She was in the small sitting room at the back of her store, The Welcome Shoppe, which was intended to be the first place tourists and seasonal residents stopped when they arrived in Lost Haven. She carried all sorts of Lost Haven collectable items: keychains, license plate frames, coasters—crap, really—but her store was always busy. She wanted to believe it was because everyone was interested in the history of Lost Haven, and her personal collection of books and essays about the small coastal town was irresistible.

She gazed at the bookshelves lining the walls of the sitting room. Signs written in her hand let folks know:

"Please feel free to read!"

"Borrow if you like!"

"Only copy in print: Please handle carefully. :)"

She probably needn't worry about that last one. No one handled the books but her, and she rarely cracked them open because she already knew everything written, sketched, and photographed within them. No sense damaging the bindings just so she could run a finger along the rough, imperfect paper, examine the graceful swoops and sudden corners of the elegant fonts, and enjoy the delicate, slightly musty scent of slowly degrading history.

As for the newer essays, well, she'd written those…and it seemed improper to constantly re-read one's own writing.

Still, Jenna felt the pull of the books. She wanted to lock the shop's front door, pour a cup of coffee and curl up on the love seat. Spend the evening with the men and women who had made Lost Haven great. Hear their voices, visit with their families, and share their dreams.

It wasn't that she didn't like real people. Some of them were nice enough and got the benefit of the doubt, at least at the beginning. Jenna had read plenty of books beyond her Lost Haven collection, including some psychology texts, and she suspected she might have a small, undiagnosed social anxiety issue.

Or most people were just rude morons with no

self-awareness or ability to take responsibility for their actions.

Maybe a bit of both.

The electronic bell mounted inside the front door jangled her away from the books. She touched a soft leather spine — *The Encroaching Dune* by Gilbert Winkle — and turned away to greet her visitor.

This was not a time for books or dreams.

No, this night was about to be ruined by something Jenna had dreaded all day, week, month: a meeting.

—

The visitor was Belma Winkle, owner of Winkle's Fine Chocolates & Sweets, one door north of Jenna's along Main Street. She often told her customers you could not trust a skinny chocolatier, and if that logic were true, Belma could be trusted with nuclear launch codes. Her hair was large with brown swirls frosted in silver and a very light green at the tips, giving her head the vague appearance of a chocolate mint cupcake.

This was not an accident.

She bustled toward Jenna, somehow managing to navigate the narrow aisle lined with driftwood picture frames and Lost Haven shot glasses without nudging either, and when she got close she flapped her hands and pursed her small mouth into an upside-down macaroni.

"Oh Jenna. Oh come now."

Jenna was confused. For a moment she thought Belma was going to cry over the reason for the meeting, and she struggled to find something to say or do to comfort the woman. Then Belma pushed past her, through the ring of chairs and leaned over the snack tray.

"See, dear, how you have my dark chocolate caramels pushed against these—what are they? Lemon bars? I suppose you could call them that...anyway, Jenna, the powdered sugar will get on the chocolate and just ruin the texture. Ruin it!"

Jenna watched while Belma plucked one of the celery sticks off the tray. She expected the woman to slide the firm, cubic chocolates away from the moist bars, but Belma mashed the celery into the powdered sugar and scooped the lemon bars away from her chocolates, piling them into a quivering yellow heap.

Belma stood up and examined her work. "There."

She turned, holding the celery like it had been tainted with Ebola, and looked for a place to drop it.

Jenna put her hand out.

"Oh, you're a saint," Belma said. She draped the stalk across Jenna's palm with a grimace, then dusted her hands together. When she turned back to the tray Jenna stuck the celery in her mouth and pulled every last bit of lemon bar off it, then crunched.

Belma jumped like someone had jabbed her with a shovel, then frowned at Jenna, who shrugged.

Belma's face softened. "Well, dear, I didn't want to even think about it, much less say it, but this could be our last night as neighbors."

Her chin started to tremble, and this time Jenna was ready.

"We'll be fine, Belma. He can't tear down the Main Street shops—they're historical landmarks."

"But his lawyers—"

"Are all going to have boats in the Lost Haven marina because of what Kavanaugh is paying them, but it won't get them this street. Now you aren't thinking about selling, are you?"

"Me?" Belma pressed a hand to her chest. "Child, Winkle chocolate has ruined teeth in Lost Haven for four generations, and I'd eat one of those lemon turds before I'd even *think* about selling."

"What lemon turds?"

The voice startled both women, making them flinch and turn in unison. Lawrence Donald stood near the cash register, scowling at them. He owned Elegant Confections, three doors down from Jenna and about half a world too close to Belma.

"The lemon turds you put out to lure hapless tourists into that dungeon you call a bakery," Belma said. "And I appreciate it, because after one taste they have to cleanse their palates with my chocolates. I hear about it all the time when they come into *my* shop to buy more."

"Why, so they can murder a dog?" Lawrence spent another moment serving Belma a withering stare, then turned to Jenna and broke into a dazzling smile full of perfect white teeth. "Jenna. Always a pleasure."

"Lawrence," Jenna said. "Would you like some coffee? Tea?"

"Nothing stronger?"

Jenna looked at the carafes, a worry line appearing between her eyebrows. "I didn't even think about that."

"It's fine," Lawrence said with a wink. "I had a little something before I left the shop."

"Well," Belma muttered, just loud enough for Lawrence to hear, "that explains your recipes."

"You two argue like my parents," Jenna said. It had the desired effect of shocking both of them into silence. Jenna lifted the rest of the celery stick in victory and was about to take a bite when the worry line reappeared. Something had been hunkering in the back of her mind since Lawrence arrived. What was it? Lemon turds...getting startled...

She pointed the frayed stalk at him. "Why didn't the bell ring when you came in?"

He peered back at the door, then looked at Jenna with a shade of pity. "The door was open when I got here, sweetie." He made an obvious effort to not glance at Belma. "I think some of your guests were raised by savages. Or Republicans."

Belma gasped. "My family goes back to the founding of Lost Haven, and even before that!"

"Yes, we all know," Lawrence said. "It's practically the town motto."

Belma huffed. "It's you new people who are the savages, painting everything crazy colors and opening a candy shop on the same street as mine—and the street's only a block long!"

"It's a long block, and I own a confectionery, not a candy shop, you sugar clown. And it's one of the founding families who's trying to tear it all down to build a hideous resort, so take that back to your family tree and hang yourself with it."

"Enough," Jenna said. "You don't have to be friends, but if you want to stay neighbors you need to learn to get along. If Mr. Kavanaugh heard you two talking like this he'd do whatever he could to turn you completely against each other."

Lawrence's eyebrows went up. "Bribes?" Jenna pointed the celery at him again, and Lawrence grinned. "I'm only joking. Unless it's a halfway decent bribe. Or cab fare for Belma."

———

It was the samples of Belma's sweets and Lawrence's confections that kept The Welcome Shoppe busy. Those, and free samples from every other baker and food shop in Lost Haven. The owners stocked the samples each morning and checked them throughout the day, and the passive-aggressive (though sometimes just aggressive) rivalries were a constant source of amusement for Jenna.

The other businesses in Lost Haven—small art shops, clothing stores, beach necessities—kept tidy displays in Jenna's store with promises of discounts and exclusive "Only in Lost Haven!" items.

Nearly everyone who had samples in the Welcome Shoppe had given Jenna a copy of their store's key, for the times when supplies ran out and she needed to re-stock at odd hours. It was a simple matter of leaving a Post-It note with something like, "Took three sailboat-shaped coasters. See you soon!"

The resulting keyring was crowded enough to make a janitor whistle with envy, and Jenna considered it her daily workout if she had to lug it more than a block.

Overall, she was happy to send visitors to the other stores; any money spent in downtown Lost Haven was welcome, but she was less than thrilled with the predictable conversations when it came to her role as town historian. Those typically went something like this:

Jenna would say, "Oh, you should try some of that

Winkle chocolate, it's the best in the state. Maybe the Midwest."

Tourist: "Mm! You're right, this is fantastic! Where can I get more?"

"Out the door and turn right, you can't miss it. And that sunset painting on the wall, yes, right above the chocolate, you can get a small print of that at the gallery next door to Winkle's."

Tourist: "Stellar! This town is simply amazing."

Then Jenna would get excited. "Oh, you don't even know. I have every history book written about Lost Haven right here, and they are *fascinating*. Please feel free to browse, sit and read, and ask any questions that come up."

Tourist: "Huh. Would you look at that. Books. Well, thanks for the chocolate!"

And off they went.

It was certainly nice to help them and the other shop owners. But it would also be nice if someone stayed with Jenna and her books, just for a little while.

—

The door chimed again as Wilford Tunney shuffled through. He was close to eighty, if not squinting at it in his rear-view, and owned the Lost Haven Art Gallery between Winkle's and Elegant Confections. It was the largest business on Main

Street—nearly double the square footage of Winkle's—and almost everyone along the block was ready to snatch it up the moment Wilford retired from the business. Or life, whichever came first.

Jenna wasn't interested in the space. The Welcome Shoppe didn't need to be any bigger, and even though she'd like to expand her reading collection for visitors, as town historian she already had all the literature about Lost Haven in her small nook. The thought of displaying them all face-out on long stretches of bookshelves was appealing, granted, but most of them had blank faces with nicks and scratches. Water stains.

She didn't need the space.

She met Wilford outside the ring of chairs and gave him a warm hug, resting her cheek on the thick turn-down collar of his black sweater. On cue, Wilford acted surprised, embarrassed, and said, "Oh, be still my heart."

He slid a wrapped peppermint out of his sweater pocket and pressed it into Jenna's hand. "For your date later tonight."

"Wilford, you know I don't have a date."

"But, Garrett...?"

"That's been over for a while now. Remember, right before Christmas?"

"That's it," Wilford dropped his hands helplessly. "There are no more true men left in this world."

"Witness," Lawrence said.

—

They all heard Sherri Lander talking before the door opened. She pushed through, the electronic bell drowned out by her laughter. Her cell phone was clamped between her ear and shoulder so her hands could focus on carrying some kind of iced coffee drink and a small, shivering dog.

"I know!" She said. "I know, right? I *know*!"

Wilford nudged Jenna's arm and whispered, "She knows."

"I know!" Jenna whispered back, fighting a wicked smile.

Sherri owned the Beach Life Fashion Boutique, on the far side of Elegant Confections. She stopped in front of the four others, who stood there blinking while she smiled at each of them and continued on the phone. "Exactly. Oh, don't I know it. Hey, hon? Hon! I have to go. Yeah, there's a thing. No, not a thing, a *thing*. M'kay, bye!"

She handed the drink to Jenna and leaned in from the waist to kiss her on the cheek, left the drink in Jenna's hand and smooched everyone whether they liked it or not.

"Hi hon. *Muah*. Hon. *Muah*. Hon. *Muah*." Then she lifted one of the dog's trembling paws—which had pink toenails—and waved at everyone. "Say hello to Mr. Wolfie!"

"Hi Wolfie," Jenna said. She scratched the dog's thin, floppy ear, and Mr. Wolfie's large eyes stared at her hand like it was an alien ship here to abduct him. Sherri treated the dog mostly like an accessory, which was a shame, but every time she set him down he rushed toward the nearest person, skidded to a halt between their feet, and hopped up and down on his hind legs until they scooped him up. It was probably best for everyone—including Mr. Wolfie—that Sherri carried him like a purse.

She did exactly that, cupping the trembling dog with one arm, and said, "Sooo, this whole thing is a bummer, right? Such a shame."

Jenna was still holding the iced drink, which was damp with condensation. She set it on the round table and wiped her hands on her jeans. "Nothing's happened yet, Sherri. We're all still fine."

"Fine?" Sherri's eyes popped wider than usual as she wiggled the cell phone. "That's not what Bart says."

"Bart," Lawrence said, in a tone that should have been followed by *Excuse me*. "What else did he say? He's sorry for what his daddy is doing to us poor peasants?"

"Oh, Harry's a sweetie," Sherri said. "He doesn't mean any harm."

Jenna shared a blank look with Wilford. Harrison Kavanaugh was absolutely *not* a sweetie, and his recent actions indicated he *did* mean harm. Or he just didn't care who he harmed, which might be worse.

Belma crossed her arms over her ample front. "Did he promise you another shop in town after he demolishes yours? Because last time I checked, there aren't any vacancies."

"Bart said not to worry about it." Sherri stepped to the table and popped one of the dark chocolate and sea salt caramels into her mouth. "So I don't."

"Problem solved," Lawrence cheered. "Let's all go home." He scowled at Sherri and sank into a corner of the love seat.

Belma took the other end of the small couch. The seam on her jeans barely grazed Lawrence's cushion.

Lawrence stared at the violation, aghast. "Are you kidding me?"

"What?" Belma said. "Folding chairs dig into my thighs. And the recliner is Wilford's favorite chair."

Wilford winked so only Jenna could see. They both knew he didn't particularly like the chair, but he enjoyed these meetings a bit more when Belma and Lawrence bickered. He dropped into the plush recliner and sighed like he'd just returned home from a tour overseas.

Sherri perched on the end of a folding chair and put Mr. Wolfie in her lap, where he curled up and shivered into a twitching nap. Jenna sat next to Sherri, with the last open seat to her right.

Lawrence cocked an eyebrow at the chair. "Late

as usual. I swear it's on purpose, some kind of power play."

"She's very busy," Jenna said.

"She also called this meeting," Lawrence replied. "The least she could do is be on time. I'll bet you one American dollar she's sweeping sand."

They were talking about Ingrid Gallagher, owner and operator of The Sanctuary Café, the last shop on the northern corner of the block. She came from one of Lost Haven's founding families and didn't really need to work, but she told Jenna she enjoyed staying busy and the sound of people talking, eating, and drinking.

And gossiping, Jenna would have added, but not out loud. Ingrid was the biggest gabber in Lost Haven, and nothing made her happier than rushing into Jenna's store, closing the door behind her with a furtive look left and right, then turning to Jenna and saying, "Guess what?!"

And Lawrence was probably right about her sweeping sand. All of the shops suffered from the constantly shifting dunes beneath Lost Haven, but Ingrid's café had it the worst. The gaps in her floorboards and the corners of her shop were always dusted with the fine grit, and she was constantly armed with a short broom for slapping it out the front or back doors.

The shifting sands were partially responsible for the legend of Sanctuary—the alleged ghost town buried beneath Lost Haven—and they were completely to blame for the lack of basements along Main Street and throughout most of the town. The ground just wasn't stable enough to dig a hole and build a foundation, so most structures sat atop posts driven into the ground, which allowed the flowing sand to move around them like a river.

Belma reached for one of her own chocolates. "Ingrid's just being dramatic. She told me she had something that was going to stop Kavanaugh in his tracks. She said—what was it—we were all safe and should consider ourselves lucky to be her friends. But she was hugging me when she said it, so I couldn't throw up."

Lawrence rolled his eyes. "Classic Ingrid, unfortunately for everyone ever."

"What did she have?" Jenna asked.

"She said it was a surprise," Belma said, "which means she has nothing. My guess? She's gonna sell to Kavanaugh."

Sherri frowned. "How would that help us?"

"It's Ingrid sweetie," Lawrence said. "Remember when she created that ordinance for separate plastic, glass, paper, and compost bins? She thought she was doing us all a favor, but all she did was cost us time and money."

Belma pointed the remaining half of the chocolate at Lawrence. "He's right. I bet her big surprise is she's doubling her price, thinking it will raise the market value for all of us."

Jenna hoped that wasn't it. She didn't want to sell at all, no matter what the payout was. But she asked, "Will it?"

Belma snorted.

Wilford shook his head. "Those families go way back. They have their own rules of business—tax write-offs, trusts, things we've probably never even heard of. Whatever Ingrid and Kavanaugh agree on won't mean a thing for the rest of us." He sighed, then leaned forward, the first of many steps for extracting himself from the deep chair. "I'll go get her."

"No no, I'll run down," Jenna said. She patted Wilford's knee and scooted through the display racks and shelves to the front door, dragging her anchor of keys from the front counter on the way by.

A little fresh air before things really got serious would be nice.

———

Lost Haven's Main Street was one long block with businesses on the east side of the narrow lane. The shops looked out at Lilac Park, an oasis of grassy picnic spots, winding paths, and hidden ponds. The park was about the size of a football field and sloped gently toward the marina to the west, and when its hundreds of lilac trees were in bloom the entire town smelled like spring in heaven.

It was early June, so the blossoms had been gone for a few weeks, but Jenna still took a moment to enjoy the lake breeze filtering through the park, where it picked up hints of peony and lily.

She turned and walked past Belma's shop. The front windows were softly lit to display the dozens of different chocolates and assorted sweets—almond crescents, oatmeal bites, magic cookie bars, and some pink marshmallow balls Jenna hadn't seen before but decided she needed to try, just so she could honestly recommend them to tourists.

Wilford's art gallery was dark except for the front windows. The first one had a vintage bicycle with a stuffed dummy on the seat, holding the handlebars. Its face was an iPad showing a loop of cars driving off cliffs.

Art, apparently.

The window on the other side of the entrance had a soft spotlight falling across a canvas painted orange with a single black dot in the bottom left corner. The small plaque next to it said $7,000.

"Good luck," Jenna muttered, and kept walking.

The display at Lawrence's Elegant Confections was breathtaking. Tiers of delicate pastries, cookies, and cakes fell from the top of the tall, narrow window like a waterfall of delight to a reflecting pool (actually a mirror) scattered with orchid petals. Also on the mirror, in a flowing script of glittering sand like it had been left by a gently receding tide, were two words: Treat Yourself.

I will, Jenna thought. As soon as she got back she'd take a heaping scoop of those lemon bars and not feel a bit of guilt about it.

Sherri's Beach Life Fashion Boutique had bronze mannequins with carved abdominal muscles and blank faces wearing day-glo bikinis and camouflage board shorts. Each one had sunglasses perched on a hairless head and carried a cell phone. For living the beach life, none of them seemed to be having any fun.

Jenna wove her way through the wrought iron tables and chairs on the sidewalk outside The Sanctuary Café and peered through the window in the front door. The café was mostly dark inside with a shaft of light cutting across the floor from the partially-open door into the back.

Jenna could smell the earthy coffee beans mingling with a bouquet of herbal teas. She knocked on the glass, expecting Ingrid to poke out from the back room and wave. The woman always seemed rushed, even when she had no reason to be, and showing up late to everything was evidence to the world of just how busy she was.

Jenna knocked again with no response. The café felt empty, no vibrations from someone walking around inside. Maybe Ingrid had gone out the back to add her trash, recycling, and compost to the multiple bins? Jenna tried the thumb latch on the door handle: locked.

She hefted the keyring and sorted through until she found the one labelled "Café." The lock turned easily and she pushed the door open a few inches. "Ingrid? We're all ready for your meeting."

Nothing.

Shoot, Jenna thought. If Ingrid had walked along the back of the shops, they would have missed each other. Ingrid was probably sitting with the others at that moment, saying she was too busy to go back out and fetch silly Jenna.

"Ingrid?"

She pushed the door open further. It thudded against something, like a rolled-up floor mat, and Jenna reached down to move it.

Then she stopped, her fingers an inch from Ingrid's open, lifeless eyes.

CHAPTER TWO

Jenna banged through the front door of her shop. Her cell phone was on the counter next to the cash register, and when she picked it up she had to stop and think for a moment before the unlock code came to her.

"Let me guess," Lawrence said from the love seat, "she's going to keep us waiting even longer."

Jenna had 9-1 dialed on the phone. To Lawrence, she said, "Well..." then dialed the other 1.

Wilford leaned forward in the recliner. "Jenna, what's wrong? You're pale as a blank canvas."

"Ingrid..." Jenna said.

Belma shook her head. "She sold out to Kavanaugh, didn't she? The one chance we had, poof!"

A female voice answered the phone. "9-1-1, what's your emergency?"

"Heather?"

"Jenna? Is that you? Honey, what's wrong?"

"Ingrid Gallagher is dead."

She couldn't hear anything from the phone after

that. Heather ran the Lost Haven Police dispatch center and asked for details about what happened, but Jenna's Welcome Shoppe had exploded in questions from Belma, Lawrence, Wilford, and Sherri. They rushed toward her in a mass—Wilford a few steps behind—making all sorts of confused noise. Mr. Wolfie howled at the ceiling fan.

Finally Heather shouted, "I'm sending Garrett!"

Jenna hung up and thought: *Oh, man. That's all I need...*

———

Belma hooked one arm and Sherri grabbed the other. They hauled Jenna back to the love seat and wedged into it with her in the middle, three gallons of people poured into a two-gallon container. Maybe three and half, with Belma.

"Calm down, sweetie," Belma said. She patted Jenna's knee. "You're going to be just fine."

"I'm fine right now," Jenna said.

"You're just in shock," Sherri said. "When it wears off we'll be here for you."

Jenna frowned. Was she in shock? It didn't feel like it, but maybe that's what shock felt like. "I'm pretty sure I'm okay."

Lawrence was perched across from her on one

of the folding chairs. "Was there, you know. A lot of blood?"

"Lawrence Donald!" Belma crowed.

"What? I want to know if she keeled over from being too dang busy all the time or if she was murdered."

Sherri put a hand to her chest. "Murdered?"

"If she was," Lawrence said, "we might all be in danger."

Wilford scoffed. "From who?"

"Um, hello," Lawrence said. "The billionaire on the hill who wants us all gone so he can build his hideous resort?"

Kavanaugh, Jenna thought. *Would he?*

She realized everyone was staring at her, waiting. "What?"

"Blood," Belma said. "Was there blood?"

Jenna flashed back on Ingrid's dead body. The blank eyes, open mouth. That was all she'd really seen before running back to her shop. She pried herself out of the love seat, went behind the counter and found the small but powerful flashlight she kept with the pens and utility knife. Everyone watched from the reading nook.

"Jenna, dear," Wilford said, "what are you doing?"

"I'll be right back," she said.

And before the protests from the nook could change her mind, she headed back to The Sanctuary Café.

—

Jenna stood among the metal tables and chairs, staring at the front door to the café. She knew there was a dead body on the other side. It was the first she'd ever seen, other than funerals, but those didn't count. Those bodies were prepped and per-fumed—they were basically dolls.

This was a *corpse*.

No, she told herself, it's *Ingrid*.

And someone may have killed her.

Jenna willed her feet to step forward. They ignored her.

She pointed the flashlight at the large window set in the front door. Maybe she could see everything without going inside…nope. The beam just reflected off the pane, turning the window into a blank screen.

"Well," she said, "here we go."

She didn't move.

The wind coming through Lilac Park—the same breeze that had carried soft tones of peonies and summertime about five minutes earlier—was now cold and heavy with damp, earthy scents. It smelled like someone was digging a hole somewhere in the dark foliage.

You're being ridiculous, she thought. *There's no one—*

"Hey Jenna!"

She gritted her teeth to keep a yelp from escaping. Lawrence, Belma, Wilford, Sherri, and Mr. Wolfie stood outside The Welcome Shoppe, huddled together like a reluctant family photo.

Lawrence shouted again: "Is it bad?"

"I..." Jenna said.

You're what? Too chicken?

"I don't want to contaminate the crime scene."

That sounded good. Legitimate.

"Didn't you already do that?" Lawrence yelled.

She made a mental note: *Get Lawrence.*

But he was right, and now they were all watching. Even more importantly, she realized there was no record of a murder in any of the books in her shop. People certainly died in Lost Haven, mostly of old age and accidents, but even those were rare. The elderly typically moved to Arizona or Florida to escape the Lake Michigan winters, and their deaths were discovered via obituaries and estate sales.

If this was indeed the first murder in Lost Haven, it would be town history. And as town historian, she had a responsibility to know the details. So it wasn't bravery or morbid curiosity that finally made her step forward and push the door open—it was duty.

And maybe a little morbid curiosity.

———

"Ingrid?"

Jenna whispered the name through a two-inch crack in the doorway. Ingrid didn't answer, which was probably the best result. Jenna reached above her head and touched the end of the flashlight to the heavy door—a spot where she hoped there would be no fingerprints to disturb—and pushed.

The door swung in. Before it could open far enough to hit Ingrid's body again Jenna hooked the flashlight around the edge of the door and stopped it. She took a deep breath. Rich coffees, tangy teas, and running underneath it all like a rip current: coppery blood.

For history, she thought. *For books.*

Then: *Never tell anyone you just thought that.*

She poked the flashlight beam around the door and looked down.

Ingrid was still there, still dead, and still staring back at her with dull eyes.

It matched exactly the image burned into Jenna's mind, so there was no shock this time. Dead Ingrid was expected, and there she was.

Hooray?

Jenna ran the beam down Ingrid's body. She wore her brown Sanctuary Café apron with a short-sleeved athletic t-shirt underneath, designer jeans, and running shoes. Ingrid had been a runner and avid yoga practitioner, and while she liked to dress casually, everyone knew her simple wardrobes cost thousands of dollars. They knew because Ingrid told them.

Jenna leaned further into the café and checked the far side of the body. No blood that she could see. Then she swept the beam over Ingrid's head again. The top of her skull seemed odd—too flat—and her thick, dark hair was splayed out in a fan shape on the floor. Through the strands Jenna caught a red gleam.

She knelt and put the flashlight directly above the hair. A small puddle of blood was hidden in the strands. Had Ingrid been shot? Bludgeoned? Jenna eased her own head down, down, until her cheek nearly brushed the floor. Her nose was a few inches away from Ingrid's ear. She couldn't tell if the odd bumps were from Ingrid's skull or her mussed hair. Jenna thought: *Maybe if I just tip-toe around to the other side...*

From four feet behind her, a man yelled, "Step away from the body and put your hands up!"

Jenna was so startled she levitated—just for a moment and without moving a muscle—then dropped back to the floor in the exact same position.

When she'd recovered, mostly, she said, "Garrett, you *cannot* do that to people."

"Sorry Jenna."

She could hear the grin in his voice. That sideways grin with the dimple that had made girls say and do stupid things all the way back to middle school. It had been cute while they were dating. Toward the end, and especially now, it was infuriating.

Jenna stood up without touching anything and stepped backward out of the café. She turned and Garrett was there. Tall, on the lanky side of lean, and in full Lost Haven Sheriff's Department regalia. Garrett Bower looked good in uniforms and knew it. He'd been an all-star for the Lost Haven Mariners in three sports as a pitcher, forward, and wide receiver, and after school had gone to the community college to play more sports and study criminal justice.

Jenna suspected he'd chosen that path partially—maybe mostly—for the uniform.

Garrett looked over her head into the café. "Ingrid's dead, huh?"

"Yes. I found her."

"Did you kill her?"

"*What?* No. Why would you ask that?"

Garrett shrugged. "You can get feisty. Maybe she chewed with her mouth open or kept changing the channels."

"Seriously? You want to bring that up now?"

"Nah, I'm just yanking your chain. You touch anything in there?"

Jenna looked back at the café. "I touched the door handle, before I knew she was dead. That's it, I think."

"Mm. What's up with them?"

Garrett didn't look down the sidewalk, but he

meant the other shop owners, who had moved as a mass of wide eyes and nervous hand-washing about two steps closer.

"We were supposed to have a meeting," Jenna said. "Ingrid wanted to talk about Kavanaugh."

Garrett's eyebrows went up. "Kavanaugh? You think…?"

"I don't even want to say it out loud, in case it isn't true. He'd ruin me."

Garrett scanned the Main Street storefronts, all the way down to her Welcome Shoppe and the other owners huddled there. "Isn't he doing that anyway?"

—

Jenna sipped a warm mug of tea in her reading nook. The other shop owners watched her closely, as if waiting for her to suddenly hurl the mug and begin her inevitable breakdown from the trauma of finding Ingrid's body.

Instead, she got a scoop of the lemon bars and started eating it.

Lawrence glanced around, fiddled with a non-existent piece of lint, and said, "Soo, what did good ol' Garrett have to say?"

"He said to come down here and wait."

"For what?"

Jenna shrugged and said around a mouthful of lemon bars, "For him to question us, I suppose."

"But why?" Sherri said. "We didn't do anything."

"Just doing his job," Jenna said. To Lawrence: "Great bars, by the way."

Belma scoffed.

Jenna said, "Do any of you know what Ingrid was going to tell us at tonight's meeting?"

"I told you—" Belma started.

"Yes, that you think she's going to sell. Wait, you *thought* she *was* going to sell. Ingrid is all past-tense now, huh?" Jenna thought about that for a moment, then shook her head. "Anyway. We were messing around before, gossiping. This is serious. Why did Ingrid call this meeting?"

Everyone looked at everyone else. No one said anything.

Jenna said, "Guys, somebody may have killed Ingrid because of it. If you know, or think you might, you could be in danger."

Wilford's bushy white eyebrows twitched as he looked around the circle. Lawrence pursed his lips and squinted, thinking hard, while Belma's mouth hung slightly open. Sherri clutched Mr. Wolfie to her chest and whispered something into his vibrating ear, then nodded.

"I don't know why Ingrid called the meeting," she said, "but I know who does."

—

S herri didn't want to say at first. "I don't want to get anybody in trouble. Especially him."

"Him," Jenna repeated. "I'm going to take a wild guess and say it's Bart Kavanaugh."

Sherri's eyes popped. "Please, you can't tell him I told you anything."

"You haven't," Lawrence said.

Sherri turned sly, nodded. "Right."

Jenna said, "Can you call him? Ask him to come down here?"

"I suppose…He doesn't really like to come around the shops—he has a name for Main Street: Stain Meat."

Wilford frowned. "What does that mean?"

"I'm not sure," Sherri said, "but he thinks it's hilarious."

"Will he come?" Jenna asked.

"I usually go visit him…" Sherri said.

Belma perked up. "Tell him something is wrong with your car."

"My car? Why?"

"Aw," Lawrence said, "so precious. Because he bought it for you, sweetie, and probably cares about it more than you."

Sherri started to protest: "He did not—"

"Everybody knows," Lawrence said.

Sherri looked around the circle. Everyone nodded.

"No one's judging you," Belma said. "If somebody wanted to buy me a Beamer, I wouldn't say no."

"How about a one-way plane ticket to Antarctica?" Lawrence said.

"How about we have two murders tonight?" Belma shot back.

Lawrence gasped in horror and reluctant admiration.

Jenna put a hand on Sherri's knee. "Don't tell Bart about Ingrid when you call. I want to see his face when he finds out."

"Why?" Sherri said.

"I hate to say it, but I think there's a chance he already knows." Jenna looked at the rest of the group. "You guys, if the Kavanaughs had something to do with Ingrid's death—especially Harrison—the resort plans are done. Main Street will be safe."

CHAPTER THREE

It was a ten-minute drive from the Kavanaugh estate up on the hills overlooking Lost Haven. While they waited for Bart, Jenna stuck her head out the shop's front door and looked up the street toward the Sanctuary Café.

Garrett's cruiser was still parked outside. A flashlight beam spilled through the windows and swept across the tables and chairs out front. Jenna thought about Garrett in there, alone with the corpse, his first murder investigation…

"I'll be right back," she said over her shoulder.

There was no one else on the street. She hurried to the café and saw Garrett inside, standing in the middle of the room and turning in a slow circle. He poked the flashlight beam into the corners and under tables as he turned, like he was watering shadows with it. The door was open a few inches.

"Garrett?"

He jumped, just a tiny bit, and Jenna felt a strum

of satisfaction. "Jenna, dang it, you need to go back to your store."

"I will, I just wanted to make sure you're okay."

"I'm fine. Now…"

"What?"

Garrett played the beam across the front windows, making sure Jenna was alone. "You think it's okay for me to turn the lights on? With fingerprints and all?"

"Probably not," Jenna said. Then, trying to keep the concern out of her voice: "Are you going to collect that stuff? The evidence?"

"Heck no, I called the state police and they told me to sit tight and wait for their crime scene team."

Jenna relaxed. Garrett was great at giving tickets to city drivers from Chicago and breaking up wrestling matches outside the bars along the lakeshore, but he couldn't boil pasta without checking the internet first.

"Maybe you should come out of there," she said.

"Yeah, I just wanted to make sure whoever did this—if it was anybody—isn't still in here, hiding or something." He crept to the door and slid through, careful not to touch anything with his bulky gun belt.

Jenna waited for him among the outdoor tables. "What do you mean, if it was anybody?"

"If she was murdered. Maybe she just fell."

"Fell?" Jenna said. She realized there was disappointment in her voice, so she hurried to cover it up: "That would be good, huh?"

"Very good," Garrett said.

Jenna nodded. It would be good, safe, and... boring. She felt terrible for thinking it, then even worse because she didn't actually feel *that* terrible.

"So do you need to come down and question us? I have some of Belma's salted chocolates."

Garrett brightened. "Oo, the dark ones?" He looked down the street, then at the door of the café, considering. "Shoot, I can't, I gotta stay here and control the scene until the state crew shows up. Probably makes us look bad if they come with all their sensitive equipment and there's a raccoon or something wandering around the body."

"I'll save some for you." Jenna fought the habit of standing on her toes to kiss him on the cheek before she left.

Garrett knew it, watching her with that sideways grin just starting to pull as she turned and walked away. She was almost to Belma's door when Bart Kavanaugh swung around the corner of the Welcome Shoppe. He'd parked on a side street, even though every spot on Main was empty. He saw her coming and stopped with a hand on the door handle.

"Hey, Jenna Jenna."

"Bart."

He was about her height and stocky, easing over the line into pudgy. He'd played some sports with

Garrett but didn't have the natural talent or desire to work—just his father's money, influence, and a town small enough that it didn't cut anybody from the squads.

He waved down to Garrett and said to Jenna, "What'd you do now?"

"I was going to ask you the same thing." She gave him a quick scan, looking for swaths of blood across his two-hundred-dollar shirt or matted in his receding hair. No such luck. He wasn't even carrying a bloody hammer, pipe, or frying pan.

So it wasn't going to be that easy.

—

B art went straight back to the nook, didn't say hello to anyone, and asked Sherri, "What happened to the car?"

"Nothing," Sherri said.

"Don't tell me nothing. What'd you do, back into a Prius or something? That's not your fault, they're too quiet."

"No, I didn't do anything, really. It was a…fib."

"A fib?" Bart looked around at the faces. Belma and Lawrence were barely suppressing smiles while Wilford looked slightly sorry for the young man.

Bart said, "If this is a surprise party, it sucks."

"Please, grab a seat," Jenna said. "Help yourself to the snacks."

Bart took a chocolate caramel and squinted at the tray. "What happened to the lemon bars?"

"Nothing," Belma said, "that's the way they're supposed to look. Just like they taste."

Everyone looked to Lawrence for a retort. He shook his head. "I don't want to get murdered next, so I'm not sassing anybody until this is over."

Bart stopped mid-chew on the caramel and tried to frown. "Murdered? What are you people talking about?"

Sherri stood up. "Honey, come sit."

She pulled Bart onto her chair and sat on his lap, then nestled Mr. Wolfie in hers. The small dog kept rooting around in Sherri's hands until he found Bart's, then licked furiously until Bart flailed him away and tried to hide his hands again.

"I can get another chair," Jenna said.

"Why?" Sherri asked.

She let it go. "Bart, something terrible has happened, and we wanted you to hear it from us. In case, you know. It involves you." This was true—Jenna did want Bart to hear it from them so she could gauge his reaction. If he assumed it was out of compassion, well, there was some of that too. Probably.

Bart said, "Is this still about Sherri's car?"

"Mother of pearls," Lawrence said. "It's a good thing you're rich."

Belma checked her watch. "Thirty seconds. A new record for your no-sass policy."

"Alas, it cannot be contained," Lawrence lamented.

Jenna cut them both off and told Bart, "This isn't about the car. Ingrid Gallagher is dead."

Bart froze with his tongue working caramel out of his teeth. "Huh?"

"She's dead. That's why Garrett is at the café right now—he's waiting for the crime scene crew to show up."

"She's right up the street?" Bart said. He glanced back at the front door, eyes wide, as if zombie Ingrid would be shambling through at that very moment.

Jenna squinted at him. Bart was either very smart or very stupid, and she found it hard to tell the difference right then.

"How'd she die?" Bart said.

Jenna shook her head. "We don't know yet. But there's some blood."

"Oh, man. I gotta tell Dad."

Now they were getting somewhere. Jenna said, "Is he around?"

"I just left him. He's back at the house, talking with the lawyers and contractors about finally tearing these old buildings down." He dropped that into the group like a stone, unaware or indifferent about what it meant to them.

"Was this a long meeting?" Jenna asked.

"Yeah, all afternoon. I just about died of boredom,

all the contract and legal talk. I was glad to get out, even if Sherri messed up the car, but this...I gotta call Dad."

He stood up, almost dumping Sherri and Mr. Wolfie onto the table, and pulled his cell phone out.

Jenna said, "They were close? Your parents and Ingrid?"

Bart paused, thinking about it. "Nah. They did the same parties and stuff, like the yacht club, but that's just because our families both go way back. She and my dad might have dated about a hundred years ago, but my old man got around, so..."

"Please tell him we're all very sorry."

"For what?" Bart said.

Jenna blinked. "For the loss of his friend?"

"Don't be sorry," Bart snorted. "Ingrid was being a huge pain in the butt with his resort—most of that meeting was about how to get around her so he could start demolition. He's gonna be thrilled."

———

Bart moved toward the front of the shop to make his call. Jenna could hear his voice, but the words were just a low mumble spiked with a few high notes.

Sherri looked after him, her mouth pulled into a sad smile. "Poor Bart."

"There's nothing poor about Bart Kavanaugh," Wilford said.

Sherri turned back and whispered, "It's just...he's always trying to impress his father, and Harry is very hard to impress. Maybe this will do it."

"Telling him about a murder?" Jenna said.

Sherri considered that for a moment, then nodded. "It's an odd family."

She left to check on Bart, leaving the others to contemplate just how odd the Kavanaughs must be. Lawrence poured himself more coffee, upending the carafe until a few drips proclaimed the need for more.

"On it," Jenna said. She checked the tea—still plenty left—and carried the empty carafe into the narrow area that ran the width of the shop behind the back wall. The room served as her office, kitchen, and warehouse, and was stacked with boxes of Lost Haven souvenirs. A tiny bathroom was tucked against one wall along with a closet that hid the furnace and water mechanicals.

She filled the coffee pot from the sink, recalling the times Ingrid scolded her about it during the Main Street meetings. She always brought her own coffee and wouldn't even refill it with Jenna's.

"I use pure, filtered, ionized mountain water for all my beverages," she'd say. "Anyone who can't taste the difference shouldn't be drinking it."

Jenna watched the impure, unfiltered, non-ion-ized—and free—water fill the pot, then dumped it into the coffee machine. She would miss Ingrid, but that was for later. Right now she needed to figure out what the Kavanaughs were up to. If they were responsible for Ingrid's murder, and now the path was clear for Harrison's resort, then—

"I thought you might need some help."

Jenna clenched every muscle and nearly threw the coffee pot.

Lawrence took a hasty step back, his hands flying up. "Not the face!"

"That's twice tonight someone's scared the heck out of me," Jenna said. She eased the coffee pot into the machine and hit the start button. "Three times, if you count Ingrid, but that wasn't her fault."

"Sorry," Lawrence said, "I wasn't sneaking around on purpose."

Then he glanced back at the door to the shop, and Jenna knew that's exactly what he was doing. He stepped closer and lowered his voice.

"Just between you and me, if Bart is involved with Ingrid's death, I wouldn't be shocked if Sherri were too."

Jenna frowned. "Sherri?"

"Think about it. Sherri is always talking about how she needs more space for her stupid beach store, and before all of this resort drama came around, Bart was going to co-sign a loan to buy out Ingrid's café. They were going to knock down the wall and expand."

"He did? What did Ingrid say?"

"She laughed in their faces," Lawrence said. "Pretty much the same thing she did to old man Kavanaugh when he came around with his resort pitch. And I heard the blueprint for the resort includes a big, juicy chunk set aside for Sherri's new store."

The coffee machine burped and sighed.

Jenna said, "Why didn't I know about this?"

"Oh sweetie," Lawrence said, "our petty gossip can't possibly hold a candle to your precious books. You gaze at them during our meetings like Belma looks at butter."

"Nooo…" Jenna said. But it was true. The books called to her, waited for her, and just about everything else was an interruption. The fact that other people were aware of it made her feel a bit embarrassed, and more than a little guilty.

Lawrence glanced back at the door again. "I'm just saying—we need to keep an eye on Sherri, and watch what we say around her. This is just between you and me."

He patted her shoulder and walked away, humming to himself and stopping once to peer into a box of driftwood remote control caddies and shudder.

—

Jenna carried the full carafe out of the back room. It was getting close to ten, the front windows showing the soft yellow light of the street lamps and peeks of the lights scattered along the walking paths in Lilac Park.

The rest of Lost Haven was either asleep or easing in that direction, but she had a feeling her shop was going to be awake and busy for a while. When she got to the nook, however, it was empty except for Wilford.

She put the coffee on the table and said, "Where is everybody?"

"I'd like to say they're calling friends and family to hear their voices and express their love," Wilford said, "prompted by this tragic event that proves just how fleeting life can be."

Moved by this, Jenna put a hand to her chest.

"But they're just gossiping," Wilford said. He flicked a thumb toward the front of the store. Down the rows, Bart and Sherri were whispering together, Belma was mumbling into her cell phone, and Lawrence was texting someone, the mad grin on his face bathed in harsh light from his screen.

"Well," Jenna said, "I'm not a bit surprised to see you here. You're above that."

Wilford chuckled. "Oh my goodness, no I'm not. I'm just waiting here for you to come back."

"Me?"

He checked the rows to make sure the others were still occupied, then crooked an arthritic but still very elegant finger at her. Jenna perched on the end of the love seat and leaned in.

Wilford watched the front of the store and spoke out of the corner of his mouth. "You know how Belma has been going to the café to get smoothies? Just about every day for a few months now?"

"To lose weight," Jenna said. Then, the automatic follow-up: "She looks great."

"No she doesn't," Wilford said. "She hasn't lost an ounce. She isn't drinking the smoothies."

"Then…"

"She's *analyzing* them," Wilford said. "Oh, she'll taste them, sure, to get the flavor combinations and the, what do they call it…mouth feel." He briefly closed his eyes and grimaced. "But she's doing research. Belma wants to open a smoothie bar here in Lost Haven, and Ingrid dying is very convenient for her. Drastic, no doubt, but convenient."

Jenna's mind reeled. She was still processing what Lawrence had said about Sherri and Bart, and now this? "Wait, where would she have this smoothie bar? If the resort goes up, her shop is gone. And there aren't any vacant businesses in town—she told Sherri that just this evening."

"And why would she say that?" Wilford asked. "She doesn't want anyone else looking around for a new space. And, I've heard from more than a few owners, she's quietly offering to buy them out once

Kavanaugh's resort check clears. She wants first dibs before the dust of Main Street even settles."

Jenna took a few moments to consider all of this. "But Ingrid? Belma wouldn't…"

Wilford's bushy eyebrows went up. "Have you ever had an argument with the woman over pink Himalayan sea salt?"

"No," Jenna admitted, "but I've witnessed a few."

"What more proof do you need? If she gets that red in the face over mere *salt*… Now, I'm telling you this for two reasons. One, you need to be careful around these people. I don't want to see anything happen to you."

Jenna flashed on Ingrid's dead body and couldn't help checking behind her. Just a glorious wall full of books, no slobbering murderer with a lead pipe, poised to strike.

"The second reason," Wilford said, "is that we need an honest record of this for the town's posterity. Who knows what the 'official' investigation will say if it turns out the Kavanaughs are involved? I'm counting on you to make sure the truth comes out."

He sat back and folded his hands.

"Now please, be an angel and pour me a half-cup of coffee, would you? With some cream? I'll be running to the lavatory all night, but I'd hate to fall asleep amidst these jackals. I might not wake up."

———

Jenna left Wilford with his creamy coffee and walked through her shop toward the front door. Bart and Sherri were still whispering near the Lost Haven shot glasses, Belma was still murmuring on the phone among the nautical wind chimes, and Lawrence was back to texting by the checkout counter. He winked as she passed.

Jenna thought: *What am I getting myself into?*

She wanted to step outside, get a bit of fresh air and check on Garrett. She had her hand on the door handle when Belma called, "Jenna, can you come look at this? I don't think the price tag is right."

Jenna frowned. Was one of the shop owners switching price tags again, trying to undercut the others? She found Belma holding one of the paper tags hanging from a wind chime shaped like an anchor, and when she leaned in to check it Belma whispered, "This isn't about the price tag. Keep your voice down and don't look around."

"Oh, come on," Jenna whispered. "You too?"

"Me too what?"

"Never mind." Jenna glanced at the cell phone. "Who are you talking to?"

Belma grinned. "Nobody. It's a *ruse*."

"A ruse?"

"Yeah. So I can observe the others while they think I'm not paying attention."

"Ah," Jenna said. "Why?"

Belma checked the aisle, left and right, then

peered through the racks to make sure no one was eavesdropping from the next lane. The shop wasn't that big, so it was slightly ridiculous that Belma thought they were having a secret meeting.

"I know you like Lawrence, but I have to tell you something about him."

Jenna waited.

Belma checked the perimeter again. "I happen to know he's been talking to Kavanaugh about being the official dessert chef for the new resort. And he'll get the job, if the resort gets built."

"How do you know this?" Jenna asked.

"I just do."

Jenna wanted to ask if she knew because she'd been talking to other business owners about buying their properties for her smoothie bar. But then Belma might know Wilford had told her, and...it was just too much to deal with.

"So I'm keeping an eye on him," Belma said, "and you should too. I saw him go into the back to help with the coffee and thought, ohmygosh, he killed Ingrid and now he's going to kill Jenna."

"What? Why would he kill me? Why would *anyone* kill me?"

"You seem a little determined to find out who the murderer is, and—"

"If there is one," Jenna interrupted.

Belma's eyes widened. "Oh, there is. And if it isn't Mr. Kavanaugh, who is it? If it's Lawrence, he'll try to stop you before you figure that out. Honey, I seriously thought he was going to brain you with the coffee pot or strangle you with the power cord."

Jenna flashed back on the little meeting with Lawrence. She'd never had the feeling he was a danger to her. Then again, Ingrid probably hadn't either…

"Hold on," she said. "If you thought he was going to kill me, why didn't you come back there and stop him?"

Belma blinked. "Oh, you can handle yourself, sweetie. And if he had tried to kill you, at least we'd be sure, you know."

"That he's a crazy murderer."

"Right."

"Thanks Belma."

Belma nodded sagely and put the phone back to her cheek. She turned away, saying, "Yes, that's right. Oh, you don't say? How about that."

———

Jenna stepped onto the sidewalk and looked toward the café. Garrett's patrol car was still there, and now a state police van with its side doors open was parked in front of it. The crime scene crew. Maybe they already knew if Ingrid had died from an accident or not.

If she'd been murdered, everyone in the Welcome

Shoppe was now a suspect along with the Kavana-ughs. Jenna was beginning to think Main Street was actually a pit of vipers, each one coiled and waiting to strike.

Then it dawned on her that *she* might even be a suspect. She had a key to the café and she'd found the body—which could be considered very convenient to an investigator.

But why would she want Ingrid dead?

No, she couldn't possibly be a suspect.

Probably.

Right?

———

She was deep in thought, trying to find any per-ceived motive she might have other than a vague dislike for Ingrid's laugh, when someone grabbed her left arm.

Jenna whirled, her right arm flailing, and socked Bart in the stomach. He doubled over, coughing and wheezing with spit flying out of his mouth.

Sherri, one step behind Bart, jumped back two more steps and let out a whispery *"Peep!"*

Mr. Wolfie trembled in her arms but seemed pleased with the whole scenario.

Jenna grabbed Bart's shoulder. "Oh my goodness, Bart, I'm so sorry! Are you okay?"

He coughed and stayed bent at the waist. "Jesus, Jenna, what was that for?"

"You startled me. It's not a good night to startle people."

Bart straightened and winced as he prodded his soft belly. "I think you popped something."

"Hopefully just a shirt button?" Jenna said. She fought to keep from smiling and glanced at the café to make sure no law enforcement had seen her devastating assault. The sidewalk was empty.

Sherri put a hand on Bart's back. "Do you want me to call your dad?"

"What? No," Bart said, then stopped to consider it for a moment. "No. I'm fine. Just...take it easy, Jenna."

"Don't sneak up on me and grab my arm the night someone was murdered, *Bart*."

He rolled his eyes. "Anyway, about that. Is it for sure? She was murdered? She didn't just fall or something?"

"I was just about to walk down and see if Garrett knows that yet."

"But you saw the body, right?"

Jenna nodded. "I found her."

Bart said, "Was she...naked?"

Sherri gasped and covered Mr. Wolfie's ears. "Bartholomew!"

"What?"

"She had clothes on," Jenna said. "Why does that matter? Or are you just being disgusting?"

Bart checked the front door of the Welcome Shoppe. It was open a crack, but no one was standing near the other side of it. He looked at Sherri, who gave a quick nod.

Bart lowered his voice. "There's a little rumor that Ingrid and Wilford were, uh, grinding coffee together. If you know what I mean."

Jenna didn't, then she did. Her mouth fell open. "*What?*"

"Shh," Bart said.

"Impossible. Wilford is too…sweet."

Bart's face split into a wide grin. "Oh, he's sweet all right."

Sherri giggled. "I think it's adorable."

"Well, it would be," Bart said, "as long as he isn't the one who killed her."

———

Jenna held her hands up, pushing the air away.

"You can't be serious. I'm having a hard enough time with Wilford and Ingrid messing around. That's…shocking. If you think he killed her, my head will explode."

"Sorry about your head," Bart said, "but we need

to know if she was murdered or not. If she was, I'm turning him in."

Jenna shook her head. "But if they were, ah jeez, doing what you say they were, why would he kill her?"

"Lover's quarrel?" Sherri offered. "That would be kind of romantic."

Bart's eyebrows went up at that.

Jenna said, "Wait, if they were in bed together, shouldn't Wilford be more upset about her death? Even if he—and I can't believe I'm saying this—is the one who killed her?"

"A crime of passion," Sherri whispered.

"Wrong," Bart said. "It was a crime of business. Dad told me Wilford is ready to sell his gallery and retire, head down to Florida or wherever codgers like him go. Dad says he's a pain in the butt to negotiate with too. Wouldn't budge on his price."

"No," Jenna said. "That can't be right. Wilford loves Lost Haven. He loves Main Street, and especially his gallery. He loves...that big soft chair in the nook."

Bart shrugged. "Yeah, well, he may have loved Ingrid too, and look what happened. She was the one thing holding up the resort, so he got rid of her."

Jenna almost said, *I could say the same thing about your father. Or you.*

But she held her tongue. Things were happening way too fast, and she didn't want to upset anyone who might be a killer.

She said, "How was Ingrid holding up the resort? She called tonight's meeting tonight to talk about that, but nobody knows the details."

"Oh, some people do," Bart said.

"Are you one of those people?"

"Nope," Bart said, "and I don't want to be. As soon as people start getting knocked off, that's when I'm officially out of the negotiations."

"Be careful, Jenna," Sherri said. "If Wilford is desperate enough to kill his intimate, tender lover, any one of us could be next if we cause trouble."

Jenna shuddered at the mental image, then asked Bart, "So who does know?"

He tilted his head toward the Welcome Shoppe. "I betcha Wilford does. And my old man, of course, but he's safe. We have gates, security cameras, and a couple panic rooms up at the estate."

"Ooo, don't forget the hunk," Sherri breathed.

"Oh, right," Bart said.

"Hunk?" Jenna said. "Hunk of what?"

Sherri's eyes flashed. "Of *man*."

"Dad's had a bodyguard following him around for the last week or so. Gotta give him credit, maybe he saw this kind of trouble coming."

Or he caused it, Jenna thought. But one thing was certain: If Harrison Kavanaugh had been in a meeting with lawyers and planners all evening, with a personal bodyguard next to him the whole time, he had plenty of witnesses to say he didn't rush down to Main Street, kill Ingrid, and return to talk about sewage lines and valet parking areas.

That would be what Kavanaugh said, anyway.

But how could she find out for sure?

Bart's pocket chirped. He pulled out his cell phone, checked the screen, and said, "Speak of the devil." He swiped the screen and put the phone to his ear. "Hey, Dad. Yeah. It's true, yeah, cops are all over the café."

Bart listened, then glanced at Jenna, a quick there-and-gone look that made her want to lean in and catch what was being said.

"Yeah, okay. I'll call you back."

He put the phone away and stood there with his hands in his pockets.

Jenna gave it two seconds. "Well?"

"Well what?"

"What did your dad say?"

"Jenna, that was a private conversation. It's rude to eavesdrop."

She resisted the urge to pop him in the gut again, then took a moment to realize she'd never hit anyone before, let alone twice in one night. She'd typically be curled up with one of her books and a cup of tea by now (and maybe a few leftover samples from the bakeries—no sense letting them get stale), and here she was smacking people around while she tried to unravel a possible murder.

Even more surprising: she was *loving* it.

Things were getting weird in Lost Haven.

—

A man's voice carried down Main Street and Jenna turned, saw Garrett standing among the tables and chairs outside the café talking to a man in white coveralls.

"Oo, *CSI Lost Haven*," Sherri said. Her eyes widened at the possibilities. "Starring, um, Kirk Cameron!"

Bart stuck his bottom lip out and nodded, impressed.

"I'll be right back," Jenna said. She started toward the café, taking her time in case Ingrid's body suddenly appeared on a gurney or swinging inside a bodybag, like a bulging black hammock. She could do without that vision on top of everything else tonight.

The breeze out of Lilac Park was there, as always, and she wrapped her arms across her stomach, cupping her elbows with her hands. The shops stretching along Main Street looked exactly as they had before, when she'd gone down to get Ingrid for the meeting, but now each one seemed to be hiding something just inside their brightly painted doors and carefully lit display windows.

Winkle's Fine Chocolates & Sweets, hiding Belma's ambitions to open a new business that would have been a direct competitor with Ingrid's Sanctuary Café.

The Lost Haven Art Gallery, with the possibility that Wilford had been having an intimate relationship with Ingrid, yet wanted to sell to Mr. Kavanaugh and retire.

Elegant Confections, and Lawrence's hidden agenda to become the baker for Kavanaugh's Lost Haven Resort, a new career built upon the rubble of Main Street.

And the Beach Life Fashion Boutique, with Sherri and Bart already designing her new store within the resort's shopping hub.

Each one of them knew Ingrid wanted to stop the development of the resort, and some of them might even know how she was going to do it. Had one of them killed Ingrid to keep her from sharing it at the meeting?

Or had Kavanaugh murdered her before she could tell them?

Jenna stopped at the edge of the café tables and waited for Garrett to finish with the state investigator. Their heads were close together, looking at the screen on the investigator's large digital camera.

Jenna glanced back at the row of shops along Main Street. Each one belonged to a friend—at least she thought so—and if she continued to dig into what happened in the Sanctuary Café, she risked losing one or all of those friendships.

And if that digging revealed the Kavanaughs were involved, especially Harrison, her life in Lost Haven would be over. Even if her Welcome Shoppe remained, it would only be a matter of time before she had to close. Her taxes would suddenly double, her electricity would go out at peak shopping moments, and the other owners, terrified of sharing her fate, would stop piling her shelves and tables with free samples.

That was how Harrison Kavanaugh did business.

The crime scene investigator walked back into the café. Jenna stared across the street to avoid any chance of seeing Ingrid's body, wherever it was now, and hoped poor Ingrid had fallen off a chair and cracked her head on the edge of a table.

It would be boring, yes, but it would also mean Jenna could keep her friends and her life in Lost Haven, even if that included a massive, gaudy resort where her precious Main Street was now.

Garrett stepped over to her, his thumbs hooked over his gun belt. "Welp, she was murdered."

Jenna closed her eyes.

———

"Darndest thing," Garrett said, looking through the cafe's front windows. The techs had the lights on, along with some powerful lamps of their own, and were taking measurements and photographs. "These guys say somebody bonked her on the head with something heavy. One shot, pow."

"That's awful," Jenna said.

Garrett turned to her. For a moment Jenna thought he was going to put his arm around her shoulders and pull her in, ruffle her up like he used to. But he didn't. "You're sure the place was locked up when you came to get her for that meeting?"

"I had to use my key to get in," Jenna said. "Why?"

Garrett frowned. "I checked the back door, and it's locked too. So whoever killed her either has a key, or they're a freaking ghost."

"Who else has a key?"

He cocked an eyebrow at her. "Besides you?"

"Don't be an idiot."

Garrett shook his head. "I don't know who has one. Be nice if Ingrid kept a nice spreadsheet with that info, huh?" He said it with a rueful smile, knowing it couldn't possibly be that easy. "Guess I'll add that to the list of things I need to find out."

"You already have a list going?" Jenna asked. "Anything I can write down for you?"

This went back to their time as a couple, when she would help Garrett with his police reports. He hated the paperwork--said it was worse than math homework--and she enjoyed the lingo and research into violation codes. For some reason, it felt really good to type the word "perpetrator."

"Nah," Garrett said, "we probably shouldn't do that anymore, especially on something this big. Might even get some media attention."

"Wow, really? Well, maybe I can add a few things to the list, since I was the one who found her. What do you have so far?"

She had to be careful. She was digging, looking for anything that would point the suspect list away from her friends and toward Harrison Kavanaugh, and she had to be as delicate as an archaeologist to keep Garrett from getting suspicious.

Garrett checked the crime scene techs to make sure they were out of earshot. "I'm ninety-nine percent sure it wasn't a ghost."

Jenna nearly laughed, then realized he was being serious. Maybe she didn't need to be that careful after all.

Garrett said, "And I need to know where all those folks at your shop were, right before the meeting."

Jenna's breath caught. "Who, exactly?"

He ticked them off on one hand: "Lawrence, Wilford, Belma, and Sherri. And you, just to keep anyone from saying I'm playing favorites."

Jenna imagined the four shop owners telling Garrett the same rumors and suspicions they'd told her. Word would get around town for sure, and just about everyone would be embarrassed. Even if they weren't killers, the damage to Main Street would be done.

Before she could stop herself, she blurted, "What about Mr. Kavanaugh?"

"Ah, Jenna," Garrett winced. "I don't know. I guess the motive is there, with the resort and all, but I think he'd just throw a pile of money at Ingrid instead of killing her. Or he'd hire somebody else to do it." He looked down at the shops, his eyes flicking from one storefront to the next.

Jenna whispered, "You think Kavanaugh paid one of them...?"

"I don't think anything. Not yet, anyway. But I want to know what they think, and where they were. Who they saw. See if their stories line up. Heck, they could be in there right now, coming up with solid alibis for each other."

More like ways to stab each other in the back, Jenna thought. Or, more accurately, clubbing each other on the head. She tried to picture sweet Wilford caving in the top of Ingrid's skull, his soft, oversized sweater flapping around him.

Or flighty Sherri, while she clutched Mr. Wolfie under one arm.

Or Belma, with...well, Belma might be able to... *No*.

She couldn't believe any of her friends were capable of murdering Ingrid just to get some cash, boost a career or pad a retirement. She wouldn't believe it unless there was hard evidence proving so, and even then she'd have to look that person in the eye while they confessed. Without that, she'd assume they were being framed.

Harrison Kavanaugh, though—he was ruthless when it came to business. She fully believed he would do whatever he could to make the Lost Haven Resort a reality. That included murder, and setting an innocent person up to take the fall.

The thought of that made her angry. That Ingrid should die—and Main Street along with her—just so Kavanaugh could make more millions and sink his claws even deeper into the town. That was unacceptable.

The more she thought about Ingrid's death and the ramifications it had for Main Street, her friends, the Lost Haven Resort, and Harrison Kavanaugh, the more she knew that he was responsible.

Now she just had to prove it.

CHAPTER FOUR

The Main Street owners, along with Bart, were still in the Welcome Shoppe when Jenna pushed through the front door. They had gathered in the nook again and Jenna heard the low conversations halt when the door chime sang.

She took a deep breath and walked past the checkout counter and the "Lost Yet?" license plate frames, repeating to herself: *One of them might already know.*

When she stepped to the edge of the nook, everyone was staring at her.

"Murdered," Jenna said. She scanned their faces for flinches, glances, smirks. Listened for false gasps or the sound of someone slowly twirling a mustache, whatever that sounded like.

She got nothing.

The group just continued to stare at her until Bart said, "Huh."

That broke whatever spell had come over them. Everyone started talking at once, and Jenna nearly stepped back from the rush of noise.

"A *murder*?" Belma crowed. "Here, in little Lost Haven?"

Sherri wrapped Mr. Wolfie even tighter. "I'll protect you, little baby!"

Bart pulled them both close with one arm. "You're staying up at the house until this is over."

"I'm getting a gun," Lawrence announced. "A shotgun. The biggest one they have."

"Who's 'they'?" Belma asked. She wasn't being mean—she sounded genuinely curious.

Lawrence shrugged. "You know. The shotgun people."

Wilford sighed. The lines on his face, which usually framed a gentle smile, had become deep, drooping furrows. "Poor, poor Ingrid. She was so full of…life."

Jenna sat on a folding chair and waited for a lull in the chatter. "Garrett wants to talk to us—each one of us—about what happened."

"Why?" Belma said.

"We're all suspects. Me included."

Wilford snorted. "That's ridiculous. We all loved Ingrid."

Bart cleared his throat and got a sharp nudge from Sherri.

There was an awkward lull in the room until Jenna said, "That's not true."

Everyone froze, stunned, and Jenna continued: "Ingrid was a pain in the butt. She was rich, rude, entitled, and completely oblivious to how her actions impacted other people. Her prices were too high and the coffee wasn't even that good. I think the main reason she ran the Sanctuary Café was to get all the best gossip, which she used to start petty fights for her own amusement."

Lawrence's hand had crept up the front of his shirt and was now pressed over his mouth. Belma's eyes couldn't get any wider without falling out of her face.

"With all of those faults," Jenna said, "she still didn't deserve to die. And if she got killed to clear the way for the Lost Haven Resort—like some obstacle that had to be removed from a construction site— that's even worse."

She didn't look at Bart, but wanted him to pass the message along to his father: Harrison Kavanaugh was on the suspect list too, whether the police agreed or not. She hoped Garrett would change his mind about that, but knowing Garrett as well as she did…

Bart's phone sprang to life on the coffee table. He glanced at the screen and answered. "Hey Dad. Yeah, we just heard."

He stood up and walked toward the front of the store, his end of the conversation fading. Jenna strained to listen—without looking like she was straining to listen—until Lawrence stretched a leg out and tapped her knee with his toe.

"That was very wicked what you said about Ingrid. And her body isn't even cold yet." His face showed severe disapproval, but his tone was one hundred precent impressed.

"Was any of it wrong?" Jenna asked.

"Heck no," Belma said. "She was a serious pain in the rear. But you're absolutely right about her not deserving to die."

Jenna checked the shop owners again—her friends—for any sign of deceit or guilt. Either they were all innocent, or one of them was a very good liar.

—§

Bart came back, slipping his phone into his pocket. "Well, that was my dad."

"We know, sweetie," Lawrence said.

Bart seemed a little foggy, like he was trying to figure out what he was saying while he was saying it. "The police, uh, Garrett called him. They want to talk to him about Ingrid's murder."

Jenna fought the urge to spring out of her chair and give the room a round of high-fives. She settled for: "Is that so?"

"Yeah," Bart said. "The police want to talk to all of us, me included, and my dad."

"Right now?" Jenna asked.

"No, tomorrow. Uh, tomorrow morning. Eight o'clock."

Wilford gave a wry smile. "All my years in Lost

Haven, this is the first time I've been in the same group as Harrison Kavanaugh. I have to say, it doesn't feel like I thought it would." He started to work his way out of the easy chair. "We should all get some sleep. I guess I'll see you folks downtown—isn't that what they call the police station in the movies?"

"Yeah, but no," Bart said. "Dad doesn't want a whole scene, him going into the cop shop and all. We're going to do this up at the house, so you're all coming up there."

Jenna frowned. "Are you joking?"

"Nope. And the cops, er, Garrett, he agreed. Said it would be good to keep things low-profile if possible."

"The Kavanaugh Estate," Belma whispered. "Horizon House. I'll have to wear my New Year's Eve dress."

Bart stuck a hand out for Sherri. "Come on, babe. Tomorrow's gonna be a long day."

He helped her to her feet and they headed for the front door. Lawrence and Belma followed, and Jenna held Wilford's arm while he slowly rose out of the bottomless chair.

"A long day indeed," he said.

They all said goodnight and Jenna locked the front door behind them. Her young employee Wendy was scheduled to open the shop Friday morning, so the eight o'clock meeting was doable. But the nerve of

Kavanaugh to assume it was doable, just because he ordered it…

She spent fifteen minutes cleaning up and venting frustration, washing dishes in the small sink and propping them in the tiny drying rack like a ceramic boobytrap, the whole time trying to imagine what the next day was going to be like.

She eventually gave up, unable to conjure even the slightest idea. She turned off the lights inside The Welcome Shoppe, locked the door again, and started the walk home.

She lived three blocks east of Main Street, away from the lake, and the gentle breeze gave her a slight tailwind. It also carried every sound that occurred behind her, and Jenna lost count of the times she turned at a soft rustling or sliding thump, expecting to see someone there, rushing to cave her skull in.

Each time, the sidewalk was empty.

And each time Jenna faced forward her pace quickened, just a bit. She told herself it was nerves, paranoia—downright silliness—but she couldn't shake the feeling that someone was watching her, tracking her.

Everyone in town knew where she lived. Take Second Street east until it dead-ends into Pine, then a slight left across the road and you're in her postage-stamp front yard. If Ingrid's murderer thought Jenna might cause trouble, it would be simple enough to pick a dark spot between Main Street and the house and wait.

Jenna walked faster and shook her head. "So stupid."

Stupid, she thought, to think anyone would go to the trouble of killing her.

Stupid, right?

She glanced back. Why were the streetlights so far apart in Lost Haven? What idiot had designed that massive flaw? Actually, she knew the answer; it was in her copy of *The Birth of Lost Haven*. Harvey Pender (1804-1866), civil engineer, had designed the streets of Lost Haven to—

Not now, nerd brain!

She shook her head again as something large and dark crawled across the sidewalk twenty feet in front of her. Jenna halted in mid-stride, her eyes straining. Her brain ditched Harvey Pender and recalled a tidbit she'd read about seeing in the dark. She turned her head to the side and used her peripheral vision to examine the would-be killer.

Jenna let out a breath she didn't realize she'd been holding. Lost Haven was known for its fat raccoons, and this beast had to be among the royal family. It dragged its belly across the sidewalk and squeezed beneath a car parked along the street. It was hard to tell with the lake breeze, but Jenna may have heard it wheeze.

She started walking again, a step faster than when she'd pulled up to let the killer raccoon bear cross.

Stupid.

So stupid.

And stupid—*very* stupid—to basically announce to a room of murder suspects that she intended to make sure whoever killed Ingrid would answer for it.

What was she thinking?

It had seemed like a good idea in the bright lights of her Welcome Shoppe. Now, on a dark street with her dark house waiting ahead, along with a night of creaks and rustles, it ranked among the worst notions she'd ever had.

Jenna treated the last block along Second Street as a runway. By the time she crossed Pine and hit the walkway leading to her front steps she was practically sprinting. She slipped through the wobbly screen door and flipped the flimsy hook latch—something she never did—and crossed the painted wooden floor in one big step.

Keys out, in, and through the front door, then a quick turn of the deadbolt before she twitched the curtain aside and peeked through the window in the door.

The porch, walkway, sidewalk, and streets—as far as she could see along Pine and down Second—were all empty.

Still, she knew, could *feel*, that somebody was in one of those pockets of shadow.

Jenna worked her way through the house, turning on every light she had, thinking that whoever was out there, she was probably going to see them tomorrow morning at eight o'clock.

§

She briefly considered taking a shower, decided that was probably the best way to invite the killer into her house, and stepped into the shelter of her non-walk-in closet to change into a t-shirt and boxer shorts.

The shirt was Garrett's, oversized for her and still smelling faintly of him, but it was the most comfortable sleeping shirt she'd ever had—no sense in getting rid of it just because that was over.

Jenna brushed her teeth and watched the mirror for any movement, and for a few seconds—less time than the shower idea got—she thought about calling Garrett and asking him to sleep over.

On the couch, of course.

For safety.

He'd love it: being needed, her wearing his shirt, being vulnerable.

Well, to hell with all that.

She plucked the largest book she could find off the living room shelves and carried it into her small bedroom. It was a coffee table book full of gorgeous photos of Rome, and she was certain the gladiator statues inside wouldn't mind being used as a blunt force weapon should someone creep close enough to the bed.

She set the alarm on her phone for seven, left the lights on and curled under the blankets. That lasted fifteen seconds. Feeling too exposed, she checked under the bed (all clear except for an alarming amount of dust) and turned off the bedroom light. Now she was in a little cave of darkness, surrounded by a fully lit house.

She got back into bed and hefted the book. Lawrence was onto something: she needed a shotgun.

Jenna got onto her side, hugging the book and staring out into the bright hallway. She expected a scowling, staring face to tilt around the far corner at any moment, and was still waiting for it when she fell asleep.

§

The alarm startled her out of oblivion. She sat straight up, confused by the daylight peeking around the curtains, the massive book next to her, and the underlying thrill of being alive.

Then she remembered:

Ingrid.

Main Street.

Kavanaugh.

She yawned and stretched, rolled out of bed and pulled the curtains open. It was a perfect June morning with a few small white clouds drifting above the rustling leaves and pastel blossoms, already bustling with honeybees.

Amazing what sunlight could do to mortal terror. Jenna vaguely remembered the fear of the previous night, but it vanished along with the darkness. No one could possibly be murdered on a day with weather like this.

She turned on some Top 40 music and got into the shower with no concern for her life, telling herself it wasn't a good day, what with Ingrid still dead and all the Main Street shop owners being suspects. When she was clean and dry she dressed in khaki shorts, a light blue tank top with a summer-weight blouse over it, and sandals.

She checked the mirror and frowned: maybe today was supposed to be more formal. Well, everything at the Kavanaughs was more formal, right? She went back to the shallow closet and pinched the seam of her one suit, a gray off-the-rack number she'd worn for job interviews before dumping everything she had into the down payment on The Welcome Shoppe.

The suit was itchy and too tight in the waist, too loose in the hips. And she never knew what to do with the buttons on the blazer.

Screw it. Things were going to be uncomfortable

enough with the murder investigation. She abandoned the suit and headed for the kitchen, bouncing a little to the music.

Not a good day, no.

But it was an *interesting* day.

§

Jenna had never been to the Kavanaugh estate, but she'd driven below it dozens of times in her muttering little '02 Accord to soak up the history. It was built near the northern edge of Lost Haven upon the highest point in the county, with a stunning view of the lakeshore and a dominating position over the other mansions that had sprouted around the base of the hill like mushrooms beneath a towering oak.

The Kavanaugh mansion was named Horizon House because of the 360-degree view, which Jenna heard provided jaw-dropping sunrises and sunsets, particularly in the winter. Nearly all of the mansions in the neighborhood had been built by Harrison Kavanaugh's grandfather during the peak of the town's lumber industry, which had earned the Kavanaughs and several other founding families their fortunes.

Those families included the Gallaghers, and Jenna drove past Ingrid's sprawling, four-story house on her way up the hill. Tall, sculpted hedges made an impenetrable privacy screen, but the gap for the driveway showed a circular parking area in front of the house and a garage the size of a small airplane hangar angling off to the right. Two dark, luxury sedans dozed in the driveway along with a state police cruiser, and Jenna recognized the golden emblem for Roderick's Funeral Home on one of the doors.

She shuddered; no matter how uncomfortable the conversations got at Horizon House, they would be better than what was happening in the Gallagher place. She passed a few more lumber-era estates and several weak imposters wedged in by Chicago millionaires, then the road curved to the left and the houses fell away.

Rolling dunes with rippling grass stretched to the north and east, broken here and there by a clump of cypress trees. The shoulder was wide enough for cars to park and let tourists out so they could take pictures of the dunes, which were not only beautiful, but also part of the legend of Lost Haven and the buried town of Sanctuary.

Jenna had to smile. She felt a little guilty about fanning the flames of that silly myth when folks came into her shop, breathless about the ghost town and endless possibilities of buried treasure, buried churches, buried dreams.

The residents of Lost Haven had a line about it: "Anyone who believes in buried Sanctuary has their head in the sand."

It was never spoken around tourists. That would be mean, and also cause them to spend less money in town. But Jenna wouldn't have said anything about it, even if she didn't own a business. It wasn't her place to pop someone else's balloon, and she loved trying to talk history with them in the nook.

If they stayed for more than three minutes they might realize there was no mention of a buried town in any of her books, but Jenna didn't think they cared about that. They cared about the adventure, the mystery of it all, and as she pulled up to the black wrought-iron gates marking the edge of the Kavanaugh estate, she knew exactly how they felt.

§

The gates were anchored by massive brick posts on both sides of the road. Landscaped grass and trees shaded the area and kept erosion down, which was ironic, considering what the Kavanaughs had done to the rest of the land. Eight-foot black iron fencing marched up the hill to her left and along the right side of the road beyond the gate.

Jenna mused that the fence alone cost more than her entire house, ten times over. She eased to a stop near the gate and waited. A camera peered down at her from one of the brick posts, and another, smaller post held an LCD screen within reach of her window.

The screen said:

NO SOLICITORS

NO TOURS

INVITED GUESTS ONLY

VIOLATORS WILL BE PROSECUTED

PUSH HERE TO CALL

Jenna frowned. She was invited, right? Bart had said they were all supposed to come...

She also realized, at that moment, she was about to enter a locked compound—basically a luxury bunker—with a bunch of murder suspects.

Was that a good idea?

Once the gate closed, that was it. She wasn't leaving unless the Kavanaughs wanted her to. Garrett would be there along with the state investigators, she assumed, but she'd never confirmed that with Garrett. What if the Main Street shop owners were all being drawn into Harrison Kavanaugh's web like fat little flies? What if—

The horn blared and Jenna bucked against the seatbelt hard enough to knock the wind out of her.

"What's the holdup?" Lawrence shouted. His 1976 convertible Corvette was an inch from her back bumper, and his head was tilted back to soak up the morning sunshine. He wore round sunglasses and looked like he'd spent an hour on his hair.

Jenna recovered. "Good morning, Lawrence."

"Mornin', hot stuff. Did you murder anyone else last night?"

"No. You?"

"Only a bottle of red wine. If I barf on a priceless rug, don't let the Kavanaughs sell me into sex slavery. Well, not to anyone cheap."

"I think they can hear you."

Lawrence considered that for a moment. "Well, nice knowing you."

Jenna said. "I'm going in."

She tapped the screen.

A deep, serious male voice immediately said, "State your purpose."

Jenna panicked, blurted: "Er, I'm invited."

"For what?"

"The...inquisition?"

The speaker paused. "Name."

"Jenna Hooper."

"Who is that behind you?"

"Lawrence Donald." Jenna felt like she was ordering executions at a drive-through.

"Tell him to wait after you pull through. The gates will close behind you, and he is *not* to attempt to follow you. Do you understand?"

"I understand." She stuck her head out the window. "Don't follow me. You have to wait your turn."

"I shall comply," Lawrence droned.

The gates parted. Jenna's car vibrated from the power of the motors, and when the black iron stopped moving she pulled ahead.

The gates closed behind her.

No turning back now.

§

The road continued north for a short uphill stretch before a sharp curve to the west, and the hillside on her left suddenly leveled off onto a round plateau that had to be three hundred yards across.

Dozens of buried lawn sprinklers sent a fine mist over sculpted hedges, vibrant (and weedless) flowerbeds, and grass so green it looked painted. To Jenna, it looked like a yard that was to be observed but never enjoyed.

The wide asphalt driveway cut through all of it and rose on a gentle upward slope toward Horizon House. She'd never been this close before, and Jenna had to slow down so she could take it all in.

The house had at least five stories—it was hard to tell because the windows weren't all aligned or even close to the same size, though each one was bigger than her front door. The architecture was rooted in

Victorian but stretched out into Tudor and, in a few ominous spots, Medieval.

The walls were massive stone slabs carved perfectly to allow for doors and windows—even the window-sills were stone—and copper gutters etched with patina followed the dozen rooflines she could see.

The round, glass observatory perched on top of the structure was barely visible from this close, but Jenna thought she saw someone standing there, looking down at the driveway. At her.

Then the towering facade of Horizon House blocked her view. She brought her eyes down and saw Wilford's old Mercedes and Garrett's patrol car parked to the left of the wide stone steps and massive, double front doors that reminded Jenna of an unwelcoming church, and headed that way.

She pulled counter-clockwise into a crushed stone loop that ringed a small pond and fountain—all of it large enough to swallow her house and yard—and passed a narrow lane that curved around the northern side of the house and disappeared. She caught a glimpse of a massive garage with at least four over-head doors before coasting past the steps and easing to a stop, wincing as her brakes squealed just a bit.

Before she could open her door Lawrence whipped around the driveway, his tires barking on the asphalt, and parked on an arrogant diagonal next to her. He tossed his keys and sunglasses onto the passenger seat and said, "Looks like the snipers missed you too."

"So far." Jenna got out and turned in a slow circle, taking in the estate. From where she stood she couldn't see anything beyond the edge of the plateau except sky and water. It felt like she was floating on a cloud, an island untouchable by the outside world.

What would it be like to wake up here every morning? To do the same things she did at her home—eat breakfast, look for clean underwear, get bored, watch dumb TV—but do it all here?

She couldn't picture it.

"Did you just lock your car?" Lawrence asked.

Jenna came back to the driveway. "Hm?"

"You just locked your car door." He nodded toward the towering mansion. "Do you think they're going to steal it?"

"Habit, I guess. But if they want to take it into that garage and turn it into a Lexus, they can borrow the keys for a while." Jenna didn't carry a purse. She only had her phone and her keyring, with three whole keys, and stuffed everything in her pockets.

Lawrence bent an elbow toward her. "Shall we?"

She hooked her arm through. "Let's."

They walked together toward the steps. Lawrence wore a black Hawaiian shirt with subtle neon green turtles swimming along the bottom and not-so-subtle green shorts that matched the turtles.

"Thanks for dressing up," Jenna said.

Lawrence was offended. "This is my mourning shirt. Look, the turtles are sad."

"Probably because they have to be so close to those shorts."

"Said the girl wearing pleated shorts."

Jenna said, "Wait, what's wrong with pleats?"

"Oh, only *everything*."

Jenna frowned at her shorts. She paused at the bottom of the steps and told Lawrence, "I don't care. They're comfortable."

"They'd better be." He pulled her up onto the first stone stair, which was deep enough to require two steps to cross before the next rise. Lawrence said, "Do you feel like Cinderella?"

"Was she ever part of a murder investigation?"

"That was the sequel. *Cinderella and the Glass Slipper Killer.*"

"Then yes, I do feel like Cinderella."

"Well, you can't," Lawrence snapped. "I'm Cinderella. You be the wicked step-mother."

They both choked back laughter—very inappropriate given the circumstances—then stopped and turned when Belma's stubby white delivery van banged onto the plateau and tilted toward a parking spot.

"Never mind," Lawrence said. "The real thing is here."

They waited while Belma chucked things around in the cab, got sorted and slammed the door before churning around the back of the van toward them, her brown and mint hair quivering like meringue. She carried a purse the size of a small bed.

"Did I miss anything?" she huffed.

"Yes, we're all dead," Lawrence said.

Belma stomped up the stairs without pausing. "Good."

Jenna whispered, "Belma isn't a morning person."

Lawrence squinted after her, considering something important. "You're assuming she's a person."

They caught up to her as she pressed a button nestled in the intricate stonework framing the double front doors, which were eight feet tall and stained and lacquered to bring out the deep, robin's eye grain.

Belma stared at the door and said, "I just want you guys to know, whatever happens in here today, we're still friends."

Jenna blinked. What the heck did that mean?

Lawrence seemed even more confused. "We're friends?"

§

Five seconds later the door on the right opened. A thin man in his fifties stepped back and gestured toward the interior.

"Welcome to Horizon House."

Jenna heard a slight accent—Scottish?—and smiled at him as she moved inside. The smile faltered when she saw what he was wearing. Black suit pants with a razor-sharp crease, white shirt and black tie, which were all normal enough. But instead of a suit coat he wore a black bulletproof vest. The wide Velcro straps were all perfectly aligned and Jenna wondered if the thing had been tailored.

He noticed her staring and winked, a gesture so fast she wasn't sure it had happened.

"Precautions," he said.

Lawrence and Belma didn't notice. They were gaping at the front hall, which was worth gaping at. The ceiling was five stories high, all the way up to the roof, and massive wooden beams supported a Volkswagen-sized chandelier suspended around the third floor.

Stonework and polished wood paneling flowed up the walls around lush paintings of landscapes, epic battles, and dour people. Staircases curled up both sides of the wide room to an open landing on the second floor, and the higher floors each had exposed hallways with thick wooden railings. The intricate woodwork of the floor was mostly covered by a blue, maroon and gold rug the size of a swimming pool.

Closed double doors at the base of each staircase led somewhere grand, Jenna had no doubt. The front hall pushed toward the center of the house, and the back wall had a large opening that showed a hallway going left and right. Another opening beyond the hall led to a large open space, which Jenna couldn't see much of, but the far wall was entirely glass.

It was a brilliant, elegant design. As soon as someone stepped through the front door they could see all the way through the house to the sky and lake beyond—to the horizon. It worked like a magnet, drawing Jenna's eye and pulling her deeper into the mansion so she could see more.

It apparently had the same effect on Lawrence and Belma. The three of them looked like sleepwalkers, shuffling through the front hall with their mouths open.

"Mr. Kavanaugh and guests are in the receiving room," the man at the door said.

Jenna turned. Was he a butler? Should she call him Butler? Should she tip him? And what was a receiving room?

He tilted his head toward the back of the mansion as he swung the door closed.

"Thank you," Jenna said, slightly embarrassed about her ignorance, her open mouth, and her pleated shorts.

§

The receiving room was sunken three steps lower than the hall and large enough to receive an entire house. The decor carried the same timeless accents of wood and stone in the front hall yet had a contemporary feel, with heavy leather furniture placed around low glass tables.

The room was two stories high and seemed to stretch the width of the mansion, but Jenna could see subtle, inlaid doors along the left wall on both sides of a massive stone fireplace. A polished wooden bar ran down most of the right wall, ending at an opening into a very formal dining room.

Wilford sat in one of the leather chairs with a cup of tea. He lifted it in greeting. Bart Kavanaugh and Sherri were perched on the edge of a couch, whispering. The other people in the room were all standing and staring at the newcomers.

There was Garrett, in full uniform and looking slightly uncomfortable next to a man Jenna didn't recognize. He wore a suit and had a lined, golf-tanned face with a paler frame where his wraparound sunglasses would go.

They were half-turned toward Harrison Kavanaugh, a lean man in a gray suit and blue tie that made his eyes glow. He had a full head of groomed white hair and a narrow face that had always reminded Jenna of a fox.

The man slightly behind him and to the left, whom Jenna had never seen before, was at least a foot taller than Kavanaugh and three times as wide. He looked to be in his early thirties and his vast shoulders, phone pole neck and small ears seemed carved out of the same piece of oak. Jenna remembered Bart saying something about a bodyguard the night before, but this guy looked like a hired goon, even with the perfectly tailored suit.

Jenna stared, knowing she was being rude but unable to help it. The man stared back with no expression. He didn't even blink.

Kavanaugh stepped forward. "Find the place okay?"

Bart snorted.

Lawrence said, "Is the bar open?"

"Always," Kavanaugh said. "McTavish will make whatever you like."

The man in the tactical vest waited behind the bar. Jenna hadn't seen or heard him come in from the hall, but there he was, hands folded in front of him, waiting.

Lawrence slopped down the steps. "Bloody Mary, and make her bitter and angry at life."

"Certainly," McTavish said. His hands went to work behind the bar but his eyes lifted to Belma and Jenna. "And for the ladies?"

"Large double-shot latte with extra foam and French vanilla syrup," Belma challenged.

"Skim or whole milk?"

Belma blinked. "Skim."

McTavish cocked an eyebrow at Jenna.

"Just coffee, please."

"Cream, sugar?"

"Oh, I can get it, just show me where it is."

Bart snorted again and whispered something to Sherri, who covered her mouth.

McTavish gave her a reassuring smile. "It's no trouble at all, but help yourself to the tray at the end of the bar."

Feeling more self-conscious than she had since middle school, Jenna started down the three steps into the room. She briefly imagined herself arriving for a swank ball in a dress she'd needed a loan for, making a grand entrance, and promptly falling on her face because of the stairs. It made her wonder why someone would put them there.

She glanced at Kavanaugh and saw him watching her, scrutinizing, and realized: *Of course.* The darn steps were deliberate—he could stand there without a care while everyone coming in had to pause, focus on not breaking an ankle, and try to look classy while doing it.

Well, despite her shorts and tank top, Jenna didn't much care for appearing classy—and she certainly didn't appreciate being manipulated by Kavanaugh and his architecture.

She forced a calm, breezy expression on her face, stared back at Kavanaugh, and navigated the steps without falling. She didn't even lose a sandal.

There, how's that for elegance, buster? Take that right in your stupid fox face.

Kavanaugh's mouth twitched to the side—Disappointment? Anger?—then he turned to say something to the tan guy.

Swollen with accomplishment, Jenna pillaged the coffee tray. It had thick white mugs, a heavy carafe, steel pitchers of various creams, and a bowl of chunky, irregular sugar cubes. They were sand-colored with large crystals, and Jenna wondered if there was such a thing as handcrafted artisan sugar cubes. She dropped three in her coffee and faced the room.

Kavanaugh seemed to be waiting for her. His mouth twitched again, then he said, "Let's get this nonsense over with."

§

Jenna sat on a long couch with the window wall to her right. Belma and Lawrence both joined her when their drinks were ready, and the couch had enough room for all three of them to lay down and not be legally cuddling.

Kavanaugh held a hand out toward the tan guy. "This is Detective Olson from the state police. He's investigating Ingrid's death, and he's going to find out who killed her."

"Hopefully," Olson said. He smiled and nodded to everybody.

"You will," Kavanaugh said, like it wasn't an

option. "Garrett is going to assist. He knows all of you, and—"

"Holy cats."

Kavanaugh stopped and looked at Jenna, who had just taken her first sip of the coffee. It had a flavor and richness she could only describe as *utterly divine*, and she struggled to keep the obnoxious phrase from burbling out of her.

"Sorry," Jenna said. "Please continue."

Lawrence scowled at her from behind his drink and hissed, "Get it together."

Kavanaugh cleared his throat. "Olson and Garrett are going to interrogate you individually in the den."

"It's not an interrogation," Olson said with a shaky grin. "Just a conversation. Just talking. Nobody here is under arrest, and if at any point you want to have a lawyer present, just say so."

Garrett looked more uncomfortable than Jenna had ever seen him, including when she'd dragged him to *Open Togas*, the documentary about female sexuality in Roman times at the Lost Haven Film Festival.

"It'll be whatever it needs to be," Kavanaugh said, "and nobody needs a lawyer. You all just need to tell the truth."

He told the room: "This is a tragedy, a disgrace. Ingrid was a friend and a prized member of this community, and her murder will not go unpunished."

Jenna sipped her coffee and squinted at him over the rim. Was he sincere, or blustering? Trying to make the killer nervous, or campaigning to point fingers away from himself? She raised her hand.

Kavanaugh had his mouth open to say more, but when he saw Jenna's hand he clamped it into a grim line and pointed at her.

"Are you going to talk to Detective Olson?"

Garrett's eyebrows went up and he gave her a sharp head shake, just once.

Kavanaugh didn't notice. "I'll be consulting with him throughout the day, yes."

"No," Jenna said, "I mean as a suspect."

The room was silent. Belma looked like she wanted a bowl of popcorn to go along with the show. Bart glared at her from his couch, ignoring Sherri's attempts to soothe him. Wilford gave her a brief, sympathetic look before turning to Kavanaugh, waiting for the man's response. Lawrence whispered, "Oh boy," into his drink.

"Why would I be a suspect?" Kavanaugh said.

"Well, because..." Jenna briefly considered running through the reasons, then thought better of calling out a possible murderer in his own home, which she couldn't leave. "Isn't that why we came here, instead of the police station? To avoid rumors in town about, well, you?"

Kavanaugh's tongue flicked out, just a brief flash. "I'm doing this for you people, and for the town. Not me. We want to resolve this as quickly as possible and move on, and somebody here has information that will make that happen." He swept the room with his eyes, boring into everyone. "I already spoke to Olson, so don't concern yourself with that. Now, any more pointless questions?"

"Who's the side of beef?" Belma said.

Kavanaugh frowned. "The what?"

Belma wiggled a finger at the bodyguard, a wicked grin playing on her lips.

Kavanaugh glanced at the huge man. "He's invisible. Ignore him."

He pointed to the door to the right of the fireplace. "Now, my den is completely soundproof, so whatever you say in there stays in there. Unless it's a confession, which would obviously become public knowledge. In fact, it would be very convenient and save us all a lot of time if whoever killed Ingrid would just confess right now."

He waited. Nobody moved or spoke.

"If that had actually worked," Olson said, "I'd have retired immediately."

Kavanaugh gave a curt nod. "Have it your way, people. We'll waste the day. As I said, the den is soundproof, but I don't want everyone out here gawking when you suspects come and go, so you have most of the estate to entertain yourselves. Don't go above the second floor, and stay out of this room unless you're getting something from McTavish or coming to talk to Olson. We all clear on that?"

Everyone nodded except Wilford. "Can I stay

here? I have my back to the door, and I don't hear that well anyway."

"No," Kavanaugh said. "And you just volunteered to go first. I don't want you dying before Olson gets a crack at you."

Olson winced.

Kavanaugh said, "That's it, people. Let's get moving. Wilford, into the den. The rest of you," he flicked his hands toward the rest of the house, "scatter. And don't steal anything."

CHAPTER FIVE

Jenna had no idea where to go, so she followed Bart, Sherri, Lawrence, and Belma up the three steps and into the front hall. For the first time, she noticed Sherri was dog-free.

"Where's Mr. Wolfie?"

"He likes to sleep in," Sherri said. Bart took her hand and they started toward one of the staircases.

Lawrence said, "So what is there to do in this castle?" He was almost done with his drink, rattling the glass to shake everything loose from the ice cubes.

"Nothing, really" Bart said. "We have a game room, indoor pool, a gym. Uh, there's the movie theater, the library..." He looked at Sherri. "What else?"

"Outside is nice."

"Oh yeah, the gardens and stuff. The beach. But I don't think my dad wants anyone leaving the estate, so, you know. Stay away from the fences."

Jenna hadn't heard much of the last part. "You said library?"

"Yeah, second floor, take a left."

Jenna felt pulled that way but didn't want to run—might seem rude.

Belma said, "Does the pool have a Jacuzzi?"

Bart hesitated. "Yeah."

"Does it have a dress code? I didn't bring my suit."

Bart grimaced and yelled, "McTavish!"

The man appeared in the entry to the receiving room. "Sir?"

"Belma needs a bathing suit. A one-piece."

"Right away, sir. Anyone else?"

"Why not," Lawrence said. "But can you just hold onto it for me? I need a few more drinks before I'll be ready to share water with Belma."

"You just want to pee in the pool with no witnesses," Belma said.

Lawrence shrugged and finished his drink.

"I'll leave a stack of assorted suits and robes in the pool room," McTavish said. He pointed down the hallway to his left. "Simply follow the hall to the end and take the stairs down." He dipped his head and left.

Belma wandered down the hallway. Bart and Sherri headed for the stairs.

"What are you guys going to do?" Jenna said.

"I have some things to do up in my rooms," Bart said. He put extra emphasis on the plural. "But they're on the third floor, family only. Sorry."

They started up the stairs.

Jenna asked Lawrence, "How about you?"

"First, I'm getting another drink. I'll plan my next event based on how strong it is. Let me guess: you'll be in the library."

Jenna's feet did a little tap dance.

Lawrence turned back toward the receiving room, and the bar. "If I see you in there, it's because I'm lost."

"You're missing out," Jenna said. She went up the stairs as fast as she could without spilling any coffee, and was sure she could smell the books before she was halfway up.

§

The hallway at the top of the stairs was open on both sides, looking down into the front hall and the receiving room. Lawrence was behind the bar fixing his own drink, which would probably be a lot more powerful than the first.

Jenna paused and watched him pick through the dozens of bottles. She'd seen him drink before, but never drunk. Was he trying to get there because of nerves? Guilt? Or was he just taking advantage of free high-end booze?

She considered going back down and talking to him about Ingrid, maybe bring up the rumored job at Kavanaugh's resort, but the library was right there...

She glanced to her left. A set of double pocket

doors was partially open and she caught a sliver of leather-bound spines. That did it. Besides, it was probably better to let Lawrence pickle a bit more, get anything he might be hiding to float up to the top.

§

The hallway was wide enough for four people to walk arm-in-arm. High ceilings were framed with intricate, polished crown moulding, and wall sconces cast a soft yellow light that showed doors along both sides down to a tall, curtained window at the end of the hall.

The double doors were first on the left, and Jenna eased them further apart and stepped through with a thrilling mix of trepidation and giddiness. She held her breath. The room felt heavy and soft, insulated from the outside world by the rows and rows of books lining the walls.

Thick wooden shelves ran floor-to-ceiling. They were filled with dark, hardcover spines bound in leather and cloth, the titles and author names pressed in gold and silver foil. Book sets with their perfect alignment of blue, maroon, and brown stripes on the spines, along with ascending volume numbers left-to-right, were so satisfying to Jenna's book nerdiness she actually felt her neck flush.

Two wide, free-standing shelves stood in the

middle of the room, parallel to the door and tall enough she could barely reach the highest row. The bronze bust of a man—maybe Theodore Roosevelt?—was perched atop the nearest shelf smirking at her, along with a globe that looked old enough to not include most of Antarctica.

Intentional or not, the width of the shelves was genius. They were wide enough to block the far wall and give that area a sense of complete privacy, yet still allowed one to stand in the doorway and see the far corners and be irresistibly drawn to them.

The far right corner held a straight-backed chair and built-in reading desk below a tall window bundled in thick curtains. The desk had a yellow legal pad and a pen set, perfect for taking notes, but Jenna was drawn to the far left corner. A deep, plush chair was tucked there, close to the only other window in the room. She pictured herself on a December day, curled in the chair beneath a heavy blanket with snow brushing against the glass, sipping hot chocolate and lost in the pages.

Mrs. Jenna Kavanaugh...

She shuddered. As amazing as it would be to have this library every day, it wouldn't be worth spending any time with Harrison Kavanaugh.

But as town historian, did she have any power to commandeer a personal library? Common sense told her the answer was no, but these books *were* gorgeous, so...maybe?

She walked the perimeter of the room making mental notes of which books she wanted to spend time with. When the list hit double digits she took her phone out and started jotting the titles down so she wouldn't forget, and she was so engrossed in the prospect of reading them all she didn't hear the two men enter the library.

"Who are you texting?"

Jenna fumbled the phone, her thumbs jabbing nonsense onto the screen below her perfect list. Harrison Kavanaugh stood in the doorway, his bodyguard looming to the side, still unblinking.

Jenna said, "What? No one, jeez. You can't do that to people."

"Wrong," Kavanaugh said. "What are you doing in here?"

Jenna frowned. What would anyone be doing in a library? She was basking in the books.

"Are you lost?" Kavanaugh said. "No, hold on. You have those cute little bookshelves in your shop, don't you? And you're the, what, town recorder."

"Historian," Jenna said.

"That's what I said. You like my personal selection?"

I love it, she thought.

Outwardly, she shrugged. "I'm still perusing."

Kavanaugh said, "I hope you don't have any plans to record any of this for the town's history. The faster Lost Haven forgets about all of this, the better."

"Why is that?"

He nodded at the phone. "Are you taking notes?"

"Only on books."

To the bodyguard: "Check the phone."

The bodyguard stepped forward with his hand out.

"I'm just writing down book titles," Jenna said.

"Right," Kavanaugh said.

The bodyguard didn't say anything, just kept his hand out.

Jenna held the phone up to his face. "There, see? I'd let you hold it but you might smash it by accident."

The bodyguard peered at the screen. He turned and told Kavanaugh, "Books. She doesn't have a signal in here anyway."

"Good," Kavanaugh said. "I don't want you calling or messaging anyone—especially the other people here—while this is going on. I'll confiscate phones if I have to. And don't take any notes. None of this will ever leave my house."

He turned and left.

The bodyguard glanced at Jenna's phone screen again, one eyebrow up.

"Satisfied?" Jenna said.

"Hardly." He started after Kavanaugh. Over his shoulder, he said, "You don't have any Aurelius or Seneca on your list."

§

J enna fumed.

She stalked the bookshelves, scowling at the innocent spines and muttering into thin, crisp pages as she examined fonts and first sentences. First sentences were an accurate indicator of an author's worth, in her opinion. But no matter how many times she read the opening lines in these books, she couldn't focus long enough to get from the opening word to the last. She was too angry.

Check my phone, huh?

Tell me not to message anyone?

Order me not to record anything for the town's history? To not do my job?

And worst of all: *Question my reading list?*

She slapped a leather-bound copy of Marcus Aurelius' On Stoics shut and shoved it into its slot. Just a bunch of natterings about trying to stay cool.

What does that big lump know about books?

She stepped away, then went back and patted the book, apologizing for the rough, unfair treatment. It wasn't the book's fault Kavanaugh and his goon were dangerous morons.

Jenna stopped, took a deep breath. The books and her frustration were distracting her from something very important: Kavanaugh thought he was being smart, but everything he said and did only reinforced her suspicions that he was responsible for Ingrid's death.

And he wasn't going to get away with it.

Jenna went to the wide doorway, looked left and right. Lawrence was probably wandering around with his second drink—maybe he was tipsy enough to spill something against Kavanaugh.

But first things first.

She added Aurelius and Seneca to her reading list, closed the app before anyone could see it, and left the library.

§

Lawrence was in the game room, a right turn down the first-floor hallway and through a door on the right. Jenna could hear billiard balls clacking together as she got to the doorway and peeked in.

"Want some company?"

Lawrence didn't have a pool cue—he was just rolling balls across the felt, trying to knock them into pockets. "Why not?"

He stepped back from the pool table and turned in a slow circle until he found his drink on a table behind him.

"Is that number two or three?" Jenna said.

"Mm."

"Four?"

Lawrence tipped it until ice cubes slid against his face. He set the glass down and smacked his lips. "Is poor Wilford still in the torture chamber?"

"I think so," Jenna said. "I peeked on my way by and the door is still closed."

"Gonna get in trouble with Daddy K, sneaking around like that. Can you imagine growing up in this place? All this stuff to do, and probably not allowed to do any of it. No wonder Bart's a…well, Bart."

"Yeah," Jenna said. She leaned a hip against the pool table and glanced at the doorway: empty. "Sometimes I wonder how Sherri puts up with him."

Lawrence frowned. "Only sometimes?"

"Listen, about those two—you said we need to keep an eye on them. Do you think they really had something to do with Ingrid's death?"

"I wouldn't be a bit surprised. They were both seriously miffed when she laughed off their offer to buy her little café. And then when it looked like she was going to scuttle old man Kavanaugh's resort plans…" Lawrence suddenly looked at the ceiling, peering into the corners. He grabbed a nearby lamp by the neck and stared straight into the bulb.

"What are you doing?" Jenna said.

He blinked at a giant framed photo of some horse race and whispered, "Do you think this room is bugged?"

"Bugged? By who?"

"Shush! By the owner, stupid."

"Maybe," Jenna said. "Probably."

She thought about what Belma had told her, the

possibility that Lawrence would be the head baker for the Lost Haven Resort.

"But I'm not afraid of Kavanaugh, Lawrence. What can he do? He's already trying to put us both out of business. I've got nothing to lose here. How about you?"

"Well, there is the possibility that he's a murderer, so, you know."

Jenna said, "But he was here with a bunch of lawyers all evening, including the time Ingrid was killed. That's what Bart said, anyway."

"Oh, good ol' Harrison wouldn't get his hands dirty with the manual labor part. But he'd pay somebody to do it, just like he does with everything else."

"Who do you think? The bodyguard?"

"That gorilla? I don't know—was Ingrid smashed into itty-bitty pieces?"

Jenna flashed on the body. Ingrid had been hit very hard on the top of the head, and the bodyguard was certainly tall and strong enough to do something like that. Was he a bodyguard/assassin?

She said, "I'll poke around a little, see if he was here with Kavanaugh the whole time."

Lawrence narrowed his eyes and jostled the ice cubes in his glass, deep in thought. "If the bodyguard was here, then of the other three—Kavanaugh, Bart, and Sherri—the only one who could have physically gone in and killed Ingrid is Bart."

"You don't think Sherri is strong enough? She has that stand up paddle board thingy."

"No, I mean physically able to be in the same room as Ingrid. Kavanaugh was here, and I heard and saw Sherri cleaning her store for at least an hour before the meeting, sweeping our beloved sand out. Poor thing had sand stuck to her skinny little legs, all the way up to her knees. You know how it is, the stuff never ends." Lawrence brooded at the horse photo. "Who knows, maybe it would be good to tear Main Street down and start over."

That, Jenna thought, *sounds like the Lost Haven Resort's head baker talking.*

§

B elma was in the twelve-person Jacuzzi by herself, arms spread along the tiled edge and head tipped back onto a rolled-up towel. Her chocolate mint hair was still dry and perfectly whipped.

Jenna took her sandals off and padded past the lap pool. The surface was as flat as glass and the sharp, but not unpleasant, tang of chlorine pricked at her nose. Windows along the far wall looked out over the steady whitecaps of Lake Michigan, and Jenna thought: *Screw the resort, the Kavanaughs should open this place for business. The library alone…*

She sat next to the Jacuzzi and slipped her feet in,

the initial sting fading to a lovely hot embrace that made her head roll around a little. Apparently her feet were sore and lonely. Jenna shook that off, refusing to think of Garrett's foot massages, and waited for Belma's eyes to open.

They didn't. Her mouth was slightly open and her body lolled with the rhythm of the churning water.

Oh no, Jenna thought. *Not again.*

She leaned closer, reaching for Belma's wrist. If there were no pulse, someone in this house had—

Belma snorted and opened her eyes. She saw Jenna reaching for her and panicked, splashing and screaming to get away. Jenna screamed with her and recoiled, then started laughing from the relief of not finding another corpse.

Belma recovered and patted her hair, found it still dry. "It's not funny. I thought you were here to drown me."

"Me?" Jenna wiped a tear from her eye. "Why would I do that?"

"Well, I thought *somebody* would come to drown me, I just wasn't sure who. I didn't expect it to be you, but…"

"Belma, what are you talking about?"

She touched her hair again, examined Jenna for a bit, then bobbed across the Jacuzzi to sit next to Jenna's feet and whispered, "The acoustics in here are crazy, so keep your voice down."

Jenna could barely hear her over the water jets.

She leaned down, her ear a few inches from Belma, who said, "Somebody told me—and I won't say who, so don't ask—that you want to sell The Welcome Shoppe and open a bookstore, and if Ingrid stopped Kavanaugh's resort you wouldn't get to do that."

"*What?*" Jenna said. "That's...that's..."

"Sorta true?" Belma said.

"No. Well, I would absolutely love to open a bookstore, everybody knows that. But I don't want to sell my shop, Belma. I mean, I wouldn't get to see you, or Lawrence, or Wilford, or any of the others as often as I do. That would be terrible."

"Sweetie, once the Lost Haven Resort gets built, you won't see much of us anyway. Might as well come out of it with a bookstore, right?"

Or a juice and smoothie bar, Jenna thought.

"Who told you about this?" she asked.

"I said I won't tell you."

"Lawrence?"

"I'm not telling."

"Bart and Sherri?"

"It was Garrett," Belma said.

"*Garrett?*" Jenna nearly flopped into the Jacuzzi. "Well that's...I...Isn't that illegal? For him to say something like that?"

Belma looked skeptical. "If gossip was illegal, we'd all be doing hard time."

"But it's part of a murder investigation. He shouldn't be spreading false rumors like that."

Jenna's mind was reeling. What *else* had Garrett spilled about her?

"It's not a false rumor if it's true," Belma said.

Jenna gave her a straight-on, level look. "Belma. Do you seriously think I killed Ingrid?"

Belma wouldn't meet her eyes. "Well, you *do* love books…"

"As much as you love the idea of opening a juice and smoothie bar?"

Belma gasped, inhaling Jacuzzi froth. In between hacks and wheezes she said, "Who told you about that?"

"Not so fun, huh? Don't worry about who told me. Worry about being a murder suspect."

"Me? I was getting butter from the Nelson farm last night before the meeting. You can check with them."

"I'm sure Detective Olson will. I hope you're telling the truth."

Belma choked out the last bit of hot tub residue. "So where were you last night when Ingrid was getting herself killed?"

"In my shop, getting ready for our meeting."

"Mm," Belma said. "Any witnesses?"

Jenna stood up and scuffed her feet on Belma's pillow towel to dry them off.

"Good luck not drowning."

"Hey, if somebody tries, we'll know who the killer is."

"Not if they try and succeed," Jenna said.

§

Jenna peeked around the hall corner into the receiving room, checking to see if Wilford had emerged from the den yet. No one was in there, not even McTavish behind the bar, and she was turning toward the stairway when the den door opened and Harrison Kavanaugh stepped out and saw her.

She had a brief moment of panic, as if she'd been caught eavesdropping, and had to fight the urge to flee down the hall. Instead she froze and stared at Kavanaugh, who stopped and stared back. The bodyguard was behind him, rushing to catch up, and skidded to a halt to keep from knocking the smaller man across the room.

Kavanaugh studied Jenna for a moment, then asked, "What are you doing?"

"Nothing. What are you doing? Where is Wilford?"

"None of your business," Kavanaugh snapped.

From inside the den, Wilford called, "I'm coming, Jenna, don't fret."

Kavanaugh shook his head and crossed the room to the bar. He rapped his knuckles on the polished wood. "Bourbon."

He turned and stared out the window, apparently deep in thought about something.

The bodyguard glanced at Jenna, then peered behind the bar.

"Uh, Mr. Kavanaugh, McTavish isn't here."

Kavanaugh scowled and looked for himself, confirming that McTavish was, in fact, not there.

"You get it," he told the bodyguard.

The bodyguard took a few uncertain steps behind the bar, gazing at the bottles like they were alien artifacts. "You said...bourbon?"

"Oh, for the love of..." Kavanaugh tried to brush past him but there wasn't enough room. "Well? Get the hell out of the way."

The bodyguard took one massive step out from behind the bar. Kavanaugh used a metal scoop to dig a handful of chunky ice cubes out of a bin, dumped them into a tumbler and splashed golden liquid over them. He knocked the bourbon back in one gulp and refilled the glass.

The bodyguard shuffled from foot to foot and seemed to have no idea what to say or do beyond that.

Kavanaugh was obviously upset about something. Something Wilford said? Or *didn't* say?

Jenna was still fired up from what Belma had told her, and she saw an opportunity—not only was she going to record this historic event for Lost Haven, she was going to make a little of it herself.

She said, "Shouldn't the police be the only people in the interview room with Wilford?"

There: She'd mildly harassed an upset Harrison Kavanaugh in his own home. History made.

"Shouldn't you mind your own business?" Kavanaugh said.

"This *is* my business. This is my town too, you know."

He scoffed into his drink. "You're a tenant here, not a resident. If I wanted you gone, you'd be packed tomorrow. And you may as well start now—it's only a matter of time before that little shop of yours is a stack of kindling."

"Sir," the bodyguard said.

"What?"

"Just...take it easy."

Kavanaugh gaped. He seemed unable to process what had happened. Had the hired help just told him what to do?

"Take it easy?" he said. "Listen bucko, you—"

Detective Olson laughed in the den doorway and stepped aside so Wilford could shuffle out. He patted Wilford on the shoulder and smiled about something the gallery owner had said. Garrett stood inside the den, that sideways grin on his face.

"What's so funny?" Kavanaugh said.

"Police business," Wilford said. "It's classified."

Olson laughed again, a booming *Haw*, and said, "That's right, it's classified. Oh, man. Too much."

Kavanaugh looked like he was going to chew through the bar. What had Wilford said in there?

Jenna had an unsettling thought: Was it something Garrett had said? About her? About *them*?

Olson shook her out of that nightmare. "Jenna Hooper, right?"

Jenna blinked. "Yes?"

The detective swept a hand into the den. "Please."

"Oh, I was, actually just looking for Wilford."

"He'll be here when you get out," Olson said. "This will only take a few minutes." He put on a fake stern voice and pointed. "And Wilford, don't you go anywhere, I might want to talk to you again."

"Where am I gonna go?" Wilford said.

Olson laughed again and raised his eyebrows at Jenna. "Ready?"

Garrett waited inside the den, his smile gone now.

She wasn't ready for this—she didn't have enough evidence to make sure the police were considering Harrison Kavanaugh as a true suspect. She needed to talk to Wilford, maybe even Bart and Sherri, to get a better idea of who was involved with Ingrid's death.

And she needed something to prove *she* wasn't.

But Detective Olson and Garrett were waiting, and she was nearly certain Kavanaugh and the bodyguard would be in there for some, if not all, of the interview. Jenna took a deep breath and walked down the steps, across the room, and into the den.

Behind her, Wilford said, "No, seriously, where should I go? I'll get lost and die in this place."

§

K avanaugh's den was classic tycoon chic. The exterior walls were mostly glass, overlooking the entire town of Lost Haven to the south and gradients of blue water to the horizon in the west. Jenna had the disturbing thought that if the man ever got his hands on a cannon, he could cause some serious trouble.

A massive wooden desk that looked like a varnished sarcophagus hunkered along the wall on the left, which was made entirely of built-in shelves of various sizes. Framed photographs of Harrison Kavanaugh and other people showed thin smiles and the confident posture of money. Jenna recognized the Governor of Michigan, did not recognize a bunch of judges in robes, and—wait, was that the President of the United States?

Detective Olson said, "Take a seat, Miss Hooper."

The area in front of the desk had a large, muted rug on the hardwood floor. Four leather and brass-tack chairs that looked like they usually faced the desk had been pulled into a rough circle, and ten feet behind them a long, narrow table held a partial scale model of Lost Haven. There was the marina, Lilac

Park and the amphitheater in the grassy field at its southern end, and Main Street.

But Main Street was different. Instead of The Welcome Shoppe and other small businesses, a model of Kavanaugh's Lost Haven Resort loomed like some monstrosity plucked off the Las Vegas strip and dropped into the civilized world to wreak havoc.

Because the block of Main Street was long and narrow, Kavanaugh had found the space he needed by going up. The main part of the resort was at least ten stories tall, maybe fifteen in other sections, all of it a confusing mess of pillars, balconies, and roof-top pools. Jenna approached it cautiously, afraid it might suddenly come to life and start playing carnival music.

Or she might topple it onto the floor and hack it to pieces.

She stood on the rug and faced the back of the structure from just about where her house would be on the scale model. Her sunsets would be gone, replaced by blank windows and industrial air conditioning units.

Framed sketches showed some of the attractions within the resort, rendered in black ink and colored pencil. Grinning tourists with blank eyes strolled past unsettling notions like *Kavanaugh's Man Kave*, *Bikini Lines Swimwear*, *Barty's Party Sports Bar*, and the suspiciously named *Bakery*.

"Pretty slick, huh?" Olson said. "Mr. Kavanaugh

said he's working on getting a casino into the place. If he pulls that off, you're gonna need more parking. And better roads."

"And a head of security," Garrett said. It had that tone of when he was trying to be coy but just sounded confused, and he was looking at Detective Olson with an eyebrow cocked.

Olson seemed to be blushing. "Nah, he wasn't serious about that."

"He's serious about everything," Garrett said.

"Well, anyway…" Olson left it at that. "Miss Hooper, I know you all have to get back and open your shops, so I'll try to make this as quick as possible. Let's have a seat, here."

Jenna sat with her back to the resort model. She couldn't stand to look at it for one more second. Detective Olson was on her left and Garrett sat on her right, his elbows on the chair arms and big hands laced together in front of his stomach. He did look good in his uniform, but Jenna couldn't help wondering what else he'd told Belma about her. She didn't have any secrets—well, nothing illegal, anyway—but certainly a few things she didn't want her mother knowing.

What else had he blabbed about?

And who else had he blabbed to?

Detective Olson said, "So you like books, huh?"

Jenna gave Garrett a scowl so harsh it pushed him backward.

"What'd I do?" he said.

"Nothing."

Olson said, "Hey, look, Officer Bower here told me you two had a thing going for a while, and—"

"Did he give you all the good details?" Jenna asked.

Olson blinked. "Just that he'd be happy to step out of the room if you're uncomfortable talking about anything with him present."

"Like what?"

Olson said, "Oh, I don't know, like if you were with a male friend last night at the time Ms. Gallagher was murdered."

Jenna whirled to her right. "Garrett!"

"What? How should I know?"

"We haven't been broken up very long."

"Do you want me to leave or not?"

"Are you going to tell Belma everything I say?"

Garrett frowned. "Belma? Huh?"

"Never mind. Everyone can stay. Let's just get started." She crossed her arms and stared at the shelves behind Kavanaugh's desk.

Olson and Garrett shared a look: They were both wearing guns but did not feel safe.

§

Detective Olson cleared his throat. "So, Ms. Hooper, did you like Ingrid Gallagher?"

"Yes," Jenna said. "Do I need a lawyer here?"

Garrett said, "You can have a lawyer any time you want, Jenna. I'll run and get Mr. Montross right away, just say the word. But you don't need him, because you didn't do anything. Right?"

"Of course," Jenna said. "But…"

"Go ahead," Olson said.

Jenna considered backing off, but the two men were already on their heels from her little blow-up. Might as well keep them dancing.

"But I'm afraid the person who actually killed her is trying to frame the Main Street shop owners. This person doesn't care who takes the fall, as long as it's someone else."

"Jenna," Garrett said. It was a patient tone: *Come on now. We've talked about this.*

Olson said, "Who do you think killed her?"

Jenna glanced at Garrett.

"Everything you say here is confidential," Olson said. "Isn't that right, Officer Bower?"

"Right, yeah."

Olson came back to Jenna. "Who killed Ingrid?"

"Harrison Kavanaugh," Jenna said.

She expected the detective to laugh in her face. Instead he nodded, sat back, and flipped through his small notebook and checked what he'd written.

"Mr. Kavanaugh was at his residence between the hours of 5 PM and 12 AM. The medical examiner puts Ingrid's death at right around 9:30, so Mr. Kavanaugh was here for several hours on either side of the murder. Eight people can corroborate that fact. I've talked to all of them, and six of them didn't know Ms. Gallagher had been killed before I told them. So they had no reason to lie."

Jenna said, "Is one of those eight people his bodyguard?"

Olson turned a page. "Yes. Mr. Jay Cabo was within arm's reach of Mr. Kavanaugh the entire night."

Jenna frowned. "Jay Cabo?"

"Something wrong?"

"No, I guess I just thought his name was Body-guard. *Jay Cabo* makes him seem almost...normal."

"I wouldn't know about that," Olson tapped his notebook. "But I do know he didn't kill Ingrid Galla-gher. Neither did Mr. Kavanaugh. He's a little rough around the edges, but he isn't a murderer. And where you see him trying to frame someone, maybe all he's doing is exposing the killer. Okay?"

Jenna chewed her lip and tried to look uncertain. "I suppose."

"Good," Olson said. "So, where were you during that time?"

"In my shop, closing up and getting ready for the meeting."

"Did anybody see you?"

"Some other business owners came and went," Jenna said. "They were checking their inventories, picking up leftover free samples and restocking the non-perishables for the next day—today. Which reminds me, we all have to get back to our shops soon. How long is this supposed to take?"

"As long as necessary," Olson said. "But you can leave any time you like. I mean, nobody is under arrest. Yet."

"And Mr. Kavanaugh will open the gate for me, right?"

Olson winced. "That's another matter, but he can't legally keep you here. Now, do you remember who came and went at your shop last night?"

Jenna ticked them off on her fingers. "Sally from the Pretzel Twist, Johnny from Smokestack's, Harvey from Time to Chime, Rachel from Sidesaddle, um…"

Olson made fast notes. "And these were all between nine and ten at night?"

"I closed at eight, and they were coming and going from then until nine thirty, maybe nine forty. Then I started putting out the chairs and snacks for the meeting."

"Did you see any of the other Main Street shop owners during that time?"

Jenna wanted to say yes, to get her friends off the suspect list, even if some of them (ahem, Belma) wouldn't do the same for her. But she shook her head.

"No."

"Would you say you and Ingrid were good friends?"

That took her by surprise, and a moment later Jenna realized surprise was exactly the point. He was trying to shake something loose. Well, if he wanted details…

She rambled on for a while about the gossip Ingrid liked to share, and how that and their Main Street shops had been the strongest bond between them. A shame, really, because sometimes women had a hard time finding really good friends. A few minutes into it Garrett was examining his knuckles and Olson's eyes had glazed a bit.

He was probably thinking about about an early lunch, or golf.

Jenna was thinking: *This is going pretty well. I'm the one getting interviewed, but I already know Olson has eliminated Kavanaugh and his bodyguard—no, Cabo—as suspects.*

She certainly hadn't, but it was good to know Kavanaugh wasn't being looked at by the police. It meant she'd have to watch him even more closely.

She talked a bit about how nice Ingrid's clothes were and wondered:

What else can I find out in here?

§

Jenna was mid-sentence, talking about the great job Ingrid had done with the ordinance for multiple waste bins, when Kavanaugh and Cabo entered the den. No knocking, no asking—just entering.

"What do we have?" Kavanaugh said.

Olson said, "Mr. Kavanaugh, please, I already asked you—"

"And I said I didn't care," Kavanaugh said. "If you want to run things your way, take everybody to the state police post or wherever, handcuff them to a desk, and start playing smart cop/dumb cop. This is a voluntary interview process, and I'm voluntarily involving myself."

Garrett said, "It's good cop/bad cop."

Kavanaugh turned on him. "What?"

"You said smart cop/dumb cop."

"You're right, I'm sorry. I meant to say slow cop/fired cop. Now have we made any progress?"

Olson scratched his nose and flipped a page in his notebook. "Ms. Gallagher had very nice clothes and was ecologically responsible when it came to waste receptacles."

"Good lord," Kavanaugh said. "If I'd known it was this easy to get away with murder I'd have killed a dozen people by now, starting with my ex-wife." He turned to Jenna. "Did you know about Wilford and Ingrid?"

"Mr. Kavanaugh," Olson said.

Kavanaugh ignored him. "Well?"

"What about them?" Jenna said.

"That crazy old man came in here and said they were having a romantic relationship. A summer fling, he called it. Is that true?"

"How would I know?"

"Oh, you and Wilford are always going on about art and books at your silly little Main Street meetings. If he was creaking and gasping with Ingrid, he would have told you."

"Well, he didn't. Why are you so upset about it?"

"I'm not upset," Kavanaugh said, his face turning red. He turned to Olson. "You see? Why would the old man keep it a secret if he wasn't planning something? Something terrible."

"Like a murder?" Olson said.

Kavanaugh addressed the room: "I think he's finally catching up."

"Secret affair to murder is a bit of a leap," Olson said, "but I'm looking into it."

"Right," Kavanaugh said. "You keep looking into things, and I'll let you know when I've done your job for you."

A tense, awkward silence pressed against the windows. Cabo's jaw muscles bounced—it looked like he was chewing the inside of his mouth in order to stay quiet. Olson rolled his pen across the notebook page and Garrett watched him, helpless to stop Kavanaugh from steamrolling.

Jenna shifted in her chair, unsure whether she should poke her head up. But when it came to Kavanaugh, what did she have to lose?

"Where was Wilford when Ingrid got killed?" she asked.

The detective looked at Kavanaugh. "You want to tell her, or can I?"

"Don't be sarcastic," Kavanaugh said.

Olson checked his notes. "He said he was taking a short nap after cleaning up his gallery, before the meeting started. He has a small cot in the back office. No witnesses."

"*Sleeping*," Kavanaugh scoffed. "Has anyone checked that cot for signs of Ingrid?"

"The crime scene techs are waiting for a warrant," Olson said.

Kavanaugh jabbed a finger at the door, apparently in Wilford's direction. "See? He's hiding something!"

"We just want to make sure we do this right," Olson said. "We won't go in until the paperwork is done."

"Hold on," Jenna said, sitting straight up in her chair. "I had to use my key to go into the café when I found Ingrid's body. Garrett, you said the back door was locked too, right?"

Garrett nodded.

"So whoever killed her has to have a key. Who has keys for the café?" Jenna raised her hand. "I do, but you already knew that. Who else? I don't think Wilford does."

"We're looking into that too," Olson said, "but it isn't that simple. If the doors were unlocked when the killer got there, all he or she had to do is grab an extra key from the office and lock the door on the way out."

Jenna slumped a bit.

Olson went on: "Maybe somebody made a copy of the key months ago, didn't tell anybody, and threw it in Lake Michigan after killing Ingrid."

Jenna slouched.

Olson said, "I don't think we're going to find some guy with blood splattered on his face and a glowing key hanging around his neck. Sorry."

Jenna nearly slid out of the chair.

Maybe this whole solving murders thing wasn't for her after all.

§

Olson was talking again, but something he'd just said tugged at the edge of Jenna's thoughts—what was it?

The detective was looking at her, waiting.

Jenna said, "I'm sorry, what?"

"I asked when the Main Street owners came to the meeting last night, was anybody acting strange?"

"They're all kind of strange, pretty much all the time," Jenna said.

Garrett grunted in agreement.

Olson said, "Nervous, out of breath, shaky. That kind of thing."

She ran the beginning of the meeting through her head, went around the nook and tried to remember anything out of the ordinary. "No. Not that I noticed, anyway."

"What about today? Anybody asking you to vouch for them, say you were together last night when you really weren't?"

Jenna shook her head.

Olson said, "Mr. Donald seems to be hitting the sauce a little hard. Do you think he has a guilty conscience about something?"

"I think he has access to free high-end booze and would never forgive himself if he passed it up."

"I hope he drinks it all," Kavanaugh said. "I made sure the bar was fully stocked -- it's like truth serum for some people."

"Lawrence will tell you whatever you want to know, drunk or sober," Jenna said, "and usually whether you want to hear it or not."

Kavanaugh pointed at Cabo. "Tell McTavish to make the next Bloody Mary twice as strong. I want half of it on his shirt when he comes in here."

Olson spread his hands. "Mr. Kavanaugh, that won't be helpful."

They barked back and forth, but Jenna didn't hear them. The thing that had been tugging at her mind jumped out into the spotlight: Bloody Mary. Blood splatter.

"Blood!" she shouted.

The room fell silent. Everyone stared at her except for Cabo, who checked the floor for body fluids.

"Blood?" Garrett said.

Jenna nodded. "The blood on Ingrid's head. It was on the top of her head, right? Not the back or the sides."

"That's right," Olson said, "but I'd appreciate you keeping it to yourself. You're the only non-law enforcement person who saw the body, and that detail might help us nail the killer."

"Or eliminate a suspect," Jenna said.

Everyone waited.

"Wilford was shorter than Ingrid," she said. "How could he hit her on the very top of her head, hard enough to crush her skull?"

"He could have climbed onto a chair," Kavanaugh said. "Or a table."

Jenna shook her head. "It takes him five minutes to get out of a chair. Climbing on and off of one would take a week."

"The forensics team is still analyzing the evidence," Olson said, "but I would say it's unlikely Wilford has the physical capability to be Ms. Gallagher's killer."

"But possible," Kavanaugh said.

"And unlikely," Olson repeated.

Jenna felt something in her chest loosen a bit. Wilford might not be off the suspect list entirely, but he was on the edge.

That was good enough for now.

§

Detective Olson held out a business card. "Thank you for your time, Jenna. If you think of anything else, please give me a call."

Jenna took the card and stood up. "We're all done?"

"I might have some more questions for you, but we're set for now."

Garrett stood. "I'll walk you out."

Cabo opened the door to the receiving room and held it. Before Jenna got there Kavanaugh said, "Wait outside. I have some more questions for you right now."

"About what?"

"About things I want to know."

"I already told Detective Olson everything. And I need to go open my shop."

Kavanaugh spoke through his teeth: "Just wait outside."

He pointed at Cabo again. "Go with her. And tell McTavish about the drink."

Jenna felt an outburst building in her throat, a rush of words about treating people the right way, how having money didn't mean you could constantly be a bane to society. Probably something about bad taste in books too, just to crush him, even though it was a lie.

Garrett recognized the look and hustled her to the

door. "You're almost done. Just hang on a few more minutes, okay? You did great."

He turned to go back into the den and almost ran into Cabo, who filled the doorway. Garrett's face was about level with the bodyguard's chest. He stepped back and puffed his own chest a bit.

"Just, uh, watch out for her, okay?"

Cabo nodded and stepped aside. Garrett went into the den. Cabo closed the door and looked at Jenna for a moment, seemed like he wanted to say something, then squinted and scanned the room and bar. Both were obviously empty.

"I don't see McTavish."

"Nope," Jenna said. The tirade she'd worked up for Kavanaugh still simmered, and she had to be careful not to unleash it on an innocent bystander.

"I'll go find him."

"Good."

Cabo opened his mouth to say something else, but nothing came out. His mouth stayed open and tried to form some sort of reassuring smile.

Jenna frowned.

They stared at each other, the awkwardness building.

Jenna said, "Is there a restroom nearby?"

"Oh thank God," Cabo blurted. "Take a right in the hallway, first door on the left."

"Thank you very much."

Cabo headed for the door at the end of the bar

that led to the dining room. "I'll find McTavish. Let's meet back here, okay?"

"Fine."

"Go team."

Jenna frowned again. *Go team?*

She walked through the furniture and up the steps into the hallway. She was turning right, toward the restroom, when she heard billiard balls clacking together.

Without thinking she spun on her heel and ran toward the game room.

She didn't have much time.

§

Lawrence was still at the pool table. He had a half-full Bloody Mary balanced on the rim and was trying to poke the billiard balls into the holes using the butt-end of a hockey stick. The massive flatscreen TV showed golf highlights, which to Jenna seemed like an oxymoron.

Jenna kept one ear toward the hallway and said, "Lawrence, you--"

"Shush. This is a very important shot."

He concentrated, slid the hockey stick back and forth across the webbing between his thumb and forefinger, then jabbed it against the cue ball, which corkscrewed ninety degrees to the left and hit nothing.

"Huh." Lawrence let the hockey stick clatter to the floor. "I guess I'll never be the world champion of Pockey."

"Pockey?"

"Combination of pool and hockey. Full contact and no helmets. I just made it up." He sipped his drink. "Wanna play? I bet you *stink* at it."

"No, listen, I just had my interrogation, interview, whatever it was, and Kavanaugh was in there trying to point Detective Olson at different people. You were one of them."

"Me? Why?" Lawrence spoke into his glass, which he'd tipped up to drain.

"Because you're drunk, and he thinks it's because you feel guilty."

His brow furrowed. "About being drunk?"

"No, about killing Ingrid."

"Pfft. Well, I didn't do that, so poop on him."

"Lawrence, look at me. Do you have an alibi for last night, right before the meeting? Anything that proves you didn't kill her?"

"How about my word of honor?" Lawrence yelled. He tried to slam the glass down on an end table, missed, and had to catch himself so he wouldn't crack his face on the edge. In the process he lost a shoe and farted quietly.

Jenna took the glass from him. "No more of these.

Do you have an alibi or not? I won't lie for you, but if there is anything else I can do to keep Kavanaugh from framing you, I'll do it."

"I don't need your help." Lawrence picked his shoe up and put it in his pocket like he'd planned to do that all along. "I happen to have a very good alibi for last night."

Jenna waited. "Well?"

"I can't tell you."

"Lawrence, stop screwing around."

"I mean it, I can't. I have to keep it secret, which sort of makes it the worst alibi ever, now that I think about it."

"If it's true, you have to tell Detective Olson."

"Oh, it's true." Lawrence winced.

"If you don't tell Olson, Kavanaugh will accuse you of murder. Not to mention, the *real* murderer might come after you next."

Lawrence said nothing. He just held his breath and let his cheeks puff out.

"What is it?" Jenna asked.

He let the air escape in a wave of flammable fumes. "Okay. I was--"

"There you are."

Jenna jumped and turned. Cabo loomed in the doorway holding half of an apple. The other half was in his mouth, getting pulverized.

"I thought we were gonna meet in the receiving room."

"Right," Jenna said. "I got lost."

"Been there," Cabo said. "Mr. Kavanaugh is waiting for you." He looked past her at Lawrence. "And Detective Olson would like to see you now."

"Do I have time to get another drink first?"

"Sure," Cabo said, simultaneously with Jenna's "No."

Lawrence limped around her toward the door. He glanced down at his bare foot and seemed confused by it.

"Lawrence," Jenna said.

"Hm?"

"Be careful."

"Hey babe. I'm always careful."

He tried to wink and point a finger gun at her, then ran into the door jamb.

§

Jenna followed Cabo down the hall, still simmering about Kavanaugh ordering her around.

Wait outside.

Tell me what I want to know.

Go here, do this.

Don't go there or else.

They entered the receiving room and Jenna caught a last glimpse of Lawrence before he disappeared into the den. She moved toward the steps, looking for Kavanaugh, mostly so she could tell him to stick it.

"This way," Cabo said. He walked toward the stairway to the second floor.

Jenna crossed her arms and didn't follow. "Where are we going?"

"He wants to talk in the library."

"The library?"

All those books.

The smells.

The reading chair!

"Yeah, it's private," Cabo said. "Nobody ever goes in there."

Jenna followed. "Well, I guess I should at least hear him out..."

§

Kavanaugh stood near the far-right window reading a thick leather-bound volume.

Jenna waited near the door, resisting the pull of the shelves closest to her. There was a copy of *To Kill a Mockingbird* with a dark blue cloth spine and golden foil lettering almost close enough to reach, and it begged to be drawn out, eased open, and inhaled.

Cabo stood near the wall and seemed unsure about leaning against it.

Kavanaugh hefted the book. "One of my favorites. *A Treatise on Fair Negotiations in the Lumber Industry.*"

"That sounds like the most boring book ever," Jenna said, eyeing its gorgeous paper, nearly tan with age, from afar. "How many pages?"

"Seven hundred and sixty four," he said, without having to check.

"Yep. That's a lot of boring."

Kavanaugh chuckled, closed the book, and slid it into a gap among similar spines. The sound of it sliding against the other books and thumping into place made Jenna sigh.

Kavanaugh turned to her and put his hands in his pockets. "What do you know about Lost Haven?"

"The whole town?"

"The history," Kavanaugh said.

Was this a trick question? She was the town historian...

"Everything," Jenna said.

Kavanaugh pushed his lips out and nodded. "Everything. That's good. How about Sanctuary?"

A sharp, unexpected laugh escaped Jenna before she realized he was serious.

"Sanctuary? Do you want to know about Neverland and Atlantis too?"

Kavanaugh waited.

Cabo said, "What's Sanctuary?"

Jenna laughed again, a bit of nerves in it this time.

"Go ahead," Kavanaugh said. "Tell him."

Jenna blinked. "Uh, well, Sanctuary is a mythical ghost town that used to be on the shores of Lake Michigan, right where Lost Haven is now. The story goes that it was built by the first families who settled here: the Gallaghers, Welbournes, Minks, and, Kavanaughs."

"The Kavanaughs should have been listed first," Kavanaugh said. "But go on."

"The families—led by the Kavanaughs, according to the story—began clear-cutting the forests around the town to build their mansions, saloons, the marina, a casino—"

"A church," Kavanaugh said.

"A brothel," Jenna added. "And a nice big bank to hold all the money they were making from selling the rest of the lumber to all the towns and cities growing along the coast, especially Chicago."

"That's a lot of lumber," Cabo said.

Jenna nodded. "And the families were so busy watching the lumber float away and counting the money that came back, they didn't notice that taking all the trees away left the sand dunes free to creep toward the town. Every year the sand got closer, and one day the families had to start sweeping it off the boardwalks. Then they had to scoop it out of their doorways. Then they had to keep their windows shut so it wouldn't pour over the sills."

"Wait," Cabo said. "The whole town got *buried*?"

"That's the legend," Jenna said. "The families

moved onto houseboats and watched the town disappear under the sand. Guess what they did next."

Cabo shrugged.

Jenna stared at Kavanaugh, who responded with a tiny smile that didn't quite reach his eyes.

"They cut down more trees," she said, "and built Lost Haven on top of the buried town."

Cabo looked down at the floor. "Are we…"

"It's just a story," Jenna said, "meant to add some intrigue to the town and bring in tourists. To be honest, the founding families were smart to come up with it. The residents play along—heck, if tourists are there when I'm sweeping the sand out of my shop, I'll say something like, 'They must be doing some cleaning down there in Sanctuary, ha ha.' It's all in good fun, and it's helped keep this town alive for a long time. Even without a hideous resort."

Kavanaugh ignored the jab.

"Wait a minute," Cabo said. "On the way into town, I saw a billboard. Something about the Church of Sanctuary."

"'See the last remaining proof of Buried Sanctuary,'" Jenna quoted.

Cabo snapped his fingers. "That's it."

"The Nelson farm," Jenna said with a wry smile. "Morrie Nelson put that sign up years ago and tells every tourist he can find he has the last vestige of the Sanctuary Chapel poking out of the dune on his property. He has a hurricane fence around it and only charges five bucks to take a picture."

Cabo looked back and forth between Jenna and Kavanaugh. "Well why doesn't somebody dig it up?"

Jenna said, "He tells the tourists it's protected by the Lost Haven Historical Preservation Society—not true, by the way—and everyone in town knows it's actually part of a chicken coop he tore down and dumped at the base of the dune."

Cabo frowned. "Chicken coop?"

"It's fake," Jenna said.

"Well that's…rude. Why doesn't anybody here call him out?"

Jenna shrugged. "He's feeding his family, and the tourists love it."

"So this whole Sanctuary thing is a hoax to sucker tourists out of their money."

"Mmm," Jenna tilted her head side-to-side. "Hoax is a little harsh. Like I said, it's just a fun legend. It also makes the founding families seem like evil, heartless tycoons, which is actually pretty accurate."

Kavanaugh smiled again, and this time his whole face lit up.

It looked like he was proud.

§

Kavanaugh said, "What a great history lesson,

Jenna. When my resort is finished, how'd you like to be a tour guide?"

Jenna didn't respond.

"Head tour guide?" Kavanaugh said.

"How about I start by guiding where you can stick your head?"

Kavanaugh glared.

Jenna glared back.

Cabo stepped away from the wall, directly into the path. Jenna was a bit surprised he didn't burst into flames from the intensity.

"Knock it off, both of you," he said.

"Excuse me?" Kavanaugh said. "You don't tell me what to do."

"You're both being immature," Cabo said, looking back and forth between them. "And Mr. Kavanaugh, you hired me to protect you, and I will, but if you pick a fight with a nice young lady half your size, and she takes you down, you kinda have it coming."

Kavanaugh was flabbergasted. His mouth opened and closed a few times before he finally sputtered, "I'm finding your replacement as soon as these people are out of my house."

Cabo shrugged. "That's your choice. But I'm also trying to protect your reputation. Bad reputations attract bad people. Bad people do bad things, like try to kill other people, and that makes my job harder. Do you see the cause and effect here?"

Kavanaugh examined the bodyguard, looking him over head-to-toe like he'd never seen such a thing in his life. Jenna watched it all with pure, unmasked delight.

"You're not from here," Kavanaugh said. "You don't know the first thing about my reputation or how to conduct business with these people."

He stepped forward and poked a finger into Cabo's chest.

"And if you dare try to tell me what to do again, your job will become harder than you could ever imagine. Because guess what? Your *job* will be scraping barnacles off of oil rigs in the Arctic Ocean."

Kavanaugh turned to Jenna and smoothed the front of his suit.

"Is that everything you know about Lost Haven and Sanctuary?"

Jenna blinked, momentarily off-balance from the rapid lane change. "Of course not."

"But generally speaking, that's the snapshot of your knowledge."

He made it sound so pitiful.

"I guess."

"I thought so. If Detective Olson is done with you, you can leave any time you like."

He swept past her to the door. Cabo followed, his jaw muscles working.

In the hallway Kavanaugh turned and said, "McTavish put some food out, please help yourself.

I'd stay away from the carbs though." He shot a withering glance at Cabo. "Half my size, huh?"

He shook his head and left.

§

Jenna found Wilford, Lawrence, and Belma picking through a spread of cold cuts, cheese, and artisan rolls. Plates of olives, pickles, and warm pastry puffs ran along the bar, ending with an assortment of crackers next to a crock of Schuler's cheese. It seemed Kavanaugh's rule about no one being in the receiving room was over.

Did that mean the interviews were done? The den door was closed, and Jenna didn't see Garrett or Olson.

McTavish smiled at her from behind the bar. "M'lady. A beverage?"

Jenna briefly considered the hard liquors lining the back of the bar.

Who was she kidding? One sip, a shudder, and possible gagging wasn't going to help.

She took a deep breath. "Water is fine, thank you."

Wilford offered her a cracker with bright orange cheese spread over it, and she tossed it into her mouth.

"You survived the inquisition," he said, his eyes twinkling. "Bart and Sherri are in there now."

"Together?"

"I don't think our poor detective had a choice in the matter."

Around a mouth full of ham and roll, Lawrence said, "They're basically one person anyway. Joined at the hip and the brain stem."

Jenna glanced at McTavish, hoping he wasn't uncomfortable with that kind of talk about a Kavanaugh. Or worse, going to report it. He'd found a non-existent water spot on the wooden bar and worked at it with a soft towel. The grimace of effort did a fine job of hiding his amusement before he slipped into the dining room and disappeared.

Belma was wrapped in a thick white robe—with possibly nothing underneath—and left moist footprints on the wooden floor. Apparently no one had tried to drown her in the Jacuzzi. Not very hard, at least.

She asked Lawrence, "So are they going to arrest you for that shirt or what?"

"It's not illegal to look this good," he said, spraying some fresh cracker bits down onto the flamingos. "Are they going to arrest you for killing Ingrid?"

"Nope. But I told Mr. Detective in there I'd be happy to wear his handcuffs after some dinner tonight and tell him all the dirty little secrets he wants to know."

Lawrence shook his head. "Please. I'm trying to eat."

"Wait," Jenna said, "you've both been in the

den? Lawrence, I knew you were going, but Belma, you too?"

She nodded.

"That was fast."

Belma shrugged. "I told them what I knew—nothing—and where I was. At the Nelson farm getting butter, just like I told you."

Jenna wanted to ask Lawrence what he'd said to Detective Olson and Garrett, but didn't want to put him in a bad spot in front of the others.

Instead, she said, "What did you guys think of the model in there?"

"Hideous," Wilford said. "It wouldn't be so bad if the architecture and design were somewhat acceptable, but it looks like a prison for NASCAR fans."

Belma nodded. "Five bucks says it falls over during the first winter storm. That wind coming off the lake will push it right onto your house, Jenna. Flop."

Jenna hadn't thought of that. She'd been too devastated at the loss of her sunsets. She pulled away from the idea of being crushed to death by a honeymoon suite and watched Lawrence out of the corner of her eye. "And how about those sketches of the shops inside? Kavanaugh's Man Kave?"

"Oh, the decor," Wilford shuddered. "If the taste here is any indication, the entire Midwest will soon be sold out of antique golf equipment and photographs of cigars."

Lawrence turned away at the mention of the sketches to scan the cheese selection, which he'd already pilfered three times since Jenna walked in. Well, if he wasn't going to come clean about the Bakery...

Jenna said, "I couldn't help noticing Bart and Sherri both had nice-looking spots drawn up for them. Barty's Party Sports Bar and, what was it? Bikini Line Swimwear?"

"Ha ha," Lawrence said without turning around. And it wasn't a laugh; he actually said *ha ha*. "That's just what this town needs. Drunk sports fans with buffalo sauce on their faces running around in new bikinis and Speedos. We're all doomed."

"Speaking of bikinis," Belma said, "I should probably get dressed."

She headed for the stairs and caught Jenna's eye, shot a knowing look at Lawrence's back: *See?*

Wilford wandered into the dining room to look at the framed paintings, so Jenna stepped next to Lawrence and plucked one of the artisan rolls out of the basket.

"Bakery. That was an odd name, compared to the others."

"Hm? Oh, I didn't notice."

"Have you had a hard time picking out a name?"

"Whaaaaaafine." Lawrence glanced around and lowered his voice. "Who told you?"

"Nobody."

"Right. Belma's the biggest *nobody* I know. Troublemaker."

Jenna said, "What I want to know is, why didn't *you* tell me?"

"Sweetie, I'm in cahoots with the guy who's going to demolish your Welcome Shoppe. Your bookshelves. Your reading nook. I wasn't sure our friendship would survive it."

Jenna's eyes began to sting. Before the tears arrived she wrapped a startled Lawrence in a fierce hug and mumbled into his shoulder.

"We'll be fine, Lawrence. Our friendship can take a lot more than that."

Then she shoved him away.

"What it *can't* take is you going to prison for murder. Please, please tell me you didn't lie to the police about where you were last night to keep your resort bakery a secret."

Lawrence began stacking crackers, cheese, and summer sausage into an unsteady tower. "Jenna, I was here last night. Talking to Kavanaugh and the designers about what I need for the bakery. And of course the lawyers, which made me wish someone would murder *me*."

Jenna frowned. "But if you were here, why would Kavanaugh drag you through all of this? The interviews, the accusations?"

"Because I asked him to." He wrapped an arm around Jenna's shoulders and pulled her in so their hips bumped. "I'm a Main Street shop owner, baby. We hang together."

Jenna couldn't help smiling while Lawrence ignored his cracker tower and ate half of a pastry puff.

He chewed a few times and said, "However, Kavanaugh is a straight-up shark. If he did have something to do with Ingrid's death, I wouldn't put it past him to bring me here just in case he can frame me for it. I wasn't going to stay home and miss that."

He ate the rest of the pastry.

"Or the free food and booze," he said, shaking his head. "The man is a terrible human being, but he knows how to throw a murder investigation."

§

Jenna had just finished assembling a tidy plate of cheese, fruit, pickles, and a sandwich bigger than her face when the door to the den opened.

Kavanaugh strode out, followed by Cabo. Jenna could see Bart and Sherri in the den, standing with Olson and Garrett near the model of The Lost Haven Resort. They were smiling, pointing things out and laughing. Like they couldn't wait for it to be built.

Kavanaugh stopped in the middle of the receiving room. "Everyone, you can leave now. Let me rephrase that: You *should* leave now. Wilford, did you hear me? Time to go."

Wilford shuffled into the dining room entrance. "Eh?"

Kavanaugh told the room, "Detective Olson is continuing the investigation. I'm sure he'll be in touch if he needs any further information. Or to arrest one or more of you. Soon, hopefully."

"Can I finish my lunch?" Lawrence asked. He had another sandwich and a mound of the pastry puffs, which had turned out to be more addictive than heroin.

"Take it with you," Kavanaugh said. "Where is Miss Winkle?"

"Right here," Belma said. She was at the top of the three steps, her wet hair pinned up and looking like a glazed version of the usual whipped topping.

"Perfect, you can lead the way out." Kavanaugh pointed toward the front of the house. "No one is moving." He looked at Cabo. "Will you do something, please? Earn your salary."

Cabo's mouth was a tight line. "This way folks. Thank you for your time."

He stepped to the dining room and offered Wilford an arm. Wilford patted Cabo's shoulder and moved past him to the bar, twiddled his fingers over the rolls before plucking two out and stuffing them in the pockets of his sweater.

He hooked Jenna's arm as he passed and admired her plate. "Oh my. Don't let any of that spill. Here, let me assist you with the cheese…"

"Help yourself," Jenna said.

They walked up the steps together and moved as a group with Belma and Lawrence to the front door. McTavish was there. He swept the wide doors open with a small bow.

"Your presence has been lovely," he said.

Belma scoffed.

Lawrence said, "I think I might vomit."

Wilford told McTavish, "Come to the gallery. The dining room needs new art."

Jenna glanced back and saw Kavanaugh stomping up the stairs to the second level. He was in a hurry, not just to shoo everyone out of the house, but to get somewhere.

Had he learned something key about Ingrid's killer?

Was the evidence pointing at him now, and he was panicking?

Cabo followed Kavanaugh, and before he turned up the stairway he caught Jenna's eye. He seemed about to say something and Jenna paused, maybe to let Wilford and McTavish keep talking.

Maybe not.

Cabo shook his head once and went up the stairs as Kavanaugh disappeared around the corner toward the library. He was picking up speed.

What did he know?

CHAPTER SIX

To everyone's surprise, most of all Belma's, she made Lawrence spread out in the back of her van for the short trip down the hill and into town.

"I'm fine to drive," Lawrence said, making a pillow out of a fifty-pound bag of flour.

Belma shook her head. "You're barely fine to stand still without spinning off the planet."

"Are you spinning too? I thought it was just me…"

He started snoring.

"Thanks Belma," Jenna said. "He was going to have to ride with one of us—do you want to move him into my car?"

"Naw, if he wakes up and starts yapping I'll just strap him to the roof. I talked to McTavish, he said they'll bring his car down today." She checked the time on her dashboard: 11:30. "Stupid Kavanaugh. I open in thirty minutes and haven't done any prep. Lost the whole morning."

"Do you think it was worth it?" Jenna asked.

"Kavanaugh seemed like he was on to something when we walked out."

"Who knows?" Wilford said. "I'm not certain he cares a whisker about Ingrid's death. He may have orchestrated this whole interview thing just to get dirt on us, more ammunition to expedite his hideous resort and the death of Main Street."

"That would be terrible," Jenna said.

"No," Belma said, looking back at the mansion, "that would be Kavanaugh. But hey, if I squeeze any juicy tidbits out of that Detective Olson, I'll let you guys know."

She wiggled her eyebrows and climbed into the van's cockpit. Her tires squealed on the driveway as the van tilted around the circle and down the hill toward the gate.

Jenna set her food plate on top of her car and helped Wilford to his door. He opened it halfway and paused.

"I suppose you've heard a few things about Ingrid and me."

"Oh, no, I—"

"It's fine, Jenna. And it's true. I'm not ashamed or prudish about it—I just wasn't sure what you would think."

Jenna patted his arm. "I think if it made you two happy, it doesn't matter what anyone thinks."

He put his hand over hers and winked. "Thank

you. We were very happy, among several other less appropriate emotions..."

Jenna blushed and tried to say something to tilt the conversation toward less awkward. Her jaw decided to just hang there.

Wilford chuckled and eased into his Mercedes, the smell of oiled leather floating from the interior. Jenna watched him back out and roll toward the exit. She considered going back inside the mansion and confronting Kavanaugh to find out what he knew, but what was her leverage? Her right as town historian?

Would Garrett tell her anything?

Maybe, but there was a good chance Kavanaugh wouldn't tell the police everything.

What about Cabo?

Hm. He'd wanted to tell her something, she was almost certain of it.

About Kavanaugh?

Someone else?

Or just more disapproval of her reading list...

There was, of course, the possibility she was assuming way too much. Maybe Kavanaugh just had to use the restroom, the stress causing a flare-up of some digestive issue.

Or was she trying to figure out the wrong person? Kavanaugh had practically run up the stairs after he came out of the den with Bart and Sherri, so what did that mean? Did those two know something that implicated the millionaire?

Jenna began to weave an intricate web of deceit in which Bart and Sherri knew Kavanaugh murdered Ingrid and were trying to blackmail him in return for their silence.

Was he rushing upstairs to pull stacks of cash out of a secret safe? Fat bundles of money for Bart and Sherri. Maybe even Olson and Garrett, to make them forget what they knew.

Jenna shook her head.

That was slightly crazy, wasn't it?

But if Bart and Sherri suddenly left town, or Garrett started wearing jeans without holes in the butt... no, scratch that. He could win the lottery and his jeans would still be a mess.

She slid the plate off her roof and nestled it in the passenger seat on a semi-dirty beach towel that smelled like sunblock with a subtle hint of dead fish. She could stand there all day concocting possible scenarios and it would get her just about halfway to nowhere.

She checked the mansion's windows once more, hoping to see someone—maybe Cabo—waving her inside or flashing a secret message.

Empty.

Jenna idled toward the edge of the plateau, enjoying the stunning view from Horizon House. She might never get a chance to see it again from this spot. She put her sunglasses on and plugged her phone into the line-in cord, hit Shuffle.

My Sharona by The Knack. A good sign.

She coasted down and around the curve and saw the gate was open—a relief, she admitted—and was thinking about savoring her giant sandwich in the reading nook before unlocking the shop's front door when she tapped her brakes and the pedal resisted slightly before it went all the way to the floor, useless.

§

The car picked up speed and rolled through the gate, the brush-covered hill on Jenna's right and the severe drop-off into grassy dunes on her left.

Jenna tried to pump the brakes. The pedal wiggled but stayed against the floorboard. The road dropped into a steeper angle and curved to the right. The speedometer swept past forty and rushed toward fifty.

The car swerved across the center line and Jenna tried to crank it back into the right but the tires squawked and she felt the car tilt, just a bit. She took the curve at over fifty, knowing the car was going to roll over the edge and tumble into the dunes below.

She could be down there, hurt and bleeding in the shifting sands, for hours—it was impossible to see the bottom of the gulley from the road unless you stood on the edge and looked straight down.

Hours? Maybe days.

The Knack kept singing.

The curve straightened out and Jenna shot down the road. She had about two hundred yards of asphalt before the road took a severe curve to the left, almost a ninety-degree turn. Jenna saw Belma's van taking the turn at about five miles an hour, her brake lights flaring, taunting.

The drop-off on her left became a gentle slope and then a manicured lawn as she careened into the neighborhood of mansions gathered at the base of Horizon House. One of those houses was straight ahead, looming on the far side of the curve. If Jenna kept going she'd rocket through the front door.

With the straight road, Jenna risked steering with one hand and reached down, yanked the parking brake. It nearly came off in her hand—totally useless.

"Oh, come on!" she yelled, followed by some words she'd only muttered once before while cleaning out her shower drain.

She eased the car to the right shoulder, hoping the gravel and grass would slow her down. If she could get over onto the lawns and roll through a few shrubberies she'd owe some people a landscaping bill, but that was better than coming to a sudden and full stop in the front room of the house below.

In an instant she realized something she'd admired before and despised now—all of these houses had some kind of brick or stone or concrete posts and walls in the front yard. For decoration, security, and status, no doubt, and they all prevented her from escaping the road.

The speedometer crept toward sixty.

The house beyond the curve loomed.

Please, don't let anyone be home...

And there it was, on her left, one of the newer mansions built by a Chicago family. They had a wide driveway between two brick columns, an entrance that opened onto a wide circle drive and Jenna could see the angle coming up like an off-ramp.

She plowed over some lovely flowers and clipped a basket hanging from the left-side column, shot across the circular drive, past the house and garage—with a glimpse of a very surprised man inside—toward a privacy hedge along the back of the yard. The thick, manicured lawn slowed her down a bit, but not much.

The hill up to Horizon House had been terraced for these mansions, and above the hedge Jenna could see the rooflines of the lower tier. She tried to point the car between them, hoped the owners didn't have a playground or dog run set up in the gap, and crashed through the hedge—onto the roof of a large one-story garage.

She rocketed off of that, bounced hard on the concrete and fought the steering wheel to keep from bashing into the houses.

A terrible scraping noise filled the car, drowning out The Knack, and the entire vehicle shuddered. A closed gate made of dull black metal spanned the end of the driveway with tall, thick stone columns at both ends. The columns were attached to shorter, thinner stone walls that were meant to be decorative but looked like highway barriers to Jenna.

She chose the gate.

Maybe it was cheap aluminum, meant to look expensive but wasn't actually very sturdy. Or maybe the gate wasn't designed to take an impact from the inside. Either way, when Jenna's Accord hit, the entire gate popped off and stuck to her front bumper like a massive grille.

She plunged into the street, sparks and more noise screaming from the dragging gate, and slewed to a stop a few inches from another gated driveway.

Jenna blinked in the smoke and sudden silence.

Did that just happen?

She could see a few expensive, black cars in the circular drive beyond the gate (well, two gates, technically), and realized she was in front of Ingrid Gallagher's house.

The sound of an engine slowly crept into her awareness. Jenna turned to the right and saw Belma's van idling toward her, Belma's eyes and mouth a perfect series of "O" shapes through the windshield. The van creaked to a halt and Belma stared.

Jenna stared back, still not sure what had happened or what to do now.

Lawrence popped up from the back of the van and scowled through the windshield, his hair jutting at odd angles. He pulled himself to the dashboard and surveyed the catastrophe in the road, his eyes pinched together.

He leaned toward the van's open passenger window and yelled, "Jenna, quit screwing around."

Then he staggered into the back and disappeared, leaving Jenna and Belma to stare at each other some more.

§

Jenna sat in The Welcome Shoppe's reading nook, on the small couch with her feet tucked under, and sipped tea. She expected her hands to shake and spill some of the hot cinnamon spice, but they didn't. Detective Olson and Garrett watched her from chairs.

"I'll have the techs look at your car," Olson said. "There's quite a bit of damage, so I don't know what they'll be able to find, but we'll try."

Garrett said, "They're gonna find somebody cut her brake cables."

"Right," Olson said, "I'm talking tool marks, maybe figure out what they used to cut them. Then if we can find the tool, hopefully we get some prints."

"Lot of maybes and hopefullys in there," Garrett said.

Olson shrugged.

A few tourists wandered through the aisles trying on Lost Haven boat-shaped sunglasses, picking through the free samples, and completely ignoring the nook. Wendy stood behind the counter and ignored everything *but* the nook, though she was too far away to hear anything.

Jenna asked, "Does Kavanaugh have security cameras on the driveway?"

It seemed like her voice should come out hoarse, tired, but it was fine. *She* was fine, which was a bit odd.

"He does," Olson said, "but they aren't on during the day. 8 PM to 8 AM, motion-activated."

"How did he seem when he found out about my car?"

Olson smiled and shook his head. "He said it was probably the foreign manufacturing. But he was surprised, if that's what you're asking. Genuinely surprised, from what I could tell. And the bodyguard, Cabo? Man, he looked like he wanted to run down the hill and check on you."

Garrett frowned. "He did?"

Jenna had the same thought but kept it to herself and sipped more tea. "What kind of damage did I do?"

"Oh, let's not worry about that right now," Olson said. "Nobody was hurt, which is kind of a miracle."

Garrett said, "Jenna, did the evasive driving I taught you kick in?"

He'd gone down to North Carolina the year before and taken a course for high-speed law enforcement tactics, then come back and shown her what he'd learned. It seemed like a bunch of peeling out and doing donuts in a dirt parking lot.

"Absolutely," she said.

He relaxed a bit.

Olson leaned forward, serious now. "I want to focus on who's running around Lost Haven trying to kill you. And why. Now, until I see evidence to the contrary, I'm going to assume this is the same person who killed Ingrid Gallagher. Sound fair to you?"

Jenna nodded.

Olson said, "Jenna, do you know something you haven't told us? Something the killer doesn't want you to share?"

"No," Jenna said. Then: "Well, if I do, I have no idea what it is."

Olson made a quick note. "Okay, so if you don't know anything, would the killer come after you because you're *trying* to know something?"

"What do you mean?"

"Are you snooping around, asking questions, trying to figure out who killed Ingrid?"

Jenna blinked. "Is that bad?"

"Jenna!" Garrett said. "Of course it's bad, it nearly got you splattered all over some rich jerk's driveway."

"And it's interfering with an ongoing investigation," Olson said, "which I could arrest you for."

"I'm just trying to find out who killed our friend," Jenna said.

And prove Kavanaugh did it (if he did).

And keep me and my friends from getting framed.

And record the facts for the town's historical records.

And save Main Street.

No big deal.

"I can appreciate that," Olson said. "But that's my job. I carry a badge and a large gun—probably bigger than it needs to be—and they let me do a lot of things you can't do. Shouldn't do. Most of all, they protect me if somebody decides this investigation should end immediately. For example, oh, I don't know. You may have noticed nobody cut *my* brake cables."

"Or mine," Garrett said.

Jenna nodded again, thinking that might be because Olson had incentive to not find the killer.

For example, oh, I don't know, a cushy job as head of security at the Lost Haven Resort.

And Garrett…well, she felt bad for thinking it, but nobody expected him to crack the case. He was great at making sure people didn't roll through town with a loud radio, but this was beyond his abilities. Maybe if it came down to a car chase…

Olson said, "So if you are poking around, you need to stop. Hopefully we can take something good out of this busted brakes thing and keep you safer."

"And find the killer," Jenna said.

"Hm?"

"From whatever you find on my car, the tool marks, maybe some fingerprints."

"Oh, right," Olson said. "Yeah, that goes without saying."

Jenna thought, *Does it?*

§

Jenna stood in the Welcome Shoppe's doorway with her arms crossed and watched Olson and Garrett get into their cars.

Garrett paused and looked at her over the roof of his. "Be careful, Jenna. If you need anything, or if you think you're in danger, call me."

She pulled a hand out and gave him a small wave.

The two cars rolled away.

Wendy sidled toward the door. "Everything okay?"

"Just fine," Jenna said. "Thanks for taking care of the shop this morning."

She glanced at the clock: nearly three.

"And this afternoon, wow, sorry about that. I'm sure you have stuff you'd rather be doing on a summer day like this."

Wendy shrugged and held up her phone, which she was texting on while talking. "Me and my friends are all going nuts about Ms. Gallagher. And now your car? It's so crazy..."

"Completely," Jenna said, ignoring the bait.

Wendy wanted gossip, but if the killer was going after anyone who might know something—whatever that *something* was—Jenna wasn't about to put Wendy on that list.

"I got it from here, girlie. Thanks again. I'll clock you out at three, and take some of the samples to your friends."

Wendy's eyes got big. "Those macaroons…"

She skimmed past the counter, slid a medium-sized bag out and started dropping Lawrence's macaroons into it. They were probably a day old, dropped off by one of the assistant bakers before the shops opened. Jenna made plans to test the quality before they were all gone.

"Text me if you need any help," Wendy said around a mouthful. She crossed a quiet Main Street and headed into Lilac Park, probably on her way to the beach.

Jenna was a bit jealous of the carefree day Wendy had in front of her. She didn't have to worry about Kavanaugh, figuring out which one of her friends might be a killer, or keeping Main Street from turning into a monstrosity.

Or someone trying to murder her for the second time in one day.

Shoot, or getting arrested by Olson for trying to figure out who was behind all of it.

Man, Wendy had it easy.

Jenna stood in the doorway, watching Main Street

and realizing: She wouldn't trade places with her for anything.

§

J enna was in the back area refilling the cucumber mint ice water she kept near the free samples when the shop's door chime sounded. She came out to find Bart and Sherri standing by the counter, looking around.

"Hey guys."

Toenails skittered on the wood floor and Mr. Wolfie tore around the end of the aisle, rushed toward her and slid to a stop, sitting perfectly between her feet. Jenna looked down and smiled at his panting doggy face, then knelt and scratched his tiny furry ears.

"Jenna, oh my goodness," Sherri said. "We heard about your car, are you okay?"

"I'm fine, which is still kind of a surprise. Every time I think about it…"

"Oh, don't do that," Sherri said. "Whenever I get upset about something, Bart tells me to stop thinking about it. And you know what? It works."

"Meditation," Bart said.

Jenna nodded, as if any of it made sense. Bart checked his phone and Sherri nodded and smiled.

She and Jenna stared at each other until Sherri nudged Bart and tipped her head toward Jenna.

"Ah, right," Bart said. "So, we heard about your car, and thought it would be nice to offer you one from the garage. You know, while yours gets fixed. Or totaled, whatever they decide to do."

"Well, that's awful nice of you," Jenna said.

Bart grunted and went back to his phone.

Sherri beamed. "I know, right? Actually, it was Harry's idea."

That made even less sense than Bart's meditation, so Jenna said, "Harry, as in Harrison Kavanaugh?"

"He's such a sweetie," Sherri said. "Though it might have been Jay who suggested it first, let me think...Mr. Wolfie, I need to think." The tiny dog wiggled across the floor and Sherri scooped him up, then got into her thinking stance, staring out the front windows and idly scratching Mr. Wolfie's head. His tongue poked out the side of his mouth.

Jay, Jenna thought.

Jay Cabo, the bodyguard?

She thought about Garrett's thundercloud face when Olson mentioned Cabo wanting to rush out to make sure she was okay after the accident. All of which was ridiculous—Garrett's jealousy and Cabo's concern. Why would he care about her?

Bart looked up from his phone. "Anyway, we drove the car down. It's a junker, good for getting to the store and back but that's about it."

Jenna went to the front windows and looked out. Bart's convertible BMW was there, and Jenna scanned the other vehicles for a beat-up rust bucket. There was an Audi, a Jeep Wrangler with oversized tires, a Volkswagen bug, and a Prius, which she was pretty sure belonged to one of Wilford's assistants and shouldn't be taking up a Main Street parking spot.

"Did you park in the alley?"

Bart snorted. "Probably should have, save you some embarrassment. But no, it's right there. The Jeep."

Jenna blinked. The Jeep was a new model, not more than two or three years old, shiny black with mean-looking knobby tires and a chrome brush guard. A bank of round lights stood at attention along the roll bar above the windshield.

"Junker?" Jenna said.

"I used to tear up the dunes with it," Bart said. "It was fun, for about a week. Air conditioning sucks though. But Cabo had a good point—if somebody tries to cut your brakes again, just steer this baby into the wilderness and crank up the radio. Only terrestrial and Bluetooth though, no satellite. Like I said: junker."

Jenna was still trying to take it all in. "Cabo said that?"

Bart frowned. "About the radio? No, I said that. Just now."

"I heard him," Sherri said.

Jenna shook her head. "Never mind. Look, this is really nice of you all, but I can't accept it."

"Hey," Bart said, "it's a piece of crap, I know, but it's still a step up from your piece of crap, even before you took it off-roading and through a wall. Can you drive a stick?"

"Yes," Jenna said, "but no, Bart, it's too *nice*. I'd be nervous about scratching it or getting it dirty or dropping a French fry between the seats. It's just too…nice."

Bart seemed confused. "Look, I get you're probably in shock, so you're not supposed to make sense. Here are the keys."

He lobbed them in a short arc and Jenna had to catch them to avoid being struck in the chest. There were two keys, the ignition and a smaller one that she assumed went to a built-in storage box or the glove compartment.

Wait, did Jeeps even have glove compartments? Wasn't it a requirement to have rough, calloused hands that smelled like horses and surf wax before you could own one? If so, how did Bart get his?

The keys were on a small silver chain looped through an oblong piece of bright blue foam, a tiny floatation device should the keys fall overboard during a drunken yacht party.

Did she have to go to drunken yacht parties now? This was getting out of hand.

A group of three older women pushed through the

door and stood gazing at the wind chimes hanging from the ceiling before the gravity of free samples pulled them further into the store.

Bart said, "Babe, you ready?"

Sherri walked over and gripped his arm with her free hand. "You're still coming with me, right?"

"Yes, jeez, let go."

Sherri turned to Jenna. "I don't want to be in my store alone."

"Smart," Jenna said. "Whoever killed Ingrid— and tried to kill me—is still out there somewhere."

Sherri's mouth hung open for a moment. "Oh, right, the murderer. I was talking about Ingrid's ghost being right next door." She shivered. "I have a few of the girls working in the store right now, and if I walk in and they all have white hair, I'll tell you what: I'm moving to Florida."

"We're not moving to Florida," Bart said.

"Maybe you're not. I am."

He sighed. "Okay. Let's go."

Sherri touched Jenna's hand on her way out. "Oh, I have a professional question. One business owner to another."

Jenna thought: *If she asks me about exorcists...*

Sherri said, "Do you think it would be rude to move some of my beachwear display into the café windows?"

Jenna wasn't sure she'd heard that right. "The Sanctuary Café? Ingrid's café?"

"Not anymore," Bart said to his phone.

"Sherri, no," Jenna said. "I mean, yes, it would be incredibly rude. Offensive, even. And it's an active crime scene. You can't even go in there, let alone move stuff around and drag your mannequins in."

"I don't see how bikinis can be offensive," Sherri said. "Unless, you know. You don't shave. And I wouldn't mess anything up. Heck, I'd even sweep some of that sand out. Have you peeked in the windows? It's getting bad."

"Sherri, just...no. For too many reasons, you can't do that."

Sherri's bottom lip popped out. Then it started to tremble.

"What's that?" Jenna said. "What's happening? Are you pouting?"

Bart looked up from his phone and assessed the situation. "Ah, man."

"I just want a nice big display," Sherri said. "It's for the *shoppers*, not me."

"I know babe," Bart said. To Jenna: "Nice going."

"Are you serious right now?" Jenna said.

Bart steered Sherri toward the door. "Come on. We'll grab some dinner at the Marina Grill. The waiters will flirt with you, the waitresses will flirt with me. It'll be great."

Sherri sniffed—actually *sniffed*—and glanced over her shoulder at Jenna. "I'll ask Harry about the display. He understands business."

Jenna thought: *Maybe dying in a car wreck was the easy way out.*

§

For the rest of the afternoon Jenna helped customers and chatted about where they should go for dinner, the best places to watch the sunset, why the macaroons were all gone.

Every now and then she gazed through the front windows at the Jeep to make sure it was still there, still real. Once, when no one was in the Shoppe and the sidewalk was empty, she ran out and touched one of the knobby tires, ran a hand along the water-resistant upholstery, and tried the horn. It was loud, bordering on obnoxious, and she ran back into the Shoppe before anyone saw her, giggling the whole time.

§

All the while, her mind worked through the events from the night before—had it really only been last night when she'd found Ingrid's body? So much had happened since then.

She kept an eye on everyone who came in, scanning for suspicious strangers, or worse, suspicious friends. No one tried to lure her into the back alley or walked in wearing a thick trench coat to conceal a shotgun, pitchfork, or other lethal tool.

Belma stopped by to check her samples. Her arms were covered in flour and the front of her mint chocolate hair was matted to her forehead with sweat. The rest had flecks of butter in it.

"Still alive, huh?" she said.

"Yep," Jenna said. "You?"

"Nope. I'm a zombie." She dumped a few milk chocolate peanut butter cups into a nearly-empty bin and frowned at the coconut flakes mocking her from the bottom of Lawrence's macaroon basket. On her way out she stopped in front of the counter. "When your car was totally out of control, did your life pass before your eyes?"

Jenna thought about it. "No. I was too busy swearing and steering."

"Huh. I wonder if it still counts as a near-death experience."

Jenna was taken aback. "Near-death? I haven't thought about it that way."

"Well, you *did* nearly die, right?"

"I suppose so. I've just been focused on, mm, other things."

"Like what?" Belma said.

If Jenna told Belma she was trying to find Ingrid's killer and save Main Street, it would be all over town within ten minutes. Not the best way to keep it a secret from Detective Olson.

She said, "Oh, you know. Everything."

Belma nodded. "Well, everything doesn't really matter if you're a hot wet stain on your dashboard, does it?"

Jenna winced. "Jeez, Belma."

"I'm just saying. Garrett and that sweet hunk of detective Olson stopped by and asked me about your car, if I'd seen anyone messing with it. I didn't. They also said whoever tried to squish you into a sardine can is probably the same person who killed Ingrid."

"They told me the same thing," Jenna said.

Belma kept going. "So I says to them, 'Why would someone try to kill sweet little Jenna?' They don't know, or won't say. So I figure this crazy person is trying to kill all of us, wipe out the Main Street shop owners. And I ask myself, who would want to do that?"

Kavanaugh, Jenna thought.

"Lawrence," Belma said.

Jenna blinked. "Huh?"

"I told you about his bakery, and sure enough, it's right there on that stupid model in Kavanaugh's den. Lawrence wants that resort built, like right *now*."

"Belma," Jenna said, then stopped. If she spilled about Lawrence's alibi for Ingrid's murder—that he was actually at Kavanaugh's meeting at the time—it would only confirm what Belma suspected. And it would tip her off that Jenna was assembling facts, putting the story together.

"Belma, what?" Belma said.

"I don't think Lawrence has it in him to be a killer."

"Have you ever tried to sneak a peek at his cherry turnover recipe?"

"No…"

"He has the metal box wired into the electrical system. Shock you right off your feet. No joke."

Jenna didn't want to get into how Belma might know that. "Still, cutting my brake cables? I just don't see Lawrence doing something like that. And he was two drinks in before he could have slipped away to do it—by that point he couldn't even play pool right."

Belma considered that for a moment. "I will say this: When you came crashing through the gate in front of us, and he quit snoring long enough to see what was going on, he was genuinely surprised. And peeved, because you woke him up."

"Well," Jenna said, "I'm sorry?"

"So he's either a really good actor, or he was so drunk he forgot he tampered with your car."

"Or he didn't do it," Jenna said.

That didn't seem to fit into Belma's reality. Her brow furrowed and she gnawed at a thumbnail as she drifted toward the front door, mulling this new scenario in which Lawrence wasn't a cold-blooded killer.

Jenna said, "Belma?"

Belma stopped and turned.

"Were *you* surprised to see me come crashing through the gate?"

Belma smiled. "Sweetie child, if I knew the first thing about cars, do you think my van would be a pile of rolling crap? I couldn't tell a brake cable from a tire iron."

Jenna smiled back, relieved. "The look on your face when you slammed on the brakes—now *that* would have been great acting. And I just thought of something else. If you cut my brakes, you probably would have left after me. You know, with me almost smashing into your van and all."

Belma looked at the ceiling, playing it through. "You're right. I hope I would have been that smart, anyway, but I hadn't thought about it. Huh. Guess I'm not ready for murdering just yet."

She opened the door and got halfway out.

Jenna said, "Hey, what are you doing tonight?"

"Tonight? Nothing. Why, you need a ride somewhere? I don't want you borrowing my van…"

"No," Jenna said, "I think we should stay here, at the shops. Or hang out together somewhere. If someone is trying to wipe out Main Street, it'll be harder if we aren't solo, easy targets. And to be honest, I was freaked out last night at home, alone, and that was *before* someone actually tried to kill me."

Belma nodded. "Good thinking. I'll come back

down here after I close. We'll figure out what to do then."

Jenna felt something loosen in her chest, a tightness she hadn't realized was there. "Perfect. I'll tell the rest."

Belma was skeptical. "Even Lawrence?"

"Belma, if he is the killer—or if anybody else on Main Street is—what are they going to do? Massacre all of us and be the last one standing?"

She didn't seem convinced. "If anybody whips out a chainsaw, I'm not gonna try to save you. I'm out the nearest window."

"I understand."

Belma nodded and left.

§

Jenna checked the time: 7:48.

Close enough to eight to start shutting things down. She got the broom and hit the front corners first, whisking the ever-present sand out of the nooks and crannies toward the back of the shop.

Sticking together was a good idea.

Not just for safety, which probably should have been her primary motivation.

But it wasn't.

As Jenna swept, she kept a running list of the questions she wanted to ask the other Main Street owners. Wilford wasn't a suspect any longer, and Lawrence was innocent unless he was working with Kavanaugh to clear the way for the resort.

That left Belma and Sherri. And Bart, she supposed, though he wasn't a shop owner.

Even if none of them had killed Ingrid, they still might know something. And that included Wilford and Lawrence.

Jenna shook her head and kept sweeping. She needed to start writing this down so she could keep it all straight. The thought of compiling all the evidence and facts into a historical record for the town calmed her a bit—the sound of a pen rolling across paper, the gentle vibrations from the swoops and lines. Adding punctuation was like a tiny martial art.

The nook beckoned. And it would be good to jot some quick notes to make sure she didn't forget any of the details—heck, it might even help her figure out what she *didn't* know, which was probably a book all by itself.

One thing she did know: She would find the killer.

Hopefully before they had another chance to murder her.

CHAPTER SEVEN

Jenna finished closing the shop by eight fifteen. The sun was dropping toward the top of the marina, which reminded her of how The Lost Haven Resort would block every sunset until the end of time, which made her mutter some comparisons between Kavanaugh and various horse rear-ends.

She locked the front door behind her and waved to a few families walking through Lilac Park, then strolled past Winkle's Fine Chocolates & Sweets. Belma was behind the counter, ringing up what looked to be the last sale of the night for a teenage couple holding hands.

Jenna stuck her head in. "See you next door in a few?"

"Gotta clean up, then I'll be over. Don't get killed."

The teenagers shared a wide-eyed look.

"Ha ha," Jenna said, trying to play it off as a joke.

Belma nodded seriously at the couple and drew a finger across her throat. So much for that.

Jenna tried Wilford's art gallery, but the door

was locked. The spotlights in the front windows were on along with some soft security lighting inside the space. She rapped a few times on the glass and waited, heard no one walking across the wooden floor or calling to wait just a moment.

Ingrid's body thudded into her mind. The scenario was nearly identical, and Jenna peered through the glass door for any corpses waiting to be discovered. There was a long, dark lump halfway across the gallery floor with a white blob at one end that could be Wilford's face.

Jenna wasn't carrying the jangling anchor of all the other shop keys and briefly considered going back to get them. She certainly didn't want to find another body, especially Wilford's, but if he was in there on the floor, if he needed help...

If he or someone else was setting a trap, waiting to bash your head in...

She slipped her phone out and hit the flashlight icon, took a slow breath, and pressed the phone against the glass so the beam would cut into the gallery.

The dark lump was a collection of rubber tire fragments with a white headlight at one end.

Art, apparently.

She let the breath out and went back to Winkle's, where the now-pale teenagers held massive chocolate cupcakes with mousse frosting. The treats were completely forgotten as the stunned kids listened to Belma.

"...detective said her head was almost completely gone. Brains everywhere. Oh, and this one here, she nearly drove through town with her car on fire, setting the whole town ablaze. We could have all burned to death."

The couple turned to Jenna with their mouths open.

"None of that is true," Jenna said.

A sharp crack filled the shop as Belma swatted at a fly with a damp towel, making the kids jump. She sneered at the fat black insect as it flew away, untouched.

"Yeah, this killer means business."

Jenna said, "Belma, have you seen Wilford?"

"Not for a while. You think he's dead?"

Maybe, Jenna thought. But the teenagers seemed on the verge of tears, so she said, "What? No, I wanted to tell him to come over to the Welcome Shoppe."

"I'll tell him if I see him. Unless, you know..." Belma waited for the teenagers to look at her. "His head is gone."

§

Lawrence was leaning in the doorway of his bakery eating a massive croissant and scowling at the sun as it dipped toward the lake. A large flake of the croissant was stuck to his cheek, and he either didn't know or didn't care.

His eyes slid to Jenna. "I don't think I've ever been this hungover this late in the day."

Jenna suppressed a smile. "Hey, look on the bright side—it's almost bedtime. You can sleep it off and wake up fresh as a daisy."

"Ug, daisies. Don't make me puke again." He mashed another bite of the croissant into his face, showering the doorway with thin, tan snowflakes.

"Belma's going to come hang out at the Shoppe when she's done closing. You should too. We need to look out for each other until this is over."

"You mean keep an eye on each other?"

Jenna frowned. "That's the same thing I said."

"Mm, slight difference." He reached inside the bakery and came back with a bowl of melted butter and chocolate, dipped the croissant in it and took another bite. "Is this a sleepover? Should I bring my footie jammies?"

"You can stay as long as you like. Especially if you bring some of those croissants."

Lawrence shook his head, lamenting. "Jenna, I think this town is finally getting to you. Ulterior motives, manipulation, false friendships to get what you want." He wiped a non-existent tear from his eye. "I'm so proud."

"I'll see you there."

"Fine. I'll bring milk too—these puppies could soak up Belma's bathwater."

Jenna took a moment to banish that image from her mind for all of time. "Have you seen Wilford?"

"He was puttering around this afternoon, loading some stuff into his car. Not since then, though."

"What stuff?"

Lawrence shrugged. "Art, I assume. It was all bound up in bubble wrap and tape."

"You didn't offer to help him?"

"As a matter of fact I did, Miss Hasty Judgement. He said he was just fine, which was even more fine with me. If I have to bend over and pick up anything heavier than my face, I'll pass out."

Jenna crossed her arms and looked at the darkened gallery for a moment. "These things he was moving—they were heavy?"

"Jenna, Wilford makes a *pencil* look heavy. Who knows?"

She thought about that, and the fact that Wilford didn't have a cell phone. She couldn't call or text him to make sure he was okay, or find out what the heck he was up to. This was *not* a good time to be sneaking around doing suspicious things, if that's what he was doing.

"If you see him," she said, "tell him to come down to the Shoppe. His chair is waiting for him."

Lawrence grinned, and it seemed to make him turn a light shade of green. "You should make a

Bat-signal in the shape of a recliner. He'd come running from anywhere in town." He contemplated the last half of the croissant. "I need to lay down."

"You can have the whole couch to yourself," Jenna said. She was stepping away from his doorway and caught a glimpse of the display in Sherri's Beach Life Fashion Boutique. "What the…"

Lawrence pried himself off the doorframe and joined her. "What?"

"You've got to be kidding me."

"Jenna, tell me what you're seeing. Because I'm starting to think I'm going blind here." Lawrence blinked at the setting sun. "Was I *that* drunk?"

"The mannequins!"

Lawrence stared at the display windows. "Oh no…I can't see any mannequins…"

"That's the point. Sherri asked me if I thought it would be rude to expand her display into the café, and I told her yes, of course it was rude, obviously. But look!"

The edgy beach scene in the front windows was partially dismantled. The bronze mannequins were gone, along with their day-glo suits and flashing cell phones. Maybe Sherri was just reworking her own space, but after their earlier conversation, Jenna feared for the worst.

She tried the front door and found it locked, stepped next door and peered in the café windows. No mannequins, at least not so far. Sherri was probably trying to find a key, or convince Detective Olson her gaudy wares wouldn't contaminate the crime scene.

"Uh oh," Lawrence said. "I've seen that look once or twice. Sherri's gonna get it, isn't she?"

Jenna stared at the empty boutique windows and chewed down some choice words.

Lawrence said, "Well I can't miss that. I'll be over as soon as I can, and if you see her before then, Jenna? Please?"

Jenna glanced at him. "What?"

"Wait until I get there to give it to her."

§

Jenna steamed back down the sidewalk toward The Welcome Shoppe.

She had Detective Olson's card.

She could call him and warn him not to let any of the Kavanaughs get inside the café, a thought that led her to wonder if Harrison Kavanaugh was manipulating poor Sherri into contaminating the crime scene for him.

Maybe there was something in the café the investigators hadn't found yet, and Kavanaugh wanted it destroyed.

But what could Jenna do about it?

Who could she trust?

It was frustrating, bordering on infuriating.

She needed an outlet, something to unleash her wrath upon before an innocent bystander caught the full brunt.

The Jeep...

§

Jenna slapped a neon pink Post-It note on the front door of the Shoppe with a note to Belma and Lawrence: BACK SOON.

She had the foam key fob out and her hand on the Jeep's door handle, her head filling with scenes of sand dune rooster tails and scattering gulls as she tore across the beach—maybe a few June sunbathers as well, if their music was too loud—when a flash of blue caught her eye.

She glanced to her right, where Second Street crossed Main, and there it was.

Bart's convertible BMW.

And inside, Bart and Sherri.

Jenna forgot the Jeep.

"Hey!"

Bart turned and lifted a hand, nodded behind his Aviator sunglasses. Sherri was wearing a wide-brimmed sunhat and even bigger sunglasses, and she didn't even turn her head to acknowledge Jenna. Still pouting—unbelievable.

Their outfits were classic Lost Haven Marina

deck wear, and to Jenna's irritated eye, it looked like Sherri was playing up the mourning friend to garner sympathy for Ingrid's death and the trauma she'd experienced at Jenna's hands.

Ridiculous.

Bart did a rolling stop into the intersection, going straight across Main toward the southern edge of Lilac Park.

"Hey," Jenna yelled again. She walked toward the car, angling to catch it before it scooted away.

Bart cranked the stereo up and accelerated. Sherri never even glanced over, though Jenna caught a self-satisfied grin below the sunglasses. She watched the car until it disappeared behind a screen of fading lilacs, headed toward the marina.

Jenna considered following them and making a scene on the deck, but what would that accomplish? Probably exactly what Sherri wanted: Jenna would look like a big meanie right after Sherri's dear, dear friend Ingrid was murdered.

Then the outpouring of condolences, and of *course* she could move her display into the café windows, who would ever be so cruel to suggest otherwise?

Well, screw that.

She went back to the Jeep, but the visions of hooting and laughing across the beach had turned sour. Now she imagined herself screaming as the Jeep burst into flames and plummeted off a sheer cliff (she didn't know of any true cliffs in Lost Haven, but still) while

Kavanaugh watched from Horizon House, a grim smile on his face.

Jenna took a step back from the Jeep, expecting it to explode at any moment.

What had she been thinking?

The man she suspects of murdering Ingrid gives her a vehicle out of the blue, and she happily jumps in to go for a joy ride, all by herself?

And even if it wasn't a deathtrap (which it probably was), she didn't want to have anything to do with the Kavanaughs or Sherri for the rest of the night. They could all go sit at the Marina Grill and drink their fancy drinks and do whatever rich people did when they were exhausted from stomping on the rest of the world all day.

She unlocked the front door of the Shoppe, ripped the note off the glass, and slammed the door behind her.

§

Jenna was in the reading nook with a cup of creamy coffee and a legal pad and pen, outlining what she knew so far about Ingrid's death.

It was woefully brief.

She also had a series of columns with letters above them: B, B, K, L, S, W. The letters stood for the names of her suspects, in alphabetical order, and though it might stand up against a cursory glance from a toddler, she knew her secret code wouldn't fool anyone. She'd have to hide the pad somewhere before anyone arrived for the evening.

Below each letter was a list of alibis, hard evidence, solid suspicions, and personal notes about each suspect. At first Jenna resisted venting her anger into the columns for Bart, Kavanaugh, and Sherri, but stream-of-consciousness writing sometimes uncovered gems in her personal writing, so she cut loose.

When she came out of the spell and looked up, the streetlights were on and she had a cramped jumble of words stacked below Kavanaugh and about half as much beneath Bart and Sherri—although those two columns had phrases like "Stupid eyebrows" and "Walks too loudly," which probably didn't have anything to do with Ingrid's murder.

The columns for Belma, Lawrence and Wilford were strictly alibis and possible motives, except for "grumpy drunk" beneath Lawrence's name.

Taking it all in, she realized she couldn't just hide the sheet of paper—she needed to *burn* it lest anyone find it and read what she'd written about them. The top sheet and the next few, in case somebody got clever and tried that pencil rub trick or some other voodoo.

Then a thought that made her feel a bit silly: *Who on earth would give a rip about what you wrote down?*

Followed by: *Oh, I don't know, maybe the person who tried to kill me today?*

Ah, right. Carry on with the paranoia.

Jenna reviewed the notes for Lawrence and Wilford. Wilford's alibi at the time of Ingrid's death was weak—napping—but his fragile physical state was an alibi all by itself. There was no way he could have found the strength to bash Ingrid over the head hard enough to crack her skull...yet Lawrence had seen him loading unidentified, and possibly heavy, objects into his car that afternoon.

As for Lawrence, he had a solid alibi for the murder, but his motives were still in question.

The pen was poised above the sheet, and all Jenna wanted to do was start crossing off her friends so she could stop thinking of them as murder suspects.

But so far, no one was totally in the clear.

She sighed and sipped her forgotten, lukewarm coffee, then held the coffee in her cheeks, listening as someone tried to sneak in through the Shoppe's back door.

§

The first noises were quiet, hesitant, but the sound carried through the back room and to the silent nook.

A sliding and clicking.

Someone was turning the knob back and forth to see if it was locked.

Of course it was locked. And deadbolted twice, with a wide-angle peephole that let her check both sides of the door before she opened it. Jenna had purchased all of it the day she became owner of The Welcome Shoppe, helped install everything with Claude from the hardware store, and even had the setup approved by Garrett at one point.

Lost Haven didn't have much crime, but she saw no sense in tempting anyone with a flimsy door accessible by the back alley.

She heard the knob turn again, then nothing.

Was nothing good?

Or terrible?

Jenna eased the coffee mug, pad and pen onto the table and stood up. Her limited view of the front windows showed an empty street and sidewalk. Across Main Street, Lilac Park was mostly dark with dots of pathway lights winking through the foliage.

She checked the clock: 9:35.

Where the heck were Belma and Lawrence? It took time to close their shops and prep for the next morning, but weren't they usually done by now? If that was one of them at the back door, wouldn't they knock?

The knob turned again, a loud ratcheting *clack-clack*.

Now whoever was in the alley wasn't trying to

sneak in anymore—they were trying to break in. Jenna took a slow step toward the closed door to the back room, listening, reaching...

She stretched her hand toward the door and plucked her phone off the bookshelf next to it.

She bypassed 911 and called Garrett's cell phone.

He answered on the second ring. "Jenna?"

She tried to talk and realized she still had a mouthful of coffee. She worked it down, rolled her eyes and kept her voice low: "Somebody's trying to come through the alley door of the Shoppe."

"Right now?"

"Right now. They're testing the locks."

"Okay," Garrett said. "I'm across the bridge by the boat landing, I'll be there in two minutes."

Jenna could hear his patrol car's engine open up through the phone. Then his siren kicked on, and a moment later she could hear it coming from somewhere to the south of town.

"I guess I'll wait here," Jenna whispered.

"Jenna, don't you open that back door. Promise me."

"Why would I do that?"

"Just don't. Sit on the couch and stay on the phone with me."

"Okay."

Garrett paused. "Are you moving? You sound like you're moving."

"No," Jenna whispered as she opened the door to the back room and stepped through.

The door to the alley was at the other end of the room. She slipped her shoes off and padded between the storage shelves, past the small kitchen counter and sink, and stood off to the side of the door.

Garrett said, "Jenna, talk to me."

"Hold on," she whispered.

"Aw, man…" The car's engine climbed again.

The peephole was right there.

Jenna leaned past the knob and eased her eye toward the dark lens. Just a quick look.

BOOM BOOM BOOM

The door shook in its frame as someone pounded on the other side.

Jenna leaped back in case the locks or hinges gave way.

Through the phone, Garrett's voice said, "What was that? Was that knocking?"

Maybe with a battering ram, Jenna thought. She didn't even want to whisper into the phone in case whoever was outside caught a hint of it and tried even harder to get in.

BOOM BOOM BOOM BOOM

Jenna flinched again from the noise and had a vision of her door collapsing, tearing off the frame and getting trampled as the crazed murderer swarmed in. That was a bit unsettling, certainly, but it also made her mad. First her car gets totaled, now her door?

Well, screw that.

BOOM BOOM BOOM

She stepped up to the peephole and looked through. The lens brushed against her eyelashes every time the door shook from the pounding, and she had to blink, which made it hard to be sure she was seeing things correctly.

The face on the other side of the peephole was familiar, and bloody, and staring right back at her.

§

66What do you want?" Jenna said.

The face on the other side of the peephole pressed closer. "I need help. I need to talk to you."

Garrett's voice from the phone: "Who said that? Jenna, go back to the couch! I'm almost there..."

"Why me?" Jenna said to the door.

"You're the only person I can trust. Something terrible has happened."

Jenna squinted at the peephole. The tone of voice, the way his face had sagged with relief when she first spoke.

"Garrett's on his way here," Jenna said.

The eyes on the other side grew wide. "I can't trust him. Please."

Garrett yelled, "Jenna, what's going on?"

Jenna considered the phone for a moment, then told the door, "Hold on."

She stepped away and put the phone on the counter—still connected to a hollering Garrett—and slid the nearly full pot of fresh coffee out of the machine.

She held that in her left hand and turned the deadbolts with her right, then backed away from the door.

"Come in."

The knob turned and Jay Cabo stood in the doorway. His suit was wrinkled and splashed with fresh blood. The blood was smeared on his hands and specked across his face. His eyes were frightened.

"Mr. Kavanaugh is dead," he said.

§

Jenna froze. She wasn't sure she'd heard him right.

"Harrison Kavanaugh is dead?"

Cabo nodded.

Jenna's grip on the coffee pot tightened. "Did you kill him?"

"No. But I don't think anyone will believe me. I'm being set up."

"Why should I believe you? You could be here to kill me too."

Cabo's hands opened and he shook his head, unsure what to say.

"Jenna, did you open that door? Tell me you did not open that door!"

They both looked at the phone.

"Garrett?" Cabo said.

Jenna nodded.

"May I speak to him?"

"Sure," Jenna said, a tiny corner of her brain whispering, *This ought to be good*.

Cabo picked the phone up. "Sheriff Bowers?"

Jenna heard Garrett yell something but couldn't tell what it was.

Cabo winced away from the phone, then said. "This is Jay Cabo. I'm at The Welcome Shoppe with Jenna Hooper. I mean her no harm, and I didn't kill Harrison Kavanaugh."

The phone was silent except for the engine and siren, which also grew louder in the alley outside the doorway. There was a slight delay on the phone speaker, so the effect wasn't quite stereo.

Cabo handed the phone back to Jenna. "I think I need to sit down."

Jenna looked him over. She put the phone to her ear and told Garrett, "We're fine. I'll see you here in a few."

She hung up on whatever he said, stepped back and tilted her head toward the front of the Shoppe.

As Cabo moved closer she lifted the coffee pot a bit, ready to hurl it if need be.

Cabo headed for the doorway. He glanced at the steaming pot and seemed to notice it for the first time.

"Oh, no thanks. I don't drink coffee."

§

C abo fell into the recliner and closed his eyes, then jerked halfway back up and stared at the blood on his suit, checking to see if he'd gotten any on the furniture.

"Oh man, I'm so sorry. Your chair..."

"Don't worry about it," Jenna said. "I bought upholstery I can hose off. Some tourists...never mind."

Cabo stood up and let his suit coat drop down his arms. He folded the jacket and held it in his lap so it wouldn't touch anything. The front of his white shirt and tie were tacky with blood, and Jenna tried to focus on that instead of the way his muscles made the fabric jump.

Cabo pulled his tie loose and popped the top button on his collar, which had been tight enough on his neck to leave a red line on the skin.

The siren pushed through the back room and began to fill the front.

Jenna sat on the couch, her knee almost touching his. She still had the coffeepot and found a magazine to set it on. "Tell me about Kavanaugh. No, wait. You said you can't trust Garrett. He'll be here in about twenty seconds—tell me why."

"Jenna, I can't trust anybody here. I'm a complete stranger, and soon after I get to town Ms. Gallagher gets murdered. Now Mr. Kavanaugh. I see people whispering, eyeballing me, and Detective Olson and Officer Bowers had these private meetings with Mr. Kavanaugh. Who knows what they talked about? If the cops are in on these murders, I'm an easy guy to pin them on."

Jenna tried to imagine Garrett working some elaborate plot of murder and framing. She kept getting stuck, recalling how giddy he'd been when he discovered slip-on shoes with fake laces to wear on the job. And he couldn't even hide cheating on his girlfriend...

She said, "I can tell you this: If Garrett is involved, he doesn't know it."

"That doesn't mean we can trust him," Cabo said.

Jenna nodded. The "we" made her think of what he'd said at Horizon House. What was it? Ah, right: "Go team."

The siren suddenly blared and rubber squealed on concrete as Garrett turned into the back alley. Tires skidded to a halt and the siren died.

"Jenna!" Garrett yelled.

"In here."

He came through the door with his gun drawn, eyes wild. "Hands up! Get on the floor!"

"Who?" Jenna said.

"Everybody!"

"Garrett, stop shouting."

He scanned the nook, then walked past the checkout counter and across the front of the store, checking each aisle and the lock on the front door. Jenna and Cabo waited, an awkward silence between them now that they couldn't speak freely.

"No coffee?" Jenna asked him.

"Nope."

"Does anything sound good?"

"I could use a shower."

Jenna wrinkled her nose. "Sorry. Don't have one here."

Garrett finished his clearance of The Welcome Shoppe and stepped next to the recliner. He holstered his weapon but kept his hand on the butt. "Stop talking about showers. Nobody takes one until I collect some evidence." He pointed at Cabo's shirt. "Whose blood is that?"

"Harrison Kavanaugh's."

"Where is he?"

"On the floor of his library. He's dead."

Jenna put a hand to her mouth. "Oh no. The nice library?"

Cabo nodded, a grim line to his mouth.

Garrett said, "Did you kill him?"

"No," Cabo said. He looked down at the blood on his hands. "I tried to save him."

§

Garrett stepped away to call Detective Olson, then came back in less than a minute and said, "Okay. Everybody up."

"Where are we going?" Jenna said.

"Horizon House. Olson's on his way there now, and you're both coming with me."

Jenna and Cabo shared raised eyebrows.

"Why?" Jenna asked.

Garrett pointed at Cabo, then Jenna: "Because he's a suspect, and you're in danger. Safest thing is for you to stick with me."

Jenna was slightly irked at being bossed around by Garrett, but this would give her a chance to loiter around the crime scene. Besides, Horizon House was the last place the killer would be with Kavanaugh's fresh corpse inside.

"I didn't kill anybody," Cabo said.

Garrett shrugged. "We'll see."

"Am I under arrest?"

Garrett thought about that for a few seconds. He glanced at Jenna, once, and she got the feeling he wasn't just considering the legal aspects of the situation. She got a tiny dose of guilty pleasure at the thought of Garrett Bower being jealous.

"Not yet," he told Cabo. "But you're riding in the back seat."

"I'll drive separately," Jenna said.

Garrett frowned. "Jenna, your car..."

"Bart and Sherri let me borrow a Jeep. Well, they just brought it down the hill. It was someone else's idea." She turned to Cabo. "Was it Mr. Kavanaugh who thought of it, or..."

"Yes," Cabo said.

Jenna thought he was trying not to smile.

Garrett crossed his arms. "Kavanaugh gave you a Jeep? Why?"

"Maybe he felt bad about me almost dying after I left his little party this morning. Maybe it's a death-trap. Either way, this is perfect—I'll drive in front of you, and if the brakes go out or the engine explodes, I'll just roll back into your car instead of crashing through another wall. Or somebody's living room."

Jenna checked with Cabo, who nodded at the logic of it.

Garrett's mouth was slightly open. "That's a terrible idea."

Jenna stood up and twirled the key fob around a finger. "Shall we?"

§

G arrett insisted on being the one to start the Jeep. His cruiser idled in the middle of Main Street with Cabo in the back seat, watching through the passenger side window while Jenna stood with her arms crossed and Garrett gunned the Jeep a few times.

She carried her wallet, phone, and massive ring of keys, in case anyone else she knew was getting murdered and she needed to get inside to help. They would also come in handy as a ring of steel spikes, should any killing be in progress when she arrived. Hers included.

Garrett pressed the brake pedal, turned the radio on and off, cranked the steering wheel a bit, and checked inside the glove compartment. Jenna perked up—so Jeeps did have them—and leaned into the vehicle to see what was inside a Kavanaugh compartment.

A gun?

A stack of cash?

Nope: A user's manual and a pen.

Jenna slumped a bit from the disappointment. She had the exact same thing in her glove box, in addition to a stack of semi-used napkins and some foil ketchup pouches.

"Seems okay, I guess," Garrett said. He turned the headlights on, then the bank of lights along the top, which bathed all of Main Street and the shops in stark white daylight.

"Neat," he said.

He flicked the wipers across the windshield three times, then got out and adjusted his gun belt. "Just take it slow, huh? I'll be right behind you in case something goes wrong." He glanced at his patrol car and cleared his throat. "Is there, uh, anything else I should know about Cabo before I ride up there with him?"

Jenna fought a smile. Someone had just died, and things were very serious. "Like what?"

"Like was he rude to you?"

"Rude?"

"Too forward?"

Jenna couldn't help the smile now. "Forward? Do you mean did he get fresh with me? Right before we took a time machine back to the 1950s?"

Garrett scowled. "Jenna, don't give me a hard time on this. I just need to know if I should put a little fear into him."

Jenna looked through the back window at Cabo. He took up most of the back seat and had to duck his head to keep from putting a bulge in the roof. A significant portion of her wanted to see how it would go if Garrett tried to intimidate Cabo, but that would be selfish.

Maybe even mean.

She tucked it away for later and said, "He's harmless. And he was perfectly polite to me, not that it's any of your business."

"Well, he's still a suspect."

"Are we done here?"

Garrett picked at a non-existent clump of mud on the Jeep's fender. "Yeah, but I'm hoping if we take long enough, they'll have the body covered by the time we get there. Judging by the blood on Cabo's shirt, it's gonna be a messy one. You don't need to see that."

Oh yes I do, Jenna thought.

"I'll be fine, Garrett. Thanks for thinking of me, but that's not your job anymore."

"It isn't?"

Jenna squinted at him. "We broke up. Remember?"

"Well, yeah. But I'm still the sheriff. You know, protect and serve?"

"Hm."

"Hey!"

Jenna and Garrett both turned. Lawrence and Belma stood outside Winkle's Fine Chocolates & Sweets, pinned by the floodlights atop the Jeep.

Belma had a damp towel draped over her face. Lawrence covered his eyes with both hands and yelled, "What is this carnival ride doing here? Are we being abducted by aliens?"

"Sorry," Garrett said. He fiddled with the dashboard until the lights died and Main Street returned to a sane level of illumination.

Lawrence uncovered his eyes, blinked, and nudged Belma. "It's safe."

She pulled the towel off. Lawrence gave a small scream in mock horror, so Belma shoved him into a lamppost.

"Quit messing around!" Lawrence said. They both walked in front of the Jeep, wary of the lights slamming on again.

Belma poked the Jeep. "Whose is this? Garrett, why are you here? Why is that bull stud in the back of your cop car?"

Jenna said, "Guys, have you seen Wilford?"

"Oh no," Lawrence said. "Did the bodyguard kill him?"

"We don't know yet," Garrett said.

"Garrett!" Jenna said. She turned to the others. "Cabo didn't kill anybody. But Harrison Kavanaugh is dead."

Belma's mouth fell open. "Whaaaaaaat?"

Lawrence said, "Dead? What do you mean?"

"Dead," Jenna said. "Someone murdered him. We're going there now."

"Who is 'we'?" Belma said.

"Me, Cabo, and Garrett. Can you two stay here in case Wilford shows up? I'm worried about him."

"Well, if that's what you need me to do," Belma said, the relief baking off her like heat from an open oven.

Lawrence seemed in a daze. "Yeah, sure. What does this mean for the Lost Haven Resort?"

"Don't know yet," Jenna said. "Right now we need

to stop the murders. Hideous casino resorts will have to wait."

"I suppose," Lawrence said.

After an awkward silence, Garrett opened the Jeep door for Jenna. "Let's go, Inspector Hooper."

Jenna got in. The seat was supple, with a bit of bounce and excellent back support. She tossed her stuff on the passenger seat and gripped the steering wheel. It felt like power.

Don't smile, don't smile, she thought.

She kept a straight face and told Garrett, "See you up there."

"I'm still not sold on this." He walked around his cruiser toward the driver's door.

When he was out of earshot, Belma hissed, "Jenna, what the heck are you doing?"

"I'm not sure yet," Jenna whispered. She squeezed the steering wheel again. "But you two better get inside. I have no idea where this thing is going."

CHAPTER EIGHT

The sound of the Jeep's knobby tires on Main Street — every street, really — made Jenna think she was literally chewing up cobbles, concrete, and asphalt as she rolled on. She kept looking back to make sure she wasn't leaving a wake of chunks and dust for Garrett to drive through, and each time Garrett jabbed a finger forward, reminding her to watch the road.

"Serve and Protect," huh?

How about "Irritate and Patronize"?

Put that on the side of your stupid cruiser.

The Jeep wanted to GO. It didn't like puttering along through town while Jenna got used to the clutch and shifter, easing into higher gears and downshifting when the speedometer started to creep up. Whenever she accidentally goosed the gas too much, the Jeep's engine seemed to chuckle with joy. It wanted to show off for her.

She glanced back at the police cruiser again. Garrett was illuminated by the interior dash lights, but

Cabo was just a black shape against the rear window. Garrett jabbed the finger again, then actually talked through the car's loudspeaker:

"Eyes front, Jenna."

He's just trying to keep me safe, Jenna told herself. She squeezed the steering wheel and pulled to see if she could tear it off. Just testing, of course.

It held.

They were the only two vehicles on the short, straight road north of downtown that led to the base of the Horizon House hill. Soon she'd be climbing through the curves and mini mansions, along the same route she'd plummeted down just that morning. She relaxed her grip on the steering wheel and decided she should test a few more things out before that happened.

Safety first, right?

The right side of the road was scrubby grass with patches of dune sand glowing in the moonlight, and ahead a large drift of it had crept halfway into the lane. Lost Haven Public Works would brush it back off the asphalt within a day or two, but for now it beckoned like a puddle on a hot day.

Jenna gunned the engine, swerved to the right and hit the sand at an angle that would take her off the road if she kept going straight. The tires gobbled up the sand and kicked it out to the sides in glorious plumes. When she was halfway off the road she cut the wheel to the left, expecting to fishtail through the sand, slew a bit, then correct and continue on as if nothing had happened. It would be just like driving in February (if you live in Michigan and can't learn to drive on ice and snow, they make you move to Ohio).

But the Jeep didn't want to fishtail. It gripped the sand, asphalt, grass and anything else that happened to fall beneath it like a magnet to a steel plate and shot her back onto the road, where she crossed the center line and hit the sand on the far side. She cranked the wheel to the right, felt and heard the tires squawk on the asphalt as she got back into her lane, then stomped the clutch to let the beast wind down.

"What the heck was that?!"

The loudspeaker wasn't quite as loud this time. Jenna glanced back and saw Garrett had fallen behind, navigating through a cloud of dust and swaths of sand she'd left spread across the road. She gave him a thumbs-up, pointed to her eyes, then the road ahead.

Eyes front, buster.

She wanted to throw a fist in the air and hoot, but they were heading to a murder scene. Celebration was inappropriate, most likely. Not as bad as Sherri's mannequins in the café windows, but still, not cool. She settled for a tiny pat on the dashboard to let the Jeep know she was impressed.

"What should your name be?" she said.

Then caught herself: this baby wasn't hers, it was on loan from the Kavanaughs.

"Well, shoot. My first one-night stand." She patted the dash again. "Much better than I'd expected it to be."

§

The climb up to Horizon House was much different than it had been that morning.

As soon as the grade began to angle up, Jenna forgot about Garrett and his loudspeaker. The mansions, so stunning and luxurious (if a bit gaudy) in daylight seemed to loom a bit more, the curtained windows and walled yards hinting at secrets that must be kept rather than status that must be conveyed.

The curved, climbing road felt narrower, even with the Jeep's high beams knocking the darkness back. Jenna drove along the centerline to keep from hitting the gates and pillars tilting toward her.

She shook her head, chiding herself:

Stop it. So you had a little accident here, what's the big deal?

Well, it wasn't an accident. Someone tried to kill me here.

Hm. That's true.

Someone who might try again.

I see your point. Let's panic.

She didn't panic, but her stomach did tighten when the headlights swept across Ingrid's front gate and the road glittered with a million tiny pieces of glass. These were slivers and pebbles from her car too small for the wrecker's broom to collect. A puddle of clumpy gray sand showed where her poor car's oil had bled out.

The driveway across from Ingrid's was still missing a gate, and someone had put two sawhorses with a ladder across them to serve as temporary security. She made a mental note to send the family an apology letter, or a gift certificate toward a new gate from… the gate store?

Maybe flowers?

She'd have to look up the etiquette.

"Jenna, you okay?"

Garrett's loudspeaker snapped her thoughts. She realized she was stopped in front of the crash site, staring at the scarred asphalt and bits of glass, sparkling like a miniature reflection of the stars above.

She threw another thumbs-up over her shoulder, blinked the nighttime dew out of her eyes, and rolled forward over the glass and oil. The Jeep's tires didn't even notice, which was exactly what she needed.

§

She drove the rest of the way up the hill trying to ignore Garrett's headlights in her rear-view and the tour guide narration running through her head.

This is where Jenna tried the emergency brake, which also failed.

Yeah, yeah.

This is where Jenna thought about driving through shrubbery. See the burning bushes? How lovely.

Shut up.

This is just about where she first noticed her brakes didn't work, when she tried to—

The voice cut off. The gates to Horizon House stood wide open. Security lights from the hill above bathed the area in a harsh white glow, nearly blue, leaving everything outside of that aura behind a curtain of black.

Jenna crept up to the gates. The LCD screen was dark, and if the camera embedded in the post was on, she couldn't tell. This, for some reason, unsettled her more than her own accident site.

A Kavanaugh estate unguarded, open to anyone who wanted to stroll in—or, even more dire, one that needed help from anyone who *could* come—meant there had been a significant change in the order of the world.

Harrison Kavanaugh was dead.

Lost Haven would be reeling.

And who would be next?

Jenna punched the gas.

There was no time to waste.

§

The driveway and parking area were glowing under the same harsh security lighting as the open gates. It gave everything the eerie effect of having no shadow, since the lights came in equal intensity from every direction.

The spot where Jenna parked that morning was blocked off with cones and police tape—a slight reassurance someone actually was looking into her attempted murder—and she let the Jeep rumble to a stop nearby, next to what had to be Detective Olson's sedan. Behind her, Garrett pulled to the base of the stairs and turned on his cruiser's red and blue light bar. Slightly dramatic, but she had to allow this was a dramatic day.

Jenna slipped her phone into her pocket and considered the wallet and splayed ring of keys. She couldn't think of a reason she'd need either, yet, but someone was obviously comfortable skulking around Horizon House, so she didn't want to leave them out in the open. She popped the glove compartment, dumped the wallet and keys in, and tried the small key on the Jeep's ring to lock it.

The key didn't fit. She flipped it over and tried again. Nope.

Classic Bart: So many vehicles he mixed up the keys, and of course couldn't be bothered to double check. Well, if the murderer was savvy enough to figure out a lift-to-open glove compartment handle, she was screwed. Not because of the wallet, so much, unless they stole her low-limit cards and killed her credit. But if the killer got the keys, they'd have access to nearly every business in downtown Lost Haven to hide, kill, plunder, and plant evidence.

Shaking her head, she dragged everything with her and dropped out of the Jeep, muttering about Bart and Sherri caring more about their stupid mourning dinner attire than anything or anyone else.

Then she realized the dead body inside the mansion wasn't just Harrison Kavanaugh — it was Bart's dad.

Ah, man, she thought. *Okay. Maybe don't give him a hard time about the dumb key.*

§

The windows of Horizon House blazed with light. Every room was lit, driving away any hint of darkness that dared creep past the security lights and, Jenna hoped, leaving nowhere for a murderer to hide within the walls. Even the round, glass room atop the mansion blazed, like a lighthouse sending a distress signal.

Garrett and Cabo waited for her on the front steps. Cabo was on the ground level, Garrett on the first step, and he glanced at the top of Cabo's head, now just about even with his. He took another step up, looked down at the top of Cabo's head, and seemed satisfied.

Good lord, Jenna thought.

Garrett said, "Now Jenna, I want you here so I know you're safe. But Detective Olson might not want you inside, what with the crime scene and all. Why don't you wait in the cruiser for now with the doors locked, and I'll—"

Olson opened half of the massive front doors and stuck his head out. "Jenna, you're here. Come on, let's go. You have to see this. Cabo, you too. Garrett, I need you to go find Bart, let him know his dad's dead. Makes us look bad if the next of kin finds out from someone else."

He disappeared back inside, leaving Garrett standing with his mouth open.

Jenna was just as shocked—*What did she have to see at Kavanaugh's murder?*—but stayed cool.

Still, she couldn't resist. "I guess he doesn't want you inside, Garrett, what with the crime scene and all."

Cabo's mouth twitched, but he and Jenna both kept straight faces and climbed the stairs toward... well, what?

§

Olson was halfway up the wide staircase to the second floor, waving them forward as soon as they stepped inside. The car-sized chandelier suspended above the foyer was in full illumination, gorgeous and borderline painful to look at with its million dazzling points.

Jenna looked through the house into the receiving room, where the wall of windows had turned into a giant mirror because of the light inside the house. McTavish stood facing the glass, his hands clasped behind him, seeming to stare into blackness.

Jenna paused at the bottom of the stairs, feeling the need to go check on him. Touch his arm, tell him it was going to be okay, whatever was done in this scenario.

Offer snacks?

His head turned slightly, and though she couldn't be sure at that distance, she thought he looked at her in the reflection. Then he nodded, just once, a tiny bit, and went back to staring at nothing.

"Jenna, come on," Olson said. "I need you to see something."

"What is it?"

"It's in the library."

"Why me?"

"You'll see."

She took one step up and stopped. "I just want you to know: I'm not scared. I just want to be prepared for whatever you're going to show me."

"And I want you to be unprepared," Olson said. "That's the only way to get an honest reaction when you see it."

Jenna pursed her lips.

Oh, he's good.

Obviously unable to resist—Who could?—she followed Olson and Cabo up the stairs and turned the corner toward the library. Then the smell hit her. It was the same thick, coppery stench from when she'd found Ingrid's body, but multiplied by about ten.

She wasn't ready for it.

It took her back to that moment while simultaneously driving home the fact that Harrison Kavanaugh was dead in the next room, apparently with a lot of blood outside of his body.

She took a moment to stop and trace a finger along some very intricate woodwork in a sconce holder, using that same finger to hold her upright, should she start to keel forward.

She did not.

Well, if she wasn't going to pass out, she probably had to go into the library.

If things get bad, just look at the books. The books will save you.

Cabo stood outside the double doors, his hands opening and closing, opening and closing. It was odd to see someone his size nervous, maybe even scared.

"I don't want to go in," he whispered.

Jenna winced. "That bad?"

He didn't say anything.

"Do you have to go in?" she whispered.

"You shouldn't have to do it yourself."

"I'm actually alright. The smell got me for a second, but now I'm okay. Do you know why Olson wants me in there?"

"No. Unless…did you kill Mr. Kavanaugh?"

"What? No! Did you?"

"I already told you I didn't."

"I know, but you asked me, so…I just have no idea what Olson could want me for."

"Well. Let's find out."

He grabbed her hand, his left completely swallowing her right. She could feel the incredible strength in his grip, and if he got startled she figured there was an excellent chance he'd crush her bones into powder without even noticing. But for now he held her hand gently, almost carefully, and stepped into the library.

§

Olson stood near the far right corner, almost where Kavanaugh had been the second time Jenna saw the library. The detective had his hands in his pockets and was mashing a piece of gum, looking down at something between the the tall bookshelves in the middle of the room. His tanned face and the paler sunglasses area around his eyes looked even more odd in the warm yellow light of the library, almost like a reverse burglar mask.

Jenna and Cabo stopped. The copper smell filled the room, and Jenna briefly considered pulling a book and pressing her nose into the open spine. Maybe if she were alone...

Olson asked Cabo, "Is this how you left him?"

Cabo's hand briefly clenched Jenna's. "Ah, man. Do I have to?"

"I'd like to know if anyone disturbed the body after you left. You didn't happen to take any pictures, did you?"

"No. Jeez, no."

"Yeah, that would have been weird. But helpful." The gum snapped. "Come on, just a quick look."

Cabo leaned forward but his feet didn't move.

Jenna set her wallet and keys on the nearest shelf and wrapped her other hand around both of theirs. "It's okay. I'll go with you."

"Jenna, no..."

"As town historian I need to witness this myself. For posterity."

And to see if he has any baking flour or chocolate on him...

They stepped together around the shelf and looked down.

Harrison Kavanaugh was face-down on the thick carpet, his arms splayed at uncomfortable angles. His perfect white hair was a complete mess, caked with blood and what appeared to be bits of brain and skull. The entire head was misshapen, like someone had squished it from the crown and it had nowhere to go but out.

The smirking bust of someone (she still thought it might be Teddy Roosevelt) stared up from the floor next to Kavanaugh. Blood and more bits and pieces clung to the bronze face.

"Boof," Cabo said.

Olson put a hand on his arm. "You okay, big guy? If you're gonna faint, fall that way. Not on the body, please."

"I'm good," Cabo said, his voice thick. He swallowed, a dry clicking sound. "I'm good."

Jenna stared into Kavanaugh's head. Memories had lived there, along with languages, calculations, directions, book titles, and devious schemes to destroy her beloved town. Now it was just a mangled mess.

Tacky blood was pooled beneath his face and sprayed across the carpet, shelves, and *oh no*, the books! Spines were stained on every row of the narrow aisle, with large splatters across the lower books and fine specks on the upper.

"Grisly," Olson said, smacking the gum. "From what I can tell so far, he was walking or standing here, between the shelves, when somebody pushed the bust off from the other side. Bullseye, nailed him."

"Ug," Cabo said.

"Then, and I'll need forensics to confirm this,

I think they came around the corner, picked up the bust, and gave him a few more whacks, just to be sure."

"Terrible," Jenna said. "How much does that thing weigh?"

Olson shrugged. "Nobody touches it until we dust for prints, but I'd guess seventy pounds, maybe more. That's a big head."

No way could Wilford lift that, Jenna thought.

"So my first question would be for his bodyguard," Olson said. He grinned at Cabo. "Where were you?"

Cabo stared at the body. "Mr. Kavanaugh was in here, looking through the books for something. I was with him. He told me he couldn't think with my breathing and grunting going on, and had me go downstairs to get some dinner from McTavish."

"Breathing and grunting?" Olson said. "What, were you doing pushups or something?"

"I was just standing. Right there." He pointed to the shelves near the door. "I was reading Seneca. I thought I was being quiet, but who knows. Sometimes Seneca gets me fired up."

"Mm," Olson said, chewing. "So you went downstairs."

"I went downstairs and got some food in the kitchen."

"And what time was this?"

"8:47," Cabo said. "I remember looking at the

clock in the kitchen and checking my watch to make sure I was synchronized with home base."

"Nice," Olson said. "McTavish was there?"

"Yes. I asked if there were any leftovers from the thing this morning."

"The pastry puffs?" Olson said.

Cabo nodded, guilty. "Yeah. It's not my cheat day, but I needed some carbs. I was beat. I had those and some cold cuts."

"McTavish was there the whole time?"

"Pretty much. When he wasn't in the kitchen, I could hear him moving stuff around in the pantry and dining room."

Jenna listened intently. So far these were all questions she would have asked. Though she might have also asked if there were still any puffs left.

"Then what?" Olson said.

"I came back up here and found him like this. I stood right here, where I am now, and when I saw him I dropped down and rolled him — sorry, I guess that was bad — to see if he was still alive. He obviously wasn't, but I still pressed on his back a few times."

Olson frowned. "Why?"

"I don't know. I wanted to try some sort of reverse CPR, but I knew if I rolled him all the way over his brains would fall out. I wasn't thinking very clearly. So I thumped him on the back a few times, kinda shook him a little, and finally realized he was long gone."

"Interesting," Olson said. "Did you see anyone else?"

"No. I thought it was me, Mr. Kavanaugh and McTavish here. That's the only reason I left the library; I was going to be with the only other person in the house, so there's no way he could pull anything."

"Who else could get in and out at that time of night?" Olson said. "Bart and Sherri? With the security gate and access codes on all the exterior doors, nobody else would make it past the yard outside, if they got that far."

Cabo shook his head. "If they were here, I never saw them."

"Wait!" Jenna poked him in the arm. "You said 8:47?"

"Yeah. And *ow.*"

"Sorry." She turned to Olson. "I saw Bart and Sherri driving downtown around that time. They were going to dinner at the Marina Grill."

"You're sure it was them?"

"Positive. I was upset about the display in Sherri's storefront, and then I saw them all dressed up and I thought about going to the restaurant to make a scene, but then…"

Olson was blinking in the flood of words.

"It doesn't matter," Jenna said. "I saw them. They weren't here."

"Well shoot," Olson said. "I mean, that's good, because those kids are pretty decent, but it sure

230 · PENNY PLUME

would have been nice to wrap this up." He looked at Cabo. "So you sloshed the body around, compromising the crime scene and making my life miserable. Then what?"

"I stood back and tried to figure out what to do."

"911, maybe?" Olson said. "Just a thought."

"No offense, but I didn't know who I could trust. It looked really bad, me being the bodyguard, covered in blood." He looked down at the smears on his suit and shirt. "I guess it still looks pretty bad."

"Yeah, I get that. So you..."

"I went to The Welcome Shoppe."

"Ah, souvenirs!" Olson said. "The same thing everybody does after fleeing a murder scene."

"Jenna is the only person I know here who wouldn't think I killed Mr. Kavanaugh."

"And why is that?" Olson asked.

Yeah, Jenna wondered, *why is that? Because I'm not so sure...*

"She knows books. She knows I adhere to the stoic philosophies. And she saw how Mr. Kavanaugh spoke to me in such a way that, if I was going to murder him, I would have done it right then and there. But I didn't, because I'm not a murderer."

Olson's tan forehead wrinkled. He turned to Jenna. "Did that make sense to you?"

"Actually, yes."

"Huh. Well, I'll buy it for now, but I hope you don't have to convince a jury of it. We in law enforcement classify that sort of thing as 'nonsense.' So you fled the scene, went to The Welcome Shoppe, and that's about when Sheriff Bowers showed up."

"Right," Cabo said.

"You two didn't have time to conspire or come up with alibis before he arrived?"

"No," they said together.

Olson looked at each of them, back and forth, a few times. "Jenna, did it seem odd to you that he showed up at your door covered in blood?"

She considered for a moment. "A bit. But it's been an odd day."

"Well, you got that right," Olson said. "I can follow up with Sheriff Bowers for the rest, but I'll need official statements from both of you eventually. For now, though, Jenna: I didn't ask you to come in here so I could grill you while you look at this mess."

The poor books, Jenna thought, then caught herself. "Then, why?"

Olson pointed a finger gun at Mr. Kavanaugh's corpse. "He left you a note."

§

"A note?" Jenna said. "For me? Why?"

"I'm hoping you can answer that," Olson said. "It isn't even a note, really — it's more like a mini Will and Testament. Not legally binding, of course, but still…"

Jenna's breath stopped. "Did he give me Horizon House?"

Olson coughed on the gum. "This place? No. He just…no."

"Oh. I suppose that's for the best. The electricity bill alone is probably more than my mortgage."

"Yeah, you'd be shut off within a month," Olson said. "Anyway, the note is over there on the chair by the window. Don't walk through the blood and brains, please."

Jenna glanced at Cabo, her eyebrows raised.

He shrugged. "I didn't see the note."

She backed up and walked down the aisle on the right, between the shelves and the exterior wall. The legal pad was on the plush chair with one of the fat pens angled across its surface. Her throat tightened as she got closer and she realized she was holding her breath.

What could it possibly say?

Was it an apology?

A confession?

Olson and Cabo followed.

"Don't touch anything, please," Olson said. "Eyeballs only."

Jenna leaned over the chair and read the note:

I hereby bequeath to you the Jeep.
And the most boring book in
the world.
- H. Kavanaugh

Jenna read it again, then a third time, trying to make sense of it.

"He's giving you the Jeep?" Cabo asked.

"I guess so," she said, absently. She was thinking about the book.

The most boring book in the world? What did that mean? Was he being sarcastic?

"Is that legit?" Cabo said.

Olson shrugged. "Like I said, it's not legally binding, but it does seem to be his last wish. And he took the time to write 'hereby bequeath,' so he was obviously serious. As long as nobody disputes it, I don't see any problems. A Jeep and some book—quite boring, apparently—I don't think the estate is going to miss them."

"Hold on," Jenna said. "The most boring book. He's not saying that to *me*, I said that to *him*."

"Say what now?" Olson said.

Jenna turned to Cabo. "The book he was reading when we were all in here. *A Treatise on…*something. It was over there."

She pointed to the other corner and hurried that way. Olson and Cabo followed again, sharing an uncertain look.

Jenna scanned the shelf just below eye-level. The book had been brown, with a worn leather cover. She remembered the sound of it sliding and thumping home among its neighbors…there!

A Treatise on Fair Negotiations in the Lumber Industry

"This is the book," she said. "Can I touch it?"

Olson squinted at the spine. "Yikes. That *is* the most boring book in the world. Hold on."

He snapped on a pair of light blue latex gloves and reached along the top of the books to pull the *Treatise* out from the back.

"Might be prints here," he muttered. He slid the book out and lifted it with his index fingers pressed along the top and bottom of the pages, just inside the spine. Carrying it like that, he turned and set the book on its back on the small table next to the plush chair.

Touching just the bottom corner of the cover, he flipped the book open.

Nothing.

He carefully turned another page, then another.

No scrawled notes or folded, hidden messages. It was just the most boring book in the world.

"Does this mean anything to you?" Olson said.

Jenna shook her head. "Only confusion. I mean, giving me the Jeep is super nice—*super* nice—then he throws the book in as, what, a joke? Is he trying to prove something? I don't…oh, look."

She pointed to the copyright page, typeset in a lovely font that had slightly bulbous ends to its serif letters.

"I see words," Olson said. "Some numbers."

"The author," Jenna said. "Hollis Kavanaugh. That was Harrison's grandfather, one of the founders of Lost Haven."

"And the other place, right?" Cabo asked. "The first town, uh, Sanctuary."

"Well…"

"Okay," Olson said, "mildly interesting, but is it significant?"

Jenna tried to find a good answer. "If it is, I don't see how. I think he's just being rude. Rubbing my face in the fact that his family maybe wasn't so bad? His grandfather was a published author?"

Olson continued to flip through the book. The dense copy filled the pages, no white space or even chapter breaks, from what she could see. It looked more like a manifesto than a treatise.

"I don't know," Cabo said. "Writing that note was probably one of the last things he did, if not *the* last. I've seen Mr. Kavanaugh's penmanship, and that's definitely his writing on the pad, but it looks rushed to me. Not quite even with the lines, which would drive him crazy. He'd tear it up and start over."

"So he was in a hurry," Jenna said.

"I'm wondering: Did he know somebody was coming for him?"

Jenna eyed the book again. "You think this is a clue?"

"All I'm saying is, if he knew he was in danger, I don't think his final act would be to give you a Jeep and troll you with a book. Something else is going on here."

Olson turned another page. "Somebody might actually have to read this beast to know for sure."

"Oh, I'll read it," Jenna said. "That's a given. If anything jumps out, I'll let you know, but it might take a while."

Olson grimaced at the book. "I'd say about ten years. But hey, at least you'll have the Jeep to wake you up between sentences."

"Mm-hm," Jenna said. She turned to the book-shelf and scanned the other spines, looking for more volumes penned by Kavanaughs or titles that might help make sense of the odd gift.

Wood Pulp and its Many Uses

The Joy of Bandsaw Repair

Maybe the treatise wasn't the most boring book in the world...

Then she saw it.

"Detective Olson, can you pull a few more books out, please?"

He grinned. "Jenna, you got this page-turner, let's not get greedy."

"I think…these four." She pointed to the two books on either side of the gap where *A Treatise* had been.

Cabo peered at the titles. "I don't get it. These seem, ah, worse."

Jenna stepped back so Olson could slide the books out. He set them carefully on the chair, two stacks of two. He and Cabo stared at them.

"Okay," Olson said. "What about them?"

But Jenna wasn't looking at the books. She was looking at the back of the bookshelf, directly behind where *A Treatise on Fair Negotiations in the Lumber Industry* had been.

There, flush with the dark wood and painted to match the grain perfectly, was a round lock plate. In the center: a keyhole.

§

All three of them were frozen, staring at the hidden lock. Olson wasn't even chewing his gum anymore. Jenna wanted to hop up and down a few times, but it felt like a serious moment. And, of course: the corpse in the room.

After a few moments Olson cleared his throat and asked Cabo, "Have you seen that before?"

"Nope."

Olson put his gloved hands out, holding the room still. "Okay. Nobody touch anything. I'm going to look for a key, and I don't want your fingerprints getting all over the place. More than they already have, because this is a library."

He scanned the room, taking in all the nooks, crannies, and endless pages that could easily hide a key.

"Dang it. This is gonna take forever."

"Maybe not," Jenna said. She pulled the Jeep's floating fob out of her pocket and examined the smaller key. It hadn't fit the glove compartment, and now, Jenna saw, it had been carefully painted to make it look new.

She scraped with a thumbnail and the paint flaked away like a scratch-off ticket. The metal beneath was smooth, worn brass with a green patina to it. She used the Jeep's key to pick out the last of the paint, then held the small key up.

"Kavanaugh gives me the Jeep to use with this on the keyring. Then he writes a note giving me the book concealing that lock, which this key must be for. I think it's safe to say he wanted me to open it."

"I'd say so," Olson said. "Just...wear gloves. Please?"

§

Freshly gloved, Jenna stood in front of the empty shelf. One by one she slid the books out and handed them to Olson, who flipped and stacked them on the floor so they'd be in the same sequence when looking at the spines.

When the row was empty Jenna brushed the back of the shelf with her fingertips, searching for a seam or hinge that indicated the border of the hidden panel. There was nothing. As far as secret compartments went, the craftsmanship was *superb*.

Jenna lifted the key and checked with Olson. "Okay?"

"Hold on." He pulled out his phone and took a few pictures of the shelf, the books, the lock, the key.

"Okay."

Jenna slid the key in. It rolled over well-oiled pins and tumblers until it was fully seated, the engineering so finely tuned it gave Jenna the sensation that the key was returning home.

"Hold on," Cabo said.

Jenna and Olson both looked at him.

"We assume this is for a secret compartment, but what if Kavanaugh has some sort of self-destruct mechanism in this place?"

Jenna and Olson glanced at each other, barely hiding their concern for Cabo's sanity.

"Hey, you two weren't around him twenty-four-seven like I was. The past few days, when nobody

else was around, I saw some serious paranoia and…
and *furtiveness*."

"Furtiveness?" Olson said.

Cabo nodded gravely.

Olson turned to the shelves. "Anybody see a dictionary in here?"

"It means he was being shifty," Jenna said.

"Ah. Shifty I know."

"Or no," Cabo said, "an escape pod, in case of nuclear war, or climate change. Oh man, what if you turn the key and this whole room just launches up into orbit?"

"Space library," Jenna mused. "I like it."

She turned the key.

§

Jenna pulled lightly on the key to open the hidden panel. It didn't move.

But the entire bookshelf did.

It swung away from the wall on silent hinges, ghosting a hair above the carpet so it wouldn't leave any marks. Jenna stepped back, her mouth open.

Was she dreaming?

Because this…this was too good to be true.

It was a secret library.

Small, certainly—she could probably touch every wall at the same time—but the walls were paneled in dark, rich wood and lined with shelves above a small reading desk with a blotter and lamp. The chair was functional and well-used, angled toward the opening, ready for her.

The bookshelves were orderly, even with the bundles of yellowed paper in protective plastic sheaths nestled between some of the books. These looked like unfinished, unpublished manuscripts, perhaps journals.

Jenna leaned closer to examine the spines.

"Don't touch anything," Olson whispered from behind her. "Don't even step in there, please."

She didn't know why he was whispering, but it seemed right. This was a reverent moment.

She saw:

The Minks: A Family of Pelts and Scandal

The Shipwrecks of Sanctuary

Her breath caught.

These books were about Lost Haven!

The people, the stories, the *history*.

She finally found the air to speak.

"You guys, these books, they—"

Then her eyes drifted down to the blotter. The large sheet of paper there was held in place by dark, smooth stones at the four corners. A light dusting of fine sand covered the blotter around the sheet, and she saw small piles of the grit pushed toward the edges of the desk. Even more sand lurked beneath the chair.

Jenna cocked her head to read the sheet without stepping into the hidden room. The paper was ancient, flaked at the edges and rippled with water stains. A perfectly round hole with a charred rim showed where a careless spark or ember had landed. The ink might have been dark at one time, but now it was a series of faint tan lines that vanished altogether in some spots.

The shapes were slightly familiar...

Jenna leaned so far into the room she started to tip, then fall. She reached out to catch herself on something that wasn't a priceless, delicate piece of paper or book and saw no options.

The chair would tip.

The paper would tear.

The secrets would—

A hand caught her flailing arm from behind. Eyes wide, she looked over her shoulder and saw Cabo holding her wrist in both of his huge hands, keeping her from falling. He wasn't straining. In fact, it looked like he barely noticed the effort, like holding onto a helium ballon's string.

"You okay?" he asked.

"Mildly embarrassed," Jenna said. "I don't usually do the whole book trance thing around other people. Can you, uh..."

"Right, sorry." He pulled her upright, patted her sleeve flat, then didn't seem to know what to do. "There you go."

"Thanks."

Olson watched them, grinning and chewing his gum.

"What?" Jenna said.

"Nothing. Just a semi-observant detective, observing." He looked past her. "So this was Kavanaugh's, what, hidden office?"

"No, *library*," Jenna said. She turned to the desk and studied the sheet of paper again, one hand on the outer shelf to prevent another near-topple.

The faint lines, the shapes...

"Oh."

"What?" Olson said.

"Oh, no."

Cabo leaned next to her. "Bad?"

"Guys," Jenna said, "this is a map. This is Sanctuary."

§

"**S**anctuary is *real*?" Cabo asked.

Jenna just shook her head. "I...maybe? If not, why would there be a map?"

"Just so I'm up to speed," Olson said, "Sanctuary is what, exactly?"

Jenna started to talk but Cabo beat her to it.

"It's the original town here, before Lost Haven. The Kavanaughs and other founding families stripped all the trees to sell the lumber, and the sand dunes crept closer and closer until they buried everything. Then the founders built Lost Haven on top of it like nothing ever happened. That's the legend, anyway. It's supposed to be an urban myth. Well, rural myth."

Impressed, Jenna said, "Exactly."

Olson pointed at the map. "You're sure it's genuine?"

"Not at all," Jenna said. "But it certainly looks like it. The age of the paper at first glance, the shape of the land and harbor, the names of the buildings."

She leaned into the hidden room again and squinted at the faded, cursive text.

"See, First Bank of Sanctuary. Gallagher's. Shoreline Gaming House. These are all businesses mentioned in the history of Lost Haven, but it was never clear where they were. Maybe that's because they got buried."

"So why keep this in a secret room?" Cabo asked. "This sort of proof would bring the tourists in droves."

"I have no idea," Jenna said. She studied the desk and shelves above. Maybe the books and yellowed, loose papers had more information about why they all needed to be kept behind a hidden door. Her fingers wiggled at the thought of—

"Don't do it, Jenna," Olson said. "The crime scene

techs are on the way. Once they process everything, you can go crazy. Until then, no touching."

"Can I take a picture of the map?" she asked.

Olson squinted, considering the legal implications. "What are you going to do with it?"

"Just...look at it."

"Not sell it to the local newspaper, or, uh, whichever internet site would want it?"

Jenna frowned. The thought hadn't occurred to her. "Nope. Just look."

"Okay by me," Olson said. "But no pics of the dead body."

"That's not a problem."

Olson nodded. "I think I'll take a few myself, just for...what was it you said before? Posterity?"

Jenna gave a surprised smile. "That's right."

"Huh. I always thought that meant somebody's butt." Olson chewed his gum and held his phone over the desk, took a few photos, then captured the whole secret library with a short video.

Jenna did the same, but was much more deliberate about her map photos. She leaned as far as she could into the room and maneuvered her phone until the map was the only thing on the screen, or close to it, and took a dozen shots. Then she held the phone even closer and took photos of each quadrant of the map, images that provided finer detail and could be electronically stitched together later.

As she took the photos and saw how Sanctuary

might fit into the current layout of Lost Haven, she thought: *If this is genuine, it changes everything.*

§

Olson said, "Okay, you two need to scoot. The crime scene crew will blow a gasket if we're all just milling around when they show up—they hate that. But I need you to leave the key to the secret library here. I also can't believe I just said that."

"I can keep the Jeep key?" Jenna asked.

"Yeah, for now. But if the investigation expands to include that as evidence, I'll let you know."

Jenna worked the small key off the ring and offered it to Olson, who pointed at the desk beneath the window.

"It's totally worthless for fingerprints by now, but no reason to make it worse."

Jenna set the key near the lamp and edged toward the door without turning. She wanted to avoid seeing Kavanaugh's body again. And the sooner she could get a better look at the map photos, the better.

Olson said, "I'll call if you need to come back for anything. Cabo, I need those clothes for the crime scene crew."

"Sure," Cabo said. "Can I rinse the rest of the blood off?"

Olson looked at the smeared mess on his hands,

wrists, and neck. There was a swipe of crusty blood above his right eye as well, where it looked like Cabo had wiped sweat off his brow.

"Hold on." Olson took photos and video of all of it while Cabo stood, arms out, looking like he was being gently electrocuted. Then the detective pulled out a very official-looking plastic bag, filled with smaller bags, and inside those bags were small gauze pads. He used those to swab blood from different spots on Cabo's skin and suit, labeling each small baggie with the sample's location. He put all the samples back in the larger bag and pressed it shut.

"All set."

Cabo let his arms fall. "I, ah, probably shouldn't stay here any longer, right? Would that be tacky?"

Olson said, "Well, technically, the body you were guarding is slowly getting closer to room temperature, so I'd say your employment has ended. Unless Bart and Sherri want to keep you on."

Cabo closed his eyes. "Man, I suck. Is there a Worst Bodyguard Ever contest?"

Jenna tugged his sleeve. "Come on. Let's get your stuff, I'll help you find a place to stay."

"But don't leave town," Olson said. He was chewing his gum with that same grin he'd had earlier, when Cabo kept Jenna from falling into the secret library.

Jenna caught it. "What?"

"What?" Olson grinned.

"What's that smile for?"

"Oh, you know. Just detecting."

Jenna grabbed her stuff and cocked an eyebrow at him until she and Cabo were in the hallway, around the corner. Because whatever Olson was smirking about, with that dumb face of his, he was *wrong*.

§

Cabo's room was off the first floor hallway, turning left from the grand foyer. As they walked down the hall Jenna had a brief moment of panic when she thought his room might be directly beneath the library—and the corpse—and Kavanaugh's blood would be seeping through the ceiling to haunt Cabo even more.

But they kept going, all the way to the end, where Cabo opened a heavy wooden door onto a large bedroom complete with a fireplace and sitting area. The king-sized bed had four posts and a dark, velvet canopy that perfectly matched the thick rug beneath the sofa and chairs. A doorway along the left wall showed the edge of a granite countertop and part of an ornate mirror.

"Nice digs," Jenna said.

"Yeah. Most other jobs, I'm crammed into a musty motel room with three other dudes or sleeping in a truck. This is the nicest room I've ever stayed in, for work or otherwise."

They stood there for a moment, mourning the loss of the room, then Jenna said, "I'm going to talk to McTavish, see if he's okay. Meet you at the bar?"

"Yeah, I guess. Jenna, what am I going to do?"

Jenna blinked. "Shower. Change clothes. Meet me at the bar."

"No, I mean *do*. I'm a freaking bodyguard, and the guy who hired me just got killed in his own house. That doesn't look good on a resume."

"Well...can't you just...leave it off?"

"No, this sort of stuff travels like wildfire through the community. I bet the message boards are already lighting up."

"There's a bodyguard community?" Jenna said.

"Of course there is. I'm just...I'm done. That's it."

"Wrong," Jenna said. She lifted her phone. "Because I have pictures of the Sanctuary map, and the other papers on Kavanaugh's secret desk in his secret library, and you're going to help me figure out who killed him and Ingrid."

"I am?"

"You are. So get cleaned up and meet me at the bar."

"Yeah," Cabo said, a smile pulling at the corner of his mouth. "Okay."

Jenna started down the hallway, then stopped and turned. "Hey, Cabo."

"Yeah?"

"Go team."

CHAPTER NINE

McTavish was still looking out the window—or *at* the window—when Jenna walked down the steps into the receiving room. It looked like he hadn't moved an inch since she last saw him.

Jenna got to the polished bar and wasn't sure what to do next. She didn't want to disturb him if he needed to be left alone, but she also wanted to make sure he was okay. And there was something she needed...

She cleared her throat.

Nothing.

There was a bowl of mixed nuts halfway down the bar. She leaned toward it and caught the lip with her fingertips, making the bowl lift slightly and clatter back down.

Not a twitch. Was he meditating? There was something about not disturbing people when they were meditating, it would mess them up...no, that was sleepwalking. He wasn't sleepwalking, was he?

Jenna scoured her inner library for something,

anything to tip her off about the etiquette in a situation like this.

She landed on: "Hey McTavish. What's up?"

Well played.

"Evening miss." He didn't turn from the window. "Can I get you something? A lozenge for your throat, perhaps?"

"No, please. I just wanted to see if you're okay."

"Me? Oh, I'm fine. And you?" His Scottish lilt seemed to be increased by mourning. "I heard about your trip down the hill this morning—a bit faster than you'd planned, no? I'm glad you're safe."

"Yeah, that was…unplanned, thanks. But seriously, are you okay? Can I get you something? Some tea, coffee? Something out of one of these bottles? You'll have to tell me which one. I just see clear and brown. Oh, champagne, I know that one. Probably not that, huh?"

Good lord, shut up.

McTavish finally turned, a sad smile on his face. "I've not had a drink in twenty-two years, and I think Mr. Kavanaugh would be disappointed if I broke that streak today."

"Ah, sorry."

"No need to apologize. But I must admit, knowing about the mess upstairs and not being able to address it has me a tad thirsty for the stuff."

Jenna winced. "You've seen the library?"

"Indeed. Distasteful. Mr. Cabo was a bit ruffled

when he discovered Mr. Kavanaugh's state, and I rushed up to see what was going on. It was not what I expected to find. Quite a shock, really. And where is Mr. Cabo now?"

"He's getting cleaned up and packing."

"He's leaving?"

"Well," Jenna said, "I don't think he's comfortable staying here if he's, you know. No longer employed."

"Ah."

"But you're fine!" Jenna blurted. "I mean, this is your home. I didn't mean to say you should leave too because your employer is dead."

McTavish smiled again. "Actually, the Kavanaugh family is my employer, so with young Bart still here, I'm sure my services will be very much required."

"Working for Bart must be…" Jenna had already shown she had no tact, and wasn't sure why she bothered trying now. "…interesting."

This time McTavish actually chuckled. "Aye, the McTavish and Kavanaugh clans have a long history of interesting relationships. Their family used to work for mine, you know."

"*What?*"

"It's true. Before we all left the homeland. But that's for another day, I think. Are you sure there's nothing I can get for you? A coffee? I recall you were a fan of the sugar."

"No, please," Jenna said, then held up her phone. "But if you don't mind, I have some files here that

Olson might want printed out. I think I saw a printer in Mr. Kavanaugh's den this morning—would it be terribly rude to use it for two minutes?"

"Not at all. Can I assist in any way?"

"Ummm, I don't think so. Do I need any passwords?"

McTavish considered this, his eyes drifting up for a moment. "Not for what you're doing, no. I'll be right here if you require anything at all."

He turned back to the window with his hands clasped behind his back.

Jenna eased away, hoping no one else showed up before she was done.

§

Kavanaugh's den looked exactly as Jenna had seen it earlier that day. The Lost Haven Resort model still stood, a hideous reminder that the project would continue despite Kavanaugh's death.

Jenna scowled at it as she headed toward the massive desk, and a bright pink Post-It note caught her eye. It was stuck to the foam board that made the front of the shop known only as "Bakery."

"What the..."

Jenna stepped next to the model and leaned in. The note had a sloppy, tilted name scrawled on it: *Happy Mouth Creations YES!*

"Oh, Lawrence," Jenna whispered. He must have slapped it on when he'd come in to answer questions for Olson and Kavanaugh.

Jenna shook her head and went behind the desk. The computer and printer were on a smaller desk set to the left of the main, aircraft-carrier sized piece, at a 90-degree angle so Kavanaugh could swivel that way and immediately attack the keyboard.

The desk drawers begged for snooping—no, not snooping, *investigating for justice and history*—but she didn't know how much time she had. It was true that Olson might need printed copies of the photos she'd taken in the secret library, but he technically hadn't asked for them...

She was anticipating the need.

Oh, that sounded good.

After all, Kavanaugh had kept the documents behind a secret door in his personal library for some reason. A locked room within a room no one else would likely go—certainly not Bart or Sherri, no offense to them.

There had to be a reason why.

Jenna wondered if Bart even knew about the secret library, and she grimaced at the thought of his reaction when Olson told him about it. Then she imagined his reaction if he walked in and found her sitting in his dead dad's chair.

Lamenting the historical information that would

remain hidden in Kavanaugh's desk drawers, she got to work.

§

The photos on Jenna's phone were connected to her cloud account, and when she fired up the browser, logged in, and checked the photos app her recent shots from the library were already there.

She selected all of them and clicked Download.

Then, because it was right there and seemed ridiculous not to, she checked the browser history. Maybe Kavanaugh had been conducting internet searches for "How to murder café owners" or "Best places to hide evidence."

The history was completely empty.

"Poop."

Jenna clicked through the settings and found the browser was set to clear the history and cookies upon every shutdown.

Well played, Kavanaugh.

She thought about poking around the rest of the computer, but something McTavish had said made her hesitate. When she'd asked if she needed a password, he had said, "Not for what you're doing, no."

So some stuff on here required a password, and she didn't want to trip any alarms that would shut it all down and bring McTavish, Bart, Cabo, and the fire department to shame her for being nosy.

She checked the download status: 15%

Slightly irked about the passwords, she let the internet elves do their work and clicked one of the images that focused on the area of the map showing what must have been Sanctuary's Main Street. There were more structures—it looked like six compared to the five of Lost Haven—and each was labeled in that gorgeous, handwritten cursive.

Jenna zoomed in.

The building that had been where her Welcome Shoppe was now, or the remains of which were scattered in the sand beneath it, had been named…The Welcome Shoppe.

Hmm. Not exactly thrilling, but interesting.

Next door, where Winkle's Fine Chocolates & Sweets now stood, was Winkle's Funeral Parlor & Mortuary.

Oh, now we're talking, Jenna thought. *Belma is going to lose her mind.*

It struck her as a bit odd that the funeral parlor was one door down from the town's souvenir and gift shop, but death had been more common back then. Maybe it was strictly for convenience?

Hello and welcome to Sanctuary! Oh, your husband just died? Goodness me. Right this way…And here's a bumper sticker for your carriage.

Jenna checked the download again: 65% done.

Come on elves!

She glanced at the den door, expecting to see Olson or Bart or—oh man—Garrett. That would throw a serious monkey wrench into what she was trying to do.

But the doorway was empty.

Jenna went back to the photos. She was very curious about the rest of Sanctuary's Main Street, but she wanted the big picture while she had access to the computer. She selected an image that showed the entire desktop in Kavanaugh's secret library, including the smooth stones that held the map's corners in place.

The map took up nearly the entire surface, with a strip of polished desktop a few inches wide all around the parchment. It gave the elegant impression that the map was framed, except for a scrap of stark white paper peeking out in the upper right corner from beneath the map and stone. Jenna glanced at it, saw the Kavanaugh letterhead and modern fonts obviously created by a computer printer, and moved on. She wasn't interested in anything made within the last century.

With the whole map on display, Jenna let her eyes wander. Maybe something would jump out and wave, shouting, "Here! I'm the reason Ingrid and Kavanaugh were murdered!"

She checked the marina in the southwestern corner, which seemed to be clogged with shipping docks and timber lots. That drew her east of town to the lumber mills, three of them at the time the map was drawn, labeled Kavanaugh Lumber Co., Gallagher Timber, and Mink Lumber Mill No. 4.

The "No. 4" piqued her curiosity—where were the other three?—but nothing among the mills screamed murderous intent.

She checked the download: 90%

Curse the amazing resolution and large file size of these photos!

Deep breath and back to the map.

Horizon House was there, perched atop the highest point, and the cartographer had made sure to give the impression that the hill overlooking the town was more like a mountain. There were no imposter mansions clustered along the access road, but three large patches of land with structures scattered throughout were labeled Welbourne Estate, Mink Estate, and Gallagher's Retreat.

The founding families, establishing their territory.

Jenna followed the road down the hill and into downtown Sanctuary, drawn back to Main Street.

And then she saw it.

§

B odies.
  Bodies, everywhere.

She'd been so zoomed-in on Main Street the first time, she hadn't noticed them. The little markers looked like trees to her, anyway. Jenna fell back in the desk chair, blinked a few times, then stood up. The windows along the south wall of Kavanaugh's den overlooked the entire town, and she could see the lights of the Main Street shops.

But she didn't care about those.

Her eyes moved to the right, landing across the street, on Lilac Park. The gorgeous, landscaped paths, ponds, and gathering spots where children played, lovers met, and performances were applauded.

And, according to the map, where hundreds of people were buried in The Sanctuary Cemetery.

§

J enna rushed back to the computer screen.
  Had she read that right?

She zoomed in, zoomed out, panned left and right. Yep.

It was still there.

The vast majority of the large swath of land between the Main Street businesses and the marina belonged to The Sanctuary Cemetery. A small parcel along the north edge was labeled "Mink Park," but even on the fading, static map Jenna got the impression that the dead were steadily overtaking the entire plot.

The small markers were meant to be gravestones, not trees, and in parenthesis beneath "The Sanctuary Cemetery" the cartographer had written: "317 Residents as of 1896."

Jenna's stomach twisted as she thought of all the times she'd walked through the park with Garrett, stopping here and there for a little more than holding hands. They had been standing above decomposing coffins filled with sand and skeletons. Skulls were grinning up at them while they wandered the paths.

She shuddered and looked away from the map.

It was awful.

And absolutely thrilling.

She'd solved it.

§

The download indicator at the bottom of the computer screen showed 100%, all done.

Jenna wondered: *How long has that been there?*

She found the downloaded ZIP file, extracted it to a folder, and sent all of the photos to the printer. The machine instantly kicked on and started working. It was a compact laser printer, surprisingly quiet, and the first photo came sliding out within seconds.

Jenna thought about what to do next.

She could take this to Olson, tell him Kavanaugh knew that he'd be building his new resort pretty much on top of a graveyard, and if the rest of Lost Haven knew about it the project would be scrapped immediately. The state would get involved, it would be a disaster for Kavanaugh.

So…what? He'd murdered Ingrid because she found out about it too, then killed himself so he wouldn't tell anyone?

Seemed unlikely.

Jenna blew a slow breath through puffed cheeks. She knew about the cemetery, but still didn't know who killed Ingrid and Kavanaugh. Whoever it was, they could still frame one of her Main Street friends, or Cabo—possibly even her--and get away with the murders.

Or worse: kill again.

She couldn't risk telling anyone. Not even Olson. Not yet.

Not until she knew for sure who the killer was.

If she trusted the wrong person…

Jenna deleted the photo files, then the ZIP file, then emptied them from the trash bin, which was as empty as Kavanaugh's browser history. Say what you would about the man, but he kept a tidy computer.

She was on the verge of shutting the machine down when she glanced at the stack of printed map photos. She turned the top sheet face-down, and though faint, the colors still bled through.

"Hm."

Working quickly, she went back to her cloud account, found what she was looking for, and printed off five more pages.

That should do it.

Now it was just a matter of getting the maps from the den to the Jeep.

Easy.

§

Jenna walked out of the den and scanned the receiving room.

McTavish was gone and the receiving room was empty.

She'd pulled it off.

She was climbing the three steps to the hallway and foyer, celebrating her natural and cultivated international spy skills, when Bart rose from behind the bar.

"What were you doing in there?" he said.

Jenna yelled, "Hey! Bart!" and skipped four feet to the right, away from the bar, but managed to clutch the map sheets tighter rather than flinging them into the air.

"Oh, did I startle you? Sorry." He was either

very tired or very medicated, his words falling out mechanically.

Or, Jenna scolded herself, he was in shock because his father was just brutally murdered in his home.

Bart straightened all the way up and set a dark, heavy bottle on the polished wood. It didn't have a label, looked handmade, and the red wax seal around the mouth looked like it may have been created by Spanish monks. He set a thick tumbler next to it, stared at the glass for a moment, then pulled another from beneath the bar.

"Come have a drink with me," he said.

"Oh, I would, but I—"

"Dad and I were going to drink this when the resort opened. It was brought over by our ancestors when they left the homeland, and dad said the resort was the final step in establishing our new home."

Jenna glanced around her at the magnificence of Horizon House. There was no point in trying to relate. She took another step toward the door, but man...the dead father, the saved bottle, drinking alone...maybe she couldn't relate, but she wasn't a monster.

"A toast, then," she said, and walked down the steps. She set the map sheets on the floor and dropped her wallet, keys, and phone on top, trying to be overly dismissive about all of it: *Just some crap I carry all the time, nothing to see here buddy*.

Bart found a paring knife behind the bar and cut

the wax seal, taking a moment to close his eyes and smell the first notes escaping from the bottle after, what, centuries?

"What does it smell like?" Jenna asked.

Bart tipped the bottle toward her. She sniffed: Tangy pear, sweet grape, maybe, and underneath it a fiery current of paint thinner.

She blinked back tears and said, "Yum," because she wasn't sure what else to say.

"Yes, powerful." He poured two alarmingly deep glasses and nudged one toward her. The liquid was thick and crystal clear, and though Jenna knew zero facts about alcohol, this seemed ominous.

"Do you want to drink this with Sherri, maybe? Or McTavish?"

"McTavish? We don't drink with the help, Jenna. And if Sherri drank this right now she'd probably have a stroke. She's so full of Xanax I'll have to wake her up for the funeral, whenever that is. When she heard about dad, how it happened right here...she just kinda shut down. Even Mr. Wolfie picked up on it. He's upstairs on the bed with her, guarding her while she sleeps."

"I'm so sorry Bart. It's just terrible."

Bart looked into his glass of jet fuel for a long moment. Seeing, remembering, regretting, wishing...

He lifted the glass. Jenna did the same, the rising fumes making her squint.

"To my dad," he said.

"To your dad," Jenna echoed. Knowing she'd chicken out if she hesitated at all, she took a large sip and immediately regretted it. The liquid burned her mouth, sinuses, throat, lungs, and stomach, and she hadn't even swallowed it yet. She held it in her mouth, waiting for the lights to go out as she went completely and eternally blind.

And Bart still hadn't taken his drink. He held the glass near his mouth, staring across it at something only he could see.

Or maybe not.

Jenna turned, her entire head in flames, and followed his gaze across the room, through the den door, and saw what he saw.

The resort model. Towering, hideous, and Harrison Kavanaugh's dream.

Bart offered his glass in its direction.

"And to The Lost Haven Resort. Whoever killed my dad, did it to stop the resort from being built. Well guess what? That's not how the Kavanaughs handle things."

Bart raised his glass higher, and Jenna realized he was looking up, across the hall and through the ceiling, toward the library. Toward his father's corpse.

"I will build it for you, dad. A monument to everything you were, everything you would have been. Nothing will stop me."

He knocked the entire glass down and smiled.

Jenna forced her tiny sip through her spasming throat and tried not to vomit.

§

"I should stop bothering you," Jenna wheezed. The burning liquor was making the room spin, and Bart's vow to complete the resort wasn't helping.

"You're not bothering me," he said. "As long as you don't start talking about books, or…what else do you talk about?"

"Oh, that's about it, really." Her eyes drifted to the stack of paper near her feet. "Town history, of course, but that's probably even more boring."

She yearned to tell someone about the discovery she'd made—even if that someone was dull Bart— but she checked herself. Telling the wrong person would be disastrous, and it didn't feel like the right moment to crush Bart's dream of building a monument to his dead father.

When was the right moment for that?

When someone else could do it for her, that's when.

"Town history," Bart mused. "Is that what you and my dad were talking about in the library today?"

The way he asked it, a bit too casually, made Jenna wonder: *Does he know about the secret library? The map? Is he fishing to see if I know?*

"A bit," she said. "The founding families are incredibly interesting and complicated."

Bart snorted. "A bunch of rich weirdos, if you ask me. Some of the stuff..."

He poured himself another dose and held the bottle above Jenna's still-full glass, his eyebrows raised.

"Good lord no," Jenna said. "Bart, I truly wish your father and I could have had more conversations like we had today. Without the looming accusations of Ingrid's murder, of course. I have so many questions."

"Questions," Bart said. He drained the glass slowly this time, watching Jenna over the rim the entire time. He set the glass down and gave it a spin, watching it rotate a few times on the smooth wood until it came to rest.

"I have some of those myself. Like when Sherri and I pulled in and I saw the Jeep outside, then when I was right here and saw you."

Jenna's stomach suddenly went cold, despite the burning liquor. For the first time since she'd met Bart Kavanaugh, she actually saw a lot of his father in him.

"Why are you here?" Bart asked. "And what the hell were you doing in my dad's den?"

§

Well, this was awkward.

Jenna hadn't taken the time to piece together any plausible explanations for why she was doing what she was doing, other than the truth. And she couldn't tell anyone the truth.

Was she on the verge of being outsmarted by Bart? And an increasingly drunk Bart at that? If that happened, there would be three deaths to mourn: Ingrid, Harrison, and her poor ego.

"Well?" Bart said.

"I had to bring Cabo back," Jenna replied. Winging it wasn't a great strategy, but she had to be better at this than Bart…right?

"Cabo? Why was he with you?"

"He came to see me after he found your father's body."

"Why?"

"He was scared. Didn't know where else to go."

"Uh, the police? Garrett?"

"He needed help, not someone to play catch with," Jenna said.

"Nice burn."

"Thanks."

"Where is Cabo now?"

"Getting cleaned up and packing. He's not comfortable staying here."

"Because he killed my dad?"

Jenna blinked. "No. Because he feels terrible. Like it's his fault."

"It is. Whether he killed him or not."

"Not true. Your dad told him—"

"Don't change the subject. Why were you in the den?"

"I...needed a moment to myself. You know. All the death."

Bart nodded. "Certainly not the boring old Lost Haven we're used to. What's with the papers?"

"Papers?"

"The stack you were carrying out of the den. Big. White. Hard to miss."

Shoot! He noticed them! Maybe not quite ready for international spying just yet...

Jenna did some quick math: If Bart knew the truth about Sanctuary and the graveyard, he'd realize she knew about it too as soon as he saw the map printouts. And that she'd use it to stop the resort.

If he didn't know, he'd probably be shocked, dismayed, even a little curious. Then he'd realize Jenna would use it to stop the resort.

Either way, it would only complicate things.

"Oh, I brought those with me."

"You brought a stack of papers with you?"

"Yep."

"Why?" Bart said.

What a fantastic question.

Jenna shrugged. "Well, you know me and my books. I'm working on a contemporary history of

Lost Haven. Those are just some notes I've been jotting down."

"About my dad's death?"

Jenna frowned. "What? No. Gross."

"Are you going to sell the story to the tabloids?"

"What tabloids? And no, it's just historical stuff."

"Let me see."

"No."

"Why not?"

"It's not ready yet."

"Who cares?" Bart said. "Let me see."

"Bart, trust me. You'll be bored to death."

She winced before it was all the way out of her mouth.

Bart just shook his head and waited. He extended the first finger on his left hand, lifted it up, and let it fall straight down onto the bar next to his bottle and glass. Right where he wanted Jenna's stack of maps.

Well, it was fun while it lasted, Jenna thought.

She picked up the sheets and her stuff, let the keys, wallet, and phone slide off onto the bar, and dropped the papers next to Bart's finger.

"Enjoy."

Bart stared at her for a long moment. She was again struck by how much of his father she saw in him now. Was this some genetic Kavanaugh thing? When the patriarch passed away, did the next in line suddenly become a shrewd narcissist?

Well, *more* of a shrewd narcissist?

He finally looked down and saw what was on the paper.

He frowned, scanned the top sheet, then flicked it aside to check the next one.

The next.

His lips moved slightly as he read Jenna's first draft synopsis of *Wonderful Lost Haven: A Visitor's Guide.*

She'd only printed six pages of the seventy-five-page document, placing them on top of the maps just in case something like this happened, and Bart was now on page four. If he flipped another page he'd likely see the colored maps bleeding through. Jenna could already see it, but she knew what to look for.

Bart squinted at the page, leaning in...

"Jenna, you're in big trouble."

"Listen. Your dad gave me—"

Bart cut her off with a laugh. "This is absolutely terrible. Nobody will buy this. And you're right—I need to stop reading before I die of boredom. Or adverbs."

He poked the pile toward her like it was a plate of table scraps.

Jenna was torn between relief, fury, righteous offense, and confusion.

The nerve of this guy!

Jenna gathered the loose pages and tucked them under her arm.

Wait, Bart knows what an adverb is?

She collected the rest of her things from the bar.

It's just a first draft!

"I'm sorry about your father."

He grunted and took another hit of the jet fuel.

"Please tell Sherri we're thinking about you guys."

"Go on and tell her yourself. If you can wake her up."

"No," Jenna said, "I'll let her rest. But if she needs us to keep an eye on her shop for a while, it's no problem at all."

Bart snorted. "What's the point? I'm tearing all of it down as soon as I can."

§

Jenna made it out of the receiving room and into the foyer before she took a breath. She was still waiting for Bart to call her back in so he could check the pages again when Cabo emerged from the hallway, showered and dressed in a black golf shirt and khaki pants, carrying a small suitcase.

She'd only seen him in a suit before, which hinted at his size and strength but didn't showcase it. Now, the short sleeves of the golf shirt displayed biceps and forearms bigger than her legs, rippled with muscle. Jenna had a brief vision of Bart ordering Cabo to tear down Main Street himself, and Cabo having no trouble taking the structures down with his large, bare hands.

He stopped in front of her. "You okay?"

"What? Yeah. Why?"

"You're kinda staring at me."

"Oh, sorry. I was, uh, zoned out." She dropped her voice. "And I just had a little scene with Bart."

Cabo's eyes popped. He whispered, "Bart's home?"

Jenna tilted her head toward the receiving room. "I should say something to him."

"He's drinking."

"Oh boy. I'd better do it before he gets too deep in the bottle."

"Be careful. And don't get stuck talking to him— we have some work to do."

Cabo raised an intrigued eyebrow at the stack of papers in Jenna's hands. He walked to the receiving room entrance and, very gently, said, "Hey, Bart."

"Murderer!"

Cabo turned around and headed for the front door. "That went well."

§

The fresh, slightly chilly air on Horizon House's front steps was exactly what Jenna needed to put the drama with Bart behind her. She took a deep breath, smelling Lake Michigan on the breeze that wrapped around the mansion from the Great Lake.

The tail end of the cleansing breath was tainted by exhaust, and she looked down to see the state police crime scene van idling next to Garrett's cruiser. Two technicians were unloading cameras and hard plastic cases that contained…whatever they used for crushed-skull deaths.

Garrett stood with his hands on his hips, supervising. He looked up and saw Jenna and Cabo.

"Hey, finally. You guys having a party in there or what? Thanks for the invite."

"Oh yeah, it's a real blast in there," Jenna said.

She and Cabo walked down the steps. Garrett met them at the bottom, leaving the crime scene crew to actually get some work done.

"What have you been doing? Where's Olson? I'm out here by myself, nobody's talking on the radio—I got no idea what to do here."

"Well," Jenna said, "I've been getting berated by Bart, and Cabo has been washing Kavanaugh's blood off. Then getting berated by Bart."

"Yeah, him," Garrett fumed. "He and Sherri pull in here, don't even say hello, and I have no idea if I'm supposed to let them in or not. He goes straight into the garage and closes the door in my face."

Cabo said, "He's at the bar if you want to tell him to leave."

"And Sherri's passed out on Xanax," Jenna added. "Good luck with that."

Garrett considered the looming facade of Horizon House for a moment, then seemed to dismiss the idea of storming it and the people within. He frowned at the stack of papers Jenna carried, then at Cabo's bag.

"What are you two doing?"

Jenna said, "I'm finding a place for Cabo to stay, then collapsing into sleep. I'm exhausted. It's been kind of a day, you know?"

"It sure has," Garrett said. He checked his watch. "It's just past eleven, who's still open? Cabo, how about I take you to the Lost Hav-Inn? The rooms are nice enough. You'll probably fit on the bed."

Cabo looked back and forth at them, not sure what was happening. "Doesn't Olson want you to stay here?"

"He's not my boss."

"Garrett," Jenna said, "he's going to need your help. This is a great opportunity for you."

"Two people murdered and it's a great opportunity. Real nice Jenna."

"You know what I mean."

"Cabo, hop in the back of the cruiser. I'll run you over there."

Jenna turned to Cabo. "He's being stubborn. Let's go."

"Uhh...I don't want to cause any trouble here."

Garrett said, "Besides running around town

with Kavanaugh's blood all over you, terrifying the citizens?"

"I was never terrified," Jenna said.

"Sounded like it on the phone."

"I was being quiet, not scared."

"Get in the car, Cabo."

"Am I under arrest?" Cabo said.

"No. But you're being a public nuisance."

Jenna's mouth fell open. "Garrett! That is *enough*."

She tried to guide Cabo toward the Jeep with one hand. It was like pushing against an oak tree.

"Maybe I should just stay here," he said.

Garrett nodded. "Great idea."

"Nope," Jenna said. "Bart will scream at you until he passes out, then he'll scream at you in his sleep. And who knows what will happen when Sherri wakes up."

"Man..."

One of the front doors opened and Bart stuck his head out.

"Murderer! You! Bigfoot!" He slid out of the gap and staggered toward the top step. "Hey, look at me. *Look* at me! What are you looking at?"

"Oh boy," Garrett said. He hustled up the steps to keep Bart from tumbling down and giving the crime scene crew more work to do.

"This is our shot," Jenna whispered.

Cabo nodded and they both hurried to the Jeep.

Jenna got behind the wheel, and Cabo dumped his bag in the back and slid into the passenger seat.

"That was about as awkward as it gets," he said.

"Yeah, sorry about that. It's a whole thing between us."

"You two…"

"Not anymore. But he sometimes has a hard time remembering that."

"Huh. Are you really going home and sleeping?"

"Oh, no way." She shoved her wallet, phone and keys into the middle console and dropped the stack of papers onto Cabo's lap.

"We're going to a graveyard."

CHAPTER TEN

Compared to the last time Jenna drove down from Horizon House, this trip was almost ordinary. If not for the murder plots, hidden graveyards, and fate of the entire town in the balance, it would have been boring.

Still—Jenna squeezed the steering wheel like it held the secret to online dating.

Cabo had his interior light on and was flipping through the printed photos. Jenna's death grip relaxed once they were past Ingrid's mansion, the landscape apparently still operating on some sort of timer.

Cabo squinted at the faint ink on one of the sheets. "You're telling me this graveyard is still there, under the park?"

"I've never read anything in the histories of Lost Haven about a graveyard being relocated. That's big news for a town this size, back in those times, and I've read *everything*."

"Even the stuff in Kavanaugh's secret library?"

"Ohhh, I wish. Good point though. I need to

check with Olson about how soon I can get in there. Or at least remove the books and dig into those."

"You sound pretty fired up about that," Cabo said.

"You have no idea."

"So what are we going to do? Find some shovels and start digging up rotten coffins?"

"Ehhh…"

They came to a cross street on the northern edge of town and Jenna stopped. There was no traffic coming or going from any direction. Jenna tapped the steering wheel a few times.

"What?" Cabo said.

"We have to be very careful here. I'd love to rush into town, gather the Main Street folks, and tell them about the graveyard. It would delay the resort, at the very least, while the Lost Haven Historical Society figures out what happened to the burial plots."

"That sounds good," Cabo said.

"But if one of those folks murdered Ingrid and Kavanaugh, because of the graveyard, where does that put us?"

"Next on the list."

"Bingo."

"Well," Cabo said, "*you'd* be next. Once you got bumped off, I'd just bust the heck out of town, so no worries there."

"Ah, very nice. What happened to 'Go team'?"

Cabo frowned. "Doesn't sound like something I'd say."

"Hmm."

"But I have to ask: Why are you telling me all of this? I could be the killer. I'm not, but I could be. But I'm not."

"You were with Kavanaugh the entire time when Ingrid was killed. Wow, was that just last night? It seems like a month ago." Jenna shook her head. "Lawrence saw you, and there were a bunch of other people there, right?"

"Yeah, engineers and contractors. Some lawyers."

"Plenty of witnesses. It would be too risky to use that as an alibi. If one person saw you leave, you'd be toast."

Cabo nodded. "But I still could have killed Kavanaugh."

"Why would you?"

"Who knows. Let's say he insulted me one too many times."

"Well, you didn't kill him. And not because of the stoic philosophy hoopla you gave to Olson."

"That was a compliment to you!"

"I know, and I appreciate it, but he was right—it's nonsense. If he could have seen your face when you showed up at the Welcome Shoppe, he wouldn't need any further proof. I saw it."

"Maybe I'm just a really good actor."

"If that's the case, you're a grade-A psychopath and we're all screwed. But listen—if you kill me, I'll never forgive you."

"Fair enough. Same goes for you."

"Deal. No murdering each other."

They shook on it, his massive hand swallowing hers, but he was very careful to not squeeze too hard. Then they both stared out the windshield, not sure what else to say.

Cabo cleared his throat. "So we're not rushing into town?"

"Not yet. We need to be sure about a few things first."

Jenna cranked the wheel to the left, heading into the farmlands east of town.

"Where are we going?" Cabo said.

"I'm taking you to fake church."

§

It was almost 11:20 when Jenna pulled the Jeep into Nelson Farms. The bright headlights were no match for the vapor bulbs that bathed the parking area and scattered outbuildings in enough light to simulate a UFO abduction.

A square, white, two-story farmhouse stood to the left of the driveway. Tidy hedges and flowerbeds ran along the base of the house, and stone walkways led through mature trees and a weedless lawn. Beneath one of the trees, a wide bench swing with it's own support structure wandered lazily in a slight breeze.

On the right side of the parking area, the largest barn had a sign painted on the side facing the road: "Buried Sanctuary! Come see the church where the final prayers were spoken before the town was buried for all time. Donations Welcome. $5 Minimum."

The parking area was empty. Jenna pulled into a spot near the barn and let the headlights add more illumination to what appeared to be the peak of a wooden roof poking out of a sand dune. The dune and roof were surrounded by a ten-foot chain link fence with barbed wire coiled along the top.

"That's the Church of Sanctuary?" Cabo said.

Jenna smiled. "Not according to our map. But don't tell Nelson that yet. He'll just get depressed."

They got out of the Jeep and watched a porch light pop on above the farmhouse's side door. A tall, lanky man stepped out carrying a small package in one hand and what appeared to be a shotgun in the other. He walked toward them, taking his time, the walk of a man used to working hard all day, knowing the work would still be there no matter how long it took him to arrive.

Cabo whispered, "Uh, is that a shotgun?"

"He's harmless," Jenna said. "Hey Morrie!"

Morrie's heavy boots crunched onto the stone parking lot. "That you Jenna?"

"Yep. Sorry it's so late."

"Oh, we get 'em out here all hours of the night. They think the holy ghost might show up at midnight, that sort of thing." He lifted the package, which turned out to be a six-pack of beer bottles, missing two. "Beer?"

"No thanks, but don't let that stop you."

Morrie stopped in front of them and examined Cabo, his face slowly compressing into lines of dire concern.

"Now son, if you want a beer, you'll have to wait until I go to the store and steal the whole cooler. I don't have enough to fill you up to the ankles."

"I'm good," Cabo said. "What's with the scattergun?"

"Eh?" Morrie looked down, noticed the shotgun, and seemed surprised by it. "Oh, this. Sometimes the kids come out and try to climb the fence, sneak into the church there. You know, young love and all that. They call it 'finding religion.'"

"So you shoot them?" Cabo said.

"Ha! I wish. Nah, I just sneak around the side and rack the slide a few times, start hollerin'. They come outta there like bees from a kicked nest. I don't even know if this thing still works."

"Morrie," Jenna said, "I'm sure you heard about Ingrid."

"Ah, yeah. Rest in peace, she'll be missed. My wife loved those coffee things she made, the cappa-cheetos. Hard to believe something like that could happen here."

Jenna nodded. "Well, it happened again. Harrison Kavanaugh was murdered tonight, not too long ago."

"What!"

"I know. It's crazy."

Morrie looked off toward the barn. "I always thought that fella was too ornery to die. Who killed him?"

"We don't know yet. The state police are investigating, so hopefully we'll know more soon." Jenna took a deep breath. Her stomach tightened. She was possibly about to find out that one of her dear fellow shop owners was lying at best, a killer at worst. "But for now, I'm trying to make sure my friends won't be framed for any of this—Ingrid, now Kavanaugh. And whatever comes next."

"What's that got to do with me?"

Jenna said, "Did anyone from the Main Street shops come by yesterday?"

Morrie frowned. "Yesterday? Let's see. I can check the receipts in case Eunice or one of the girls did the sale, but I sold some butter and eggs to Belma."

The weight on Jenna's stomach lifted, just a bit. "Do you remember what time?"

"Oh, it was after dark. She accused me of trying to sell her store-bought eggs, like she always does, and she used the flashlight on her phone to inspect the shells. Then she got her fifty pounds of butter—"

"*Fifty?*" Cabo said.

"Oh, yeah. Folks can't get enough of our butter,

especially in desserts and the like." Morrie leaned closer, sharing a secret. "I mix seaweed from the lake in with the cows' feed. Gives the milk and butter that little something you can't quite identify."

"Nice," Cabo said, though he seemed unsure if it actually was.

Jenna said, "And you have receipts for what Belma bought, and what time?"

"Of course. This is a legitimate business operation."

All three of them turned as a Honda Civic with its headlights turned off coasted along the road toward the entrance. Two teenage faces peered out from the windshield, their wide eyes lit by the halogens.

Morrie set the beer down and pumped the shotgun. "Get outta here you horn dogs! This is a sacred place of worship!"

The Civic's tires squawked as the car leaped out of sight, the headlights popping on a hundred yards down the road.

Cabo shook his head. "Such a shame. So disrespectful."

"I know, right?" Morrie said. "They weren't gonna leave a donation, I guarantee you."

§

Jenna's stomach felt light, free, soaring as she and Cabo drove back toward downtown. She had a photo on her phone of Belma's Nelson Farms receipt, showing her purchase for eggs and butter at 9:27 PM Thursday night.

Cabo looked at it. "So there's no way?"

"No way. Olson said the medical examiner puts Ingrid's death around 9:30. Belma was the first one to the meeting last night. There would be no time for her to drive back into town, store all the eggs and butter, kill Ingrid, and show up at my shop like nothing was wrong. No way."

"What about Kavanaugh?"

Jenna chewed her lip. "I saw her around 8:15, right after I closed. She was ringing up what I figured was her last sale of the day, and she was still talking to them when I came back down Main Street. That had to be 8:30, maybe even 8:40."

"I left the library to get dinner at 8:47," Cabo said.

"Not enough time for her to get to Horizon House, sneak in, and kill Kavanaugh."

"Belma's in the clear?" Cabo asked.

"She's in the clear," Jenna said, smiling so big it almost hurt.

Cabo's phone was in the passenger-side cup holder, and the screen lit up with an incoming call: Detective Olson.

"You put him in your phone?" Jenna asked.

"Yeah. Didn't you?"

"I just kept his card…"

Cabo kept any judgements about that to himself

and took the call. "This is Cabo. Yeah. Uh…okay. Maybe ten minutes. Is that fast enough? Okay, yeah."

He ended the call and stared down at the phone.

"Good news?" Jenna said.

"I don't think so. We have to go back to Horizon House. Now."

"Did Olson find something?"

"It's more like what he *can't* find—Bart's gone missing."

§

Jenna pushed the Jeep along the dark country road, her headlights the only illumination other than the stars. The Jeep urged her to stomp it, really chew some asphalt, but she kept it reigned in.

She asked Cabo, "Olson has no idea where Bart is?"

"I don't know how hard he's looked. He just said I need to come back and make my statement, and if we see Bart wandering around, pick him up and bring him home."

"Oh, no. As drunk as he is, he could have fallen down the hill to the lake. Or tried to drive and gone right off the road."

"Or bumped into the killer," Cabo said. "If he *isn't* the killer, that is."

"He can't be, remember? I saw him and Sherri

driving through town around the time Kavanaugh was killed." The thought of aloof Sherri and her stupid mourning hat still irked her, but she shoved that aside.

"What about Ingrid?" Cabo said.

"Wasn't Bart with you at the Horizon House meeting?"

Cabo looked out the open window for a moment. "Yeah, he was. The whole time, too. He and Lawrence tried to get a drinking game going with the lawyers. It didn't work."

The mention of Lawrence brought another knot to Jenna's stomach. "Oh, please tell me Lawrence was there the entire time too."

Cabo closed his eyes, remembering. "He was."

Jenna let her breath out.

"No, wait. He left before the meeting was over. Kavanaugh was talking to the engineers about building the resort on a huge slab of concrete. Something crazy, instead of digging out the foundation. They thought it was hilarious. Lawrence said it was…what did he say… 'More boring than an empty bathtub.'"

"That sounds like him."

"Kavanaugh told him if he was bored, he can leave, so Lawrence did."

Jenna winced. "What time was that?"

"I can't say for sure, sorry. Maybe McTavish will know."

"Maybe," Jenna said, willing the time to be too

late for Lawrence to stop by the Sanctuary Café and kill Ingrid before he came to the Main Street meeting.

But...something Cabo just said was jumping up and down in her brain, raising its hand.

What was it?

She started mumbling: "Drinking game. Lawyers. Engineers. Kavanaugh."

Cabo raised an eyebrow. "You okay?"

"Hold on. Engineers. Slab. Slab?"

"Are you having a stroke? Nod if you can!"

"Slab!"

Jenna hit the brakes and slid to a halt on the shoulder. Dust swept past the Jeep as she punched on the interior lights and grabbed the stack of map photos.

"Kavanaugh was asking about building the resort on a giant slab?"

Cabo blinked in the wake of the interrogation. "I think so, yeah. I tried to pay attention but man, Lawrence was right. It was a snore fest."

"He knew," Jenna said. "Kavanaugh knew about the graveyard."

She flipped through the sheets until she found the shot of the full desktop, map, and smooth stones anchoring the corners.

"The graves must still be there, that's why he was asking about the slab. He was hoping to build his resort without digging into Lost Haven's past, literally, and unearthing the bodies. Cabo, if Kavanaugh had gotten his way, the Lost Haven Resort was going to be a tomb on top of the cemetery."

"Creepy. So, why was he murdered? We figure Ingrid was killed because she was going to stop the resort, right?"

"That's the assumption, yeah," Jenna said.

"If Kavanaugh was going to build it, why would the same killer go after him? And now, with Bart missing, maybe him too?"

It was Jenna's turn to blink. "Do you think there's more than one killer?"

"Man, I hope not. It's hard enough just finding one."

Jenna stared at the map, trying to fathom Belma and Lawrence working together as an assassin squad.

Bart and Wilford.

Belma and...Cabo?

As she worked through the timelines and crossed off possibilities, her eyes were drawn to the scrap of stark white paper peeking out in the upper right corner of the map, beneath the stone. The Kavanaugh letterhead mocked her. Below that, she could see the top of the first line of the letter, presumably the greeting to the recipient.

Or, recipients.

"Hold on a sec," she said.

She shuffled through the photos, finding a closer shot of the upper right corner of the map. The white paper was there, much larger. Jenna's book brain recognized the font—Garamond Premier—and the peaks of the capital letters gave hints to what the line said:

Greetings Lost Haven Historical Society

She let the letters cascade down in her mind, forming their curves, corners, and barbs.

"Oh, no. Oh, how did I miss this? It's right there!"

"What?" Cabo said. "The stone? Don't tell me there's blood on it."

"No, the letter!"

Cabo frowned. "What letter?"

Jenna pointed. "This one. The one from the desk of Mr. Harrison Kavanaugh, Esquire."

Cabo scanned the letterhead, the blank white area below that got cut off by the map and stone. Then he did it again, growing more and more confused.

"Is it a confession?"

"No," Jenna said, barely containing herself. "The first line, right here. The salutation. It says 'Greetings Lost Haven Historical Society.'"

"I just see a bunch of specks."

"Trust me, that's what it says."

"Okay," Cabo said. "I trust you. But what does it *mean*?"

Jenna beamed. "Kavanaugh wasn't going to build the resort."

CHAPTER ELEVEN

The gate to Horizon House was still open, and the front of the house still blazed with security lights. Every window was lit, as if someone inside needed to drive out every inch of darkness. The crime scene van sat abandoned near the stairs. Garrett's cruiser was gone.

It was an eerie setting, given the bloody murder scene inside the mansion.

Jenna didn't bother with any of that. She bolted from the Jeep, ran past the van and started climbing, the photos clutched to her chest. She called over her shoulder, "Come on!"

"I'm literally two steps behind you," Cabo said, from two steps behind.

"Well…hurry."

Cabo shook his head. "I'm still not exactly sure what we're doing."

"Just saving the town," Jenna said with a grin. "You know. No big deal."

§

Jenna pushed one of the massive doors open and headed for the stairs to the second floor. Then her manners took over and she skidded to a stop, went back to the entrance and leaned out to press the doorbell embedded in the stonework.

A deep tone sounded from somewhere within the house.

Cabo watched this with a raised eyebrow. "Really? I don't think the crime scene crew needs us to follow formalities."

"This is still someone's home," Jenna said.

"Not if Bart's dead."

"Shush!"

McTavish emerged from the first floor hallway. His posture was still flawless but he looked tired, his face dry and gray.

"Miss Hooper. Mr. Cabo. They're waiting for you upstairs."

"Thanks McTavish," Jenna said. She ran up four steps and stopped, unaware that Cabo had to grab the thick bannister to keep from bowling her over.

"McTavish, do you happen to know what time Lawrence left the meeting last night? When Mr. Kavanaugh told him if he was bored, he could leave?"

"Of course, miss. It was 9:40 PM. I can show you the log, if you like."

"No need, thank you." She turned to Cabo. "Lawrence couldn't have killed Ingrid. He's in the clear."

"Good," Cabo said. "He's funny. It would be too bad if he also killed people."

Jenna started up the stairs again.

"I beg your pardon," McTavish said, "but have either of you seen Master Bart?"

Jenna stopped again, crushed by how insensitive she was being. Poor McTavish—Harrison Kavanaugh murdered, Bart missing, people tromping through the estate and constantly in need of him—no wonder he was exhausted.

And, now that Jenna really looked at him, miserable.

She hurried back down the stairs and wrapped him in a fierce hug. Startled, he kept his posture ramrod straight for a moment before relaxing and resting his cheek on top of her head, just for a moment.

"We haven't seen Bart," she mumbled into his shoulder.

"Very good," McTavish said, straightening up. "Can I get you anything? Coffee? Tea?"

"No," Jenna said. "Please, don't worry about us. Go take care of yourself."

He patted her back and broke free from the embrace.

"I'll be in the kitchen should anyone need anything."

Then he was gone, turning the corner and disappearing down the hallway.

Cabo blew air through puffed cheeks. "Rough. Poor guy."

"Please don't let Bart be dead," Jenna said to the enormous chandelier.

Detective Olson stuck his head around the corner at the second-floor.

"Hey, you're here, good. What are you two doing, some weird version of Romeo and Juliet?"

Jenna frowned. Cabo was on the stairs, looking down at her with his arms spread on the bannister.

"Huh?" she said.

Cabo said, "O Jenna, Jenna! Wherefore art thou Jenna?"

"He's got it," Olson said.

Jenna blinked. "Guys. We're trying to solve some murders here. I mean…seriously."

She hurried up the stairway with Cabo close behind. At the top, she flapped the stack of photos in front of Olson.

"Tell me no one has touched anything in the secret library."

"No one has touched anything in the secret library."

"Good. Let's go."

Olson and Cabo stood together at the top of the stairs, watching her stride toward the library.

Olson said, "She's not messing around, is she?"

"Nope. And we need to keep up, for real, or she'll yell at us. It's very unpleasant. Come on."

§

The library's double pocket doors were fully open, sending a UFO-abduction level of light into the hallway.

Jenna stood in the doorway and saw the crime scene crew had bright, portable lights set up around the library. The two technicians wore light blue Tyvek suits and booties, surgical gloves, clear safety glasses and some sort of filter masks over their mouths and noses.

One knelt at the end of the bookcase pointing a camera around the corner, at Kavanaugh's bashed skull, Jenna assumed.

The other held a string from head-height to a splatter of blood on the bookshelf to the right of the secret library entrance.

Jenna hadn't noticed the blood there before, and if Olson had he'd left it unmentioned.

Both technicians looked over when Jenna entered.

In unison, they said, "You can't come in here."

"I'm with Olson."

"He can't come in here either," they said.

"Oh." Jenna stepped back into the hallway.

One of the voices was female, but Jenna couldn't tell who it belonged to.

"I'm Jenna. I, uh…can I ask a favor? Do you guys do favors?"

The one with the string said, "We won't destroy or plant evidence for you, if that's what you're thinking." It was the female voice. "So you can go right ahead and forget that."

"What? Oh, no, I wouldn't—"

"I'm just messing with ya," the woman said. "What do you want? A piece of skull?"

"*What?*"

The woman looked down at the other tech. "Olson said she could take a joke."

"Olson is a terrible detective," the other tech said.

"Hey," Olson said. He arrived in the doorway and stood next to Jenna, with Cabo on the other side of him.

Cabo was pale, looking everywhere but in the general direction of Kavanaugh's body, even though it was hidden by the bookshelves.

"You'll have to forgive the crime scene crew," Olson said. "The job requires a certain morbid humor, and they think everyone should join in."

"It's just life and death," the woman said. "What's the big deal?"

Olson pointed at her. "That's Tina. The guy on the floor is Gino."

"Smile," Gino said, and took a close-up photo of something on the carpet.

Olson whispered to Jenna and Cabo, "Whatever you do, do *not* ask about their improv group."

"Improv group?" Jenna said, just a bit too loud.

Olson winced.

"You want tickets?" Tina said. "I have a bunch in the van."

Gino stared, his eyes hopeful behind the shield.

"Uhh..." Jenna didn't know what else to say. "What's your group's name?"

Tina and Gino responded: "The Crime Scene Technicians."

A moment of silence passed.

"Very creative," Cabo offered.

"It's a disaster," Olson said. "Don't waste your time. You'll have more fun doing your taxes in ice water."

Tina went back to her string. "You're just mad because we won't let you join. Anyway, sweetie, you asked for a favor. What's up?"

Jenna gripped the stack of photos.

Please, please be what I think you are.

§

Jenna said, "Inside the little room there, on the desk. Is the map still there?"

Tina checked the secret library. "Map. Check."

"In the upper-right corner, is there a white sheet of paper sticking out?"

Tina leaned in. "White sheet. Check."

"Can you pull that out and bring it over to us?"

"What is it?" Olson asked.

"I don't want to get my hopes up until we know for sure," Jenna said.

But that was a lie. Her hopes were already soaring. She just needed the facts to match them.

Tina asked Gino, "You get all the film you need for this area?"

"All set."

Tina turned to Olson. "You okay with this?"

"Looks like she's running the show," Olson said.

"White sheet of paper, incoming." Tina pulled a pair of tweezers and a large clear evidence bag from her kit. She stepped into Kavanaugh's secret library, sending pangs of jealousy through Jenna's waves of hope, and started working.

Olson muttered, "Not gonna tell me what it is, huh?"

"She wouldn't even tell me," Cabo pouted.

"We'll all know soon," Jenna said. She realized she was bouncing on the balls of her feet.

"How did you know about it?" Olson asked.

Jenna showed him the printed photo on top of the stack and pointed to the white paper peeking out.

Olson looked at it. "Yeah. So?"

"The first line, the salutation. It says 'Greetings Lost Haven Historical Society.'"

Olson blinked under the intensity of Jenna's smile. He squinted at the peaks of letters peering out from beneath the map, just specks of black on the white paper. He turned to Cabo.

"Did she hit her head or anything after you two left?"

"Nope."

"Inhale any fumes? Take any schedule one narcotics?"

"She was driving. I hope not."

"You're both fired," Jenna said.

Tina emerged from the secret room with a letter-sized piece of paper sealed in the bag.

"Who wants it?"

Olson gestured to Jenna. "I think she deserves the honors. And the potential humiliation."

Tina carried the bag to Jenna like it held the Declaration of Independence. She dipped into a small bow and offered it.

"M'lady."

Jenna took the evidence bag. Tina backed away, still in a bow, then turned to continue her string work.

Olson and Cabo crowded behind Jenna, peering over her shoulders.

She began to read.

§

"Greetings Lost Haven Historical Society,'" Jenna read.

She took a moment to look at both Olson and Cabo.

"Told you."

She read on:

> It has come to my attention that the ground upon which I intend to build the luxurious Lost Haven Resort may contain historical items relevant to our town's history.
>
> Because of this, I will halt the acquisition and demolition of Main Street and Lilac Park until further investigation can be completed.
>
> I will leave this in your less-than-capable hands for now. If the process becomes delayed by ineptitude or bureaucracy, I will commandeer the investigation and complete it to my own satisfaction.
>
> Good day.
> H. Kavanaugh

Jenna pointed to the slashing signature below the typed name, and beneath that, the handwritten date.

"He signed this today."

Olson chewed his gum slowly as he caught up. "So he wasn't going to build."

"And somebody killed him for it," Cabo added. "Has to be the same person who killed Ingrid. I mean…right?"

"Yes," Jenna said. "Kavanaugh saw the map, realized he was going to build right on top of the Sanctuary Cemetery, and had to call it off."

Cabo frowned. "So how did he get the map?"

"From Ingrid," Jenna said. "Before our meeting last night, she told Belma she had something that was going to stop Kavanaugh in his tracks. That we—meaning the Main Street shop owners—were all safe and should consider ourselves lucky to be her friends."

"Humble," Olson said.

Jenna rushed on. "I think Ingrid found the map and slapped it down in front of Kavanaugh. Told him there was no way he could build his hideous resort. Not on top of a graveyard."

"So he asked his engineers about the slab," Cabo said. "He wanted to see if there was a way to build without digging down."

"Oh yeah," Olson said. "I thought that was an odd way to go. Makes sense now. I guess. But if Ingrid brought him the map—where did she get it?"

"Great question," Jenna said. "I have no idea. But

I wonder if there's more information in Kavanaugh's secret library. Something else she may have given him, or that he already had but wanted to keep…well…secret."

Olson glanced at Tina and Gino, now fully involved with a tangle of strings and numbered tags indicating blood spatter.

He shook his head. "We're not getting in there for a while, sorry. They're working on a theory that the statue—"

"Bust," Tina corrected.

"The bust," Olson glared, "isn't what killed Kavanaugh. They think somebody bashed him with something else, then tried to make it look like the bust fell on him."

"Something else?" Cabo said. "Like what?"

"Big and heavy," Tina said. "That's what we know so far."

Olson snapped his gum. "Narrows it down to about half the things on earth, give or take."

"What about her house?" Jenna said. "Can we check there?"

Another head shake. "It wasn't part of any crime, as far as I know, so that's not up to me. You'll have to check with her next of kin."

The thought of tracking down more Gallaghers and asking if she could root through Ingrid's things made Jenna wince. Uncomfortable, for sure, and a possible waste of time while Bart tried to move forward with the resort.

Bart!

"Ohhh," she said. "I don't think Bart knows about this letter. The last time I saw him, he vowed to keep the construction going."

Olson snapped his gum. "It ain't gonna be pretty when he turns up and reads it."

"*If* he turns up," Cabo said.

Jenna scowled at him. "He's not dead. Okay? He's just not."

Cabo shrugged. "I figure it's a coin toss at this point."

"That is enough of that, Jay Cabo. Talking about Bart being dead doesn't get us anywhere except depressed, so let's focus. If Ingrid had the map, where did she get it?"

"Wilford?" Olson said. "They were hubba hubba, maybe he had it stashed in his art collection."

Jenna nodded. "That's good. Now we just have to find Wilford and ask him."

Cabo opened his mouth.

"Don't you dare say it," Jenna said.

"I was going to offer to take my car and look for him, and for Bart. I wasn't going to mention anything about the likelihood of Wilford being dead."

"Cabo."

"Just like Bart."

"Can you arrest him?" Jenna asked Olson.

"My handcuffs won't fit," Olson said. He turned to Cabo. "But I do need to get that statement, so if I can steal you away from your sleuthing for a bit, let's get it done."

"Cool with you?" Cabo asked Jenna.

"Yes, go away. But give me your keys, I'll get your car ready."

Cabo dropped them in her palm. "It's in garage five, I think. Or six."

"*Six* garages?" Jenna said.

"Out of ten."

"It's enough to make you puke," Olson said. He started down the hallway. "Come on, we'll do this in the game room. I like the art in there."

Cabo touched Jenna's arm. "You sure you're good?"

"I'm fine. Sorry I snapped. And thanks for offering to look for Wilford and Bart, that will be a big help."

"Sure thing." He started to follow Olson, then turned back. "And hey, try not to drive my car through anyone's house, okay?"

§

Jenna watched Tina and Gino work for a few moments, until it felt too morbid—and before they could invite her to their improv show again—then went downstairs and cracked the front door.

All quiet.

No sign of Bart.

No sign of anyone, actually.

Jenna imagined spending winter nights here, when the world was frozen and the sun only emerged for a few hours before dropping back into hibernation. It would feel like she was the last person on earth.

Some days, that wouldn't be so bad...

No! She pushed that away. There was zero time to fantasize about days, weeks, months spent here with the gate closed and the library open. There was serious work to be done.

But maybe when it's all over...

She rolled her eyes at herself and closed the front door, walked halfway across the foyer and stopped. The light from the massive chandelier was just as bright as the hallway spillover from the crime scene lamps, and now she didn't have Olson and Cabo muttering over her shoulders.

Jenna examined Kavanaugh's letter again, looking for anything she'd missed the first time. Some of the fine sand from Kavanaugh's small desk had made the trip with the letter, and it was trickling off the paper and pooling at the bottom of the evidence bag.

She read the letter, taking her time on each word choice.

"...may contain historical items..."

Why 'historical items'?

Why not 'human remains'?

"...complete it to my own satisfaction."

Did that mean he'd just written the letter as a formality, and had planned to quickly override the Historical Society and resume construction?

Could he do that?

The Historical Society of Lost Haven didn't budge on which paint colors were acceptable on certain houses in town; Jenna couldn't imagine them letting something like this slide.

She pondered all of this, her finger and thumb squeezing and rolling the tiny pouch of sand in the bottom corner of the bag. It had probably driven Kavanaugh crazy having the fine grit scattering everywhere in his precious little space. Would he ask McTavish to clean it up, or was the room secret from even him?

Jenna grinned at the thought of Kavanaugh trying to figure out how to use a broom, slapping himself in the face and cracking the handle into a lamp while he—

The broom!

The sand!

The map!

If Ingrid brought the map to Kavanaugh with sand all over it, she must have kept it one place:

The Sanctuary Café.

§

Jenna ran down the first floor hallway to the game room, the thrill of her discovery rushing through her body. She would tell Cabo and Olson, they would go to the café and find something—she didn't know what yet, but something—that would tie everything together and bring peace and order back to Lost Haven.

Simple!

Except the game room door was locked.

Jenna frowned at the ornate knob, the solid door, the lack of any alternative entry. She pressed her ear to the door and could hear Cabo's voice but not what he was actually saying.

She thought: Is it rude to interrupt an official statement?

Probably.

What if it's for a break in the case?

Jenna lifted a hand to knock but a muffled sound from within the room made her hesitate.

Was that…a sob?

She pressed her ear to the door again.

Yes. Cabo was talking, but his voice hitched with sobs. When he paused, Jenna could hear Olson talking softly, probably consoling him.

Jenna stepped back from the door, suddenly embarrassed for intruding upon the private conversation. She needed to get away. If Cabo wanted to tell her about how the statement went, that was fine, but she didn't want him to know she'd eavesdropped.

She turned down the hallway and ran smack into McTavish with a knife in his hand.

§

"**O**h!"

Jenna leapt back and covered her mouth to keep from hollering again and broadcasting to Cabo and Olson she was right outside the door.

Then she saw the knife in McTavish's hand and uncovered her mouth in case she had to holler again.

"McTavish," she whispered.

"Miss Hooper," he whispered back.

"What are you doing?"

"Preparing some coffee and sandwiches. It's been a long day, and you folks need some nourishment if you're to keep going."

"Why do you have a knife?"

He glanced down at the blade, which was dull and rounded at the end.

"It's for spreading mayonnaise."

"Okay, that sounds about right."

"May I inquire about something?"

"Sure."

"Why are we whispering?"

Jenna checked the game room door: Still closed, voices still murmuring within. She turned McTavish and led him down the hallway to the end, where the space widened a bit to allow for several doors, all closed, and the open stairway to the lower levels.

She kept her voice low, but didn't quite whisper. "Cabo is in there with Olson giving his official statement about—well, you know."

"Yes. Master Kavanaugh."

"Right. I wanted to check in on them, but it sounds pretty intense. I was trying to sneak away when you caught me."

"Ah. The proverbial red hand."

Jenna smiled. "Busted."

"If you'll forgive me for being so bold, it appears that your red hands are holding official evidence."

"Oh, this." Jenna examined the front and back of the paper inside the plastic bag, like she'd never seen it before. "I'm just holding it for Detective Olson."

"Do I recognize Master Kavanaugh's letterhead?"

"Hm. Yeah, I think so. But you're right, I shouldn't be carrying this around. I'll take it back right away."

"Very good," McTavish said. He gave a brief smile, but his eyes were locked on the letter.

"And I need to get Cabo's car out of the garage," Jenna said, changing subjects as smoothly as sandpaper on gravel. "Can you point me in the right direction? I'd probably wander around here for days without some help."

McTavish reached past her and opened one of the doors. Cool air flowed in, carrying the unmistakable smells of gasoline, oil, and new tires. He hit a light switch, but all Jenna saw was a few steps leading down into a long, off-white hallway with about twelve doors along the right wall.

"The bays are separated to allow for individual climate control," McTavish said. "I believe Mr. Cabo's auto is in number six."

"Well," Jenna said. "Okay. Thanks McTavish."

"My pleasure, Miss."

He stood, waiting.

Jenna cleared her throat. "No word from Bart?"

"I'm afraid not. It isn't uncommon for him to do this sort of thing, but the timing is unfortunate."

"True," Jenna said. "Cabo is going to look for him. That's why he needs the car."

"Very good."

"Yep." Jenna took a step toward the door. "Okay. See ya."

"Mind the stairs."

She went down the steps and started walking past the numbered doors, pretending to count them, but in truth she was waiting for McTavish to tackle her and rip the letter from her hands.

Don't do it, McTavish, she thought.

Poor, sweet McTavish.

Don't be the one.

The door closed behind her.

Jenna glanced back, prepared to drop, pivot, sprawl—whatever it took to fight him off—but the hallway was empty.

§

The door to garage number six opened with a soft hiss of warm, dry air.

It was pitch black inside, and Jenna had a moment of panic as she reached around the door jamb for the light switch: McTavish had rushed through another secret passage within Horizon House and was waiting for her just inside the door, his butter knife poised to strike her fumbling hand.

She was certain of this until the moment the lights flooded the space, revealing a blue Prius, a rolling metal tool chest, and nothing else. The walls and ceiling, which had to be ten or twelve feet high, were lined with a matte gray paneling that looked like it could be hosed off.

Jenna scolded herself.

A butter knife? Really?

And McTavish?

Come on.

Get it together.

But the man did lie to her. This had to be the wrong garage, because there was no way Jay Cabo drove a Prius. Would he even fit inside?

It couldn't be a Kavanaugh vehicle either—Harrison and Bart driving a Prius was about as likely as Lawrence and Belma eloping.

Was it Sherri's? She had her own Beamer, courtesy of Bart, but was this hers too?

Jenna moved to garage seven, opened the door and hit the light. A shark-gray Jaguar crouched in the garage, looking like it was gliding along at ninety miles-per-hour just sitting still.

Jenna frowned at the machine. Too flashy for Cabo, and she had seen Harrison Kavanaugh tooling around town in it.

She killed the light, closed the door and went to garage five.

The hallway light spilling through the open door showed the front bumper of Bart's convertible BMW.

"You again," Jenna grumbled, remembering Bart and Sherri rolling across Main Street while she tried to get their attention. But no, they were too busy playing the mourning socialites to bother with her.

She hit the light switch.

Nothing happened.

She toggled it again and stepped into the garage, looking for another switch.

Something crunched under her shoes.

Jenna stepped back and saw glittering glass scattered across the smooth, painted concrete. The shards were small and thin, some of them curved.

Broken light bulb, Jenna thought.

She glanced up, and in the light from the hallway could barely see the ceiling socket just inside the door. Someone had left a broom—obviously unused—leaning against the wall on the side of the door opposite the switch.

Jenna pictured Bart and Sherri pulling in, seeing the broken glass, and leaving the broom where McTavish was sure to see it so he could get to work.

She shook her head.

Rich people.

She looked for a place to set Kavanaugh's letter, found no flat surfaces within the swath of light, and ended up tucking it into the back of her shorts. She was careful not to crease it—it was evidence, after all—and felt very sophisticated and ladylike as she grabbed the broom and started sweeping the shards into a pile, wondering how the bulb had broken in the first place. The ceiling was too high for someone to hit it with an errant hand, and light bulbs didn't just explode.

Did they?

Note to self: Exploding light bulbs—still a thing? Ever a thing?

She pulled more glass into the pile, then had a thought: What if the broom wasn't there for cleaning?

She tapped the bristles on the floor to knock any shards out, then reversed the handle and reached toward the ceiling. The broom was long enough to touch the socket. Even a half-hearted swing would be enough to shatter a light bulb.

So if that's what happened, she wondered, who did it?

And why did they want it dark in this garage?

She stepped toward the driver's side of the car, and when she left the doorway the light from the hall fell across the Beamer's hood and spilled into the front seat.

That's when she saw Sherri's body.

§

Jenna froze.

She didn't even breathe.

Sherri's body was in the passenger seat, slumped against the door. The wide-brimmed black hat was still on her head, tilted down to hide her face.

Jenna was grateful for that. The body was enough of a shock. If Sherri's dead eyes looked at her in this dark garage the way Ingrid's had in the café, she might still be clinging to the ceiling.

Maybe she's not dead.

Maybe she's sleeping.

Jenna clung to that idea instead of the ceiling. Bart said she was full of Xanax—did she stumble back to the car in a barbiturate stupor and pass out?

"Hey Sherri," Jenna said.

"Sherri!"

Nothing.

"Ah, man. Okay."

It didn't even cross her mind to go get Cabo,

Olson, or McTavish. If Sherri was dead, she was dead. If she wasn't, she might need immediate help.

Jenna took a deep breath and stepped back around the front of the car, still holding the broom. More glass crunched under her shoes and she watched the body for any stirring.

Nope.

Jenna moved along the passenger side and stopped just in front of the door. She could feel her heartbeat in her throat, pushing against her windpipe and making it hard to breathe.

"Sherri, if you're messing with me, and you're about to jump up and scare me, I will never forgive you. Ever."

Still nothing.

"Okay then. I hope you're not dead, but I also hope you don't give me a heart attack."

She reached out with the broom handle and stuck it under the hat brim.

Nudged it up, and back.

And stared into the flat, dead eyes of one of Sherri's mannequins.

§

Jenna blinked.

Her heart still slammed in her chest, and now her brain spun around.

A *mannequin*?

It was hard to tell in the weak light, but it looked like the bronze mannequin had flesh-colored paint or makeup smeared across its face. The black hat and clothing covered the rest of the shiny surface.

Jenna stepped back from the car. At a glance, anyone would think it was Sherri in the passenger seat. Especially if Bart was driving the car through town with the top down, supposedly on the way to a swanky dinner at the Marina Grille.

Sherri hadn't been in the car with him.

Jenna's mind reeled.

Where was she, then?

Was she here, killing Harrison Kavanaugh?

Was she dead?

And where was Mr. Wolfie?

Jenna had a brief moment of guilt when she felt more concern about the poor little dog than Sherri, then pushed it aside. The dog was nicer than Sherri, but neither deserved to be murdered.

She stared at the mannequin and thought about what to do next.

Bart was missing, possibly on the run because he'd killed Ingrid, his father, Sherri, and Mr. Wolfie.

Also possible: He was dead.

Okay.

She knew exactly what to do next.

She would—

The garage door opener kicked on, a low, heavy

thrum that made her hop sideways three times with the broom in front of her like a pogo stick.

Blinding security lights from the driveway flooded the garage. Jenna lifted a hand against it, squinting at the black shapes moving toward her.

"Get back! I have a broom!"

"Jenna," Cabo said, "are you okay? Are you hurt?"

She tried to look at him, but he was just a dark silhouette with a dazzling halo of light behind him.

"Hurt? Me? No. Why? There's a mannequin in here."

Cabo rushed into the garage. "Mannequin? No, Jenna, you need to come out here."

"Why? What happened?"

"Just...come on. It's bad."

§

Cabo rushed Jenna out of the garage and to the right, into the circular driveway in front of the house.

Olson and McTavish were both near the bottom of the front steps, looking at her with concern.

"Don't make those faces," Jenna said, near panic. "What happened?"

Cabo led her past them, practically dragging her toward the Jeep. Then they went by that, onto the soft grass that went all the way to the southern edge of the estate's plateau.

"McTavish saw it from the den," Cabo said. "He came and got us. Garrett's already there."

"Garrett?" Jenna said. "Is he okay? Cabo, what is going on?"

They ran between two hedges sculpted to look like longbow archers, surreal in the harsh white security lights, then they were at the tall fence that surrounded Horizon House.

Lost Haven nestled below. First the winding road through the mansions, then scattered homesteads along the semi-straight road into downtown, and finally the town itself, soft lights and mature trees wrapped by Lake Michigan on the right and the Lost Haven Marina as the coast curved inland.

From here, Jenna realized, in the dark, the entire town looked like a question mark. Which was appropriate, because she had endless questions.

"Okay, what? Who? Where?"

Then she saw the flashing fire trucks.

The smoke.

The fire.

A gout of orange flames curled above the trees downtown, lashed toward the stars, and retreated.

Jenna gripped the steel bars of the fence.

"Is that Main Street?"

"It is," Cabo said. "It's The Welcome Shoppe."

CHAPTER TWELVE

Jenna sprinted across the lawn to the Jeep.

Olson and McTavish met her there.

"Jenna, there's no reason to go now," Olson said. "The fire department is there, Garrett is there. He knows you're safe. Let them handle it."

Jenna yanked the Jeep's door open and pulled her phone out of the middle console. Sixteen missed calls, all from Garrett, Lawrence, and Belma, with two voicemails and nine text messages. Four from Garrett, two from Lawrence and two from Belma.

She was trying to wrap her head around it all when the phone vibrated in her hand. The screen said: Lawrence Donald

Jenna answered. She could hear vehicle engines and people shouting in the background. "Lawrence! Are you okay?"

"Sweetie, are *you* okay? Where are you?"

"Horizon House. Are you on Main Street?"

"Across the street from my shop. Oh, Jenna, what happened?"

"I don't know, but I'm on my way. Have you seen Belma? Wilford?"

"They're both here. We tried to spray water inside Belma's hideous shop but the fire people told us to scram. They were *not* nice about it."

Jenna walked in a circle, clutching the phone. "Belma's shop is burning too?"

"Not yet," Lawrence said, "but her display is totally melted. Now I get what they mean when they say 'a cleansing fire.'"

Jenna heard Belma screech "*Hey!*" in the background.

"And Wilford is okay?"

"Seems fine. But he said Florida is looking better and better."

"Lawrence, listen carefully. Have you seen Bart or Sherri down there?"

"Nope."

"Okay, hold on."

Jenna pressed the phone against her stomach and found McTavish standing near the back of the Jeep.

"Do you know for a fact that Sherri is passed out in Bart's room?"

McTavish blinked. "For a fact? No, I haven't personally seen her in there. Is she in danger?"

"I need you to go check on her," Jenna said. "Right now."

McTavish turned and was gone.

"Jenna, what's going on?" Olson said.

"Has anyone been in the library except us and the crime scene techs, since we opened Kavanaugh's secret library?"

"No," he said.

"And you've been in there the whole time, or they have, right? It's never been left empty?"

"Nope. Why?"

"Go check the garage. Bart's convertible." She brought the phone back up to hear Lawrence saying:

"...but I mean, are you surprised? Why should they care if her shop burns down? They'll just buy another one from Amazon and have it flown in by helicopter."

"Lawrence, if you see Bart or Sherri, stay away from them."

"More than usual?"

"Yes. Tell Belma, tell Wilford. And tell Garrett to watch for them. If he sees them, he needs to be careful. I think one of them is the killer."

Lawrence yelled, "Jenna thinks Bart or Sherri is the murderer!"

"Lawrence! Keep it down!"

"Oo, was that bad? That was bad, wasn't it? Sorry."

"Just stay away from them both," Jenna said. "I'm on my way down."

"Take it slow," Lawrence said. "You know, none of that no-brakes business."

"Yeah, I got it. And...Lawrence?"

"Yes?"

"Did they manage to save any of my books?"

"Oh. Oh, sweetie," Lawrence said.

§

Jenna ended the call and saw McTavish running down the front steps. The fact that he was wearing black slacks and polished loafers didn't seem to impede his stride or speed one bit.

Cabo reached out, hesitated, then put a massive hand on Jenna's shoulder. Even without any strength or pressure, it felt like carrying a sandbag.

"How are you doing?" he said. "How can I help?"

"I'll tell you in about six seconds."

McTavish arrived looking like he'd just stirred from a bit of tea. No huffing and puffing, not a crease out of line. Behind him, Olson hustled back from the garages, his eyes wide.

McTavish said, "Miss Sherri is not in her quarters. It seems no one has slept in the bed since last night—I change the linens and make the beds every morning, and the covers are undisturbed."

"Mr. Wolfie?" Jenna said.

"I did not have the pleasure of being snarled at, licked, or shed upon. He was not there."

Olson stepped into the conversation. "Okay, that's messed up. Who put that thing in Bart's car?"

"What thing?" Cabo said.

Jenna quickly told him and McTavish about the mannequin, along with her theory that Sherri hadn't been in the car when she saw it cross Main Street.

Olson said, "So she could be missing since, what, eight fifteen?"

"If not before," Jenna said.

"Along with Mr. Wolfie," Cabo added.

Olson pulled his phone out. "We have to find Bart."

"I think he just set fire to my shop," Jenna said, "so that's where I'm starting."

§

Main Street was bright, soaked, and crowded. It was after one in the morning, but on a Saturday, so the lakeshore bars and restaurants hadn't closed down yet and the patrons were rushing through Lilac Park, some with cocktails in-hand, to watch the show. The folks who lived near downtown were more subtle about it at first, clustering in groups in their bathrobes and pajamas, but they slowly drifted toward the park as well to join the crowd.

Jenna parked the Jeep across from the Sanctuary Cafe with two wheels bumped on the curb. She had a brief rush of the creeps when she stepped out and realized there could be a coffin—with a corpse inside—directly beneath her, but quickly forgot it when she saw her poor, beloved Welcome Shoppe.

She'd spent the entire trip down from Horizon House hoping everyone had it wrong—it was just smoke, a small fire near the coffee pot easily snuffed out—but when she saw the wall of flames crawling out of the shattered front window she knew it was all gone.

Her books, her sofa, Wilford's plush chair, the license plate frames, all the tacky driftwood art that must have served as perfect kindling for the inferno.

Gone.

Cabo stood next to her. No one had noticed them yet; the spectacle of her burning shop was too popular.

"Jenna. I'm so sorry. I saw your collection when I was in there, when I came to see you. After I found Mr. Kavanaugh. Those books had to be valuable."

"Maybe," Jenna mused. "Just to me."

"Hey. Sentimental value is still valuable."

"The only copies in print," Jenna said with a small, sad smile. "Please handle carefully."

"Devastating," Cabo said.

"Yes. But also fantastic."

"Um," Cabo said.

Jenna pulled Kavanaugh's bagged letter from under the back of her shirt. "I think Bart set fire to my shop because he knows about this letter, and the map of Sanctuary, but not where it came from."

"I want to know where that letter just came from," Cabo said.

"Don't worry about it. But Bart doesn't know that *we* know about the map. He thinks it's still safe and sound in his father's secret library."

"No, but...we saw it in there. With Olson."

"Bart doesn't know that," Jenna said. "He doesn't know that his father gave me the key to the hidden door, then left a clue about how to open it that only I could figure out. Now Bart needs to make sure there isn't any other proof about the Sanctuary Cemetery so he can build the Lost Haven Resort. What's the best way to do that?"

"Fire," Cabo said. "But the map didn't come from your shop. Did it?"

"Nope."

Jenna pointed to the Sanctuary Cafe.

"It came from in there. Come on."

§

Jenna used her janitor's keyring to open the cafe's front door. Earthy coffee and light tea aromas flowed out, a welcome change from the smoke and exhaust. She and Cabo slipped inside, then closed and locked the door behind them.

The lights from Main Street and the emergency vehicles coming through the plate glass windows provided more than enough illumination to see the tables and chairs in the main area.

The chairs were still upside-down on top of the tables, just like Ingrid had left them after she was done sweeping and mopping, except for those closest to the door. Those tables had been moved by the crime scene technicians so they could maneuver around the spot where Ingrid's body had been, which was where Jenna was standing now.

She glanced down, had a quick flash of Ingrid's lifeless eyes staring up at her, then skipped to the right and shook off another round of the creeps.

"You okay?" Cabo said.

"Yeah. Just…a lot of dead bodies around here lately."

"Are you sure you don't want to go down the street?"

"And what? Watch my livelihood burn to the ground? Inhale the burning memories? No thanks. I'd rather do something productive. Like save the rest of the town."

"Fair enough."

Cabo stepped to the L-shaped coffee bar, which ran along the back half of the right wall and the entire back wall. Just yesterday, the entire length had been a flurry of activity, energy, and gossip. Now it was empty, still, and cold.

"So what exactly are we looking for? And how do you know the map came from here?"

"Ingrid had the map," Jenna said. "It had to be her. She showed it to Kavanaugh and he was forced to write this letter."

She lifted the evidence bag.

"And with the map, came the sand. Look in any corner here and you'll see it. Ingrid always had it the worst of any of us shop owners, so no matter where she hid the map, the sand would have found it. Now we just have to do the same."

"Because…"

"Because we need all the proof we can find to use against Bart and his resort."

"I'm confused," Cabo said. "Isn't Bart a murderer? How can he build the resort from prison?"

"This is Lost Haven," Jenna said. "He's a Kavanaugh. So far there has been zero evidence showing he killed anybody, and if something does turn up, I don't think we'll ever know about it."

"You can't be serious."

"You saw how many lawyers Kavanaugh had at his meeting last night, and that was just for a stupid building. Imagine how many show up to keep the heir to the Kavanaugh fortune out of jail."

"There were a lot of lawyers," Cabo admitted.

"See?"

"Okay. So what am I looking for?"

Jenna started opening decorative tea tins and peering inside. "Books. Maps, obviously. Any sort of deed or paperwork. Old money. Gold."

"Gold?"

"The First Bank of Sanctuary printed its own money. People traded gold for cash. And I'll give you one guess on who owned the bank."

"The Kavanaughs," Cabo said, leaning over the coffee bar to check underneath.

"Ding ding."

Cabo straightened up and turned in a slow circle. "If I was going to hide something, I wouldn't put it out here. Not where some random customer might stumble across it."

He pointed to a door along the back wall, behind the bar's display case of scones and muffins that were probably just on the brink of being inedible.

"Storage?"

Jenna nodded. "And a small office. It's just one room, combined space."

Cabo hopped up to sit on the bar, spun his feet over, and dropped down on the far side.

"That was very graceful," Jenna said.

"Shh. I'm supposed to be a meathead."

Jenna saw the flash of his smile in the semi-darkness. It was hard to tell, but he might have winked at her too.

Did people still wink?

"And don't tell anybody about the Prius either, okay?"

Jenna gasped. "That *is* your car!"

"It's amazing. I love that little machine."

She found herself grinning and tried to frown it down, because this was serious business, which only made it worse. She glanced at Cabo to see if he was struggling with the same problem.

He stood in the doorway to the storage room, facing away from her, completely still.

"Did you find something?"

He didn't answer.

"Cabo?"

"Come here," he whispered. "Very carefully."

The bar had an opening near the back-left corner of the café. Jenna rushed there as fast as she could without knocking anything over, then followed the bar until she stood next to Cabo's left arm. He had the storage doorway half-open, and his body filled the entire gap.

"What is it?" Jenna said, trying to peek around him. "Please don't say it's another dead person. Is it Sherri?"

Cabo lifted a finger to his lips and eased backward, opening the storage room door as he went.

Jenna looked inside and could not believe what she saw.

§

It was a hatch.

Ten or so narrow floorboards were stacked

under the small desk, set aside to expose the subfloor in the middle of the room. A square, hinged panel of the subfloor was open, showing a vertical passageway leading straight down.

An orange extension cord plugged into one of the outlets snaked across the floor and dropped into the shaft. Jenna could see the top of an aluminum ladder leaning against the far wall.

"Where does that go?" Cabo whispered.

Jenna just shook her head. "Main Street doesn't have basements. The sand is too unstable."

She slid down to her hands and knees and eased closer.

"Careful," Cabo said. He tried to move with her but the room was too cramped. "Here, let me look first. Make sure it's safe."

Jenna waved him off.

"You're not my bodyguard. I can't afford you."

She stopped a foot away from the edge and leaned forward.

Looked down.

She stayed there for a moment, trying to make sense of what she saw. Then she leaned away and sat on her heels.

"Oh, my."

Cabo was crouched in the doorway behind her, ready to spring forward or yank her away from the hatch.

"Oh my what? What is it?"

Jenna turned to him and smiled. "It's an attic."

§

Cabo blinked.
"An attic."

Jenna nodded, her eyes shining.

"I'm gonna need more help here," Cabo said.

"It's the First Bank of Sanctuary. Remember the map? It was set right where the café is now. Supposedly buried and lost beneath the eroding sand."

Cabo leaned back, absorbing the news. "So...it was buried, but..."

"Not lost," Jenna said. "It's still there. The attic, anyway. This has to be where Ingrid found the map. *This* is why Kavanaugh wrote his letter. Not for a bunch of stupid dead bodies."

"Jenna."

"Sorry, I'm just excited." She whispered toward Lilac Park: "Sorry dead bodies."

Cabo scooted forward. "Let me see."

Jenna moved to the side of the hatch so they could both look down. The shaft was made of vertical planks secured with boards and braces all the way down, about ten feet or so, until it ended inside the room below.

The extension cord had to be connected to a light source, because they could clearly see the bottom of the ladder sitting on the wide wooden planks of the attic floor, secured between an ancient-looking trunk and a couple new sandbags.

The passageway wasn't very wide, making the angle of the ladder quite steep.

Cabo sat back. "This is making me dizzy."

"The height?"

"No, the arrangement. That's an attic. It's supposed to be up."

"Think of it like an apartment building," Jenna said. "That's the floor below."

Cabo looked down. "Nope. Still nonsense."

"Maybe it will get better once you're down there."

She swung her feet around, dropped them into the shaft and stepped onto the ladder.

"What are you doing?" Cabo said.

Jenna went down one rung. "I'm going to the First Bank of Sanctuary. Cabo, this is the proof that will stop the Lost Haven Resort for good. This is *literally* buried treasure. I'll get pictures, show them to… everybody…and this whole nightmare will be over."

"Except for the murderer," Cabo said. "And the murdered people."

"Ah, right. Except for them."

"And your burning shop."

"You're killing me. Come on. We—"

Jenna stopped and tilted her head. A cool draft rose from the attic below, brushing her bare ankles and caressing her hair.

"What?" Cabo said. "You hear something?"

"Not hear," Jenna said. "Smell."

She inhaled the breeze, which, even though it had not changed temperature, suddenly gave her chills.

"Gasoline."

§

Jenna stepped onto the attic floor of the First Bank of Sanctuary. It was solid and smooth, with a dull, faded finish, and she marveled at the craftsmanship that had gone into fitting the planks together so perfectly.

The orange extension cord powered a string of work lights, each small bulb protected in a plastic cage. These were hung from small nails driven into the rafters around the attic, showing the entire space.

It was huge.

Jenna oriented herself, facing what had to be the front of the bank. The flat roof was higher there, too high to touch, and angled slightly toward the back wall until the space between the ceiling and floor was maybe four feet. An opening in the back left corner showed narrow stairs going down.

Jenna looked up. The rafters were rough and unfinished. She could see the tool marks left by... who?

The sheer history of it all made her giddy.

Then Cabo stepped off the ladder and ruined it.

"Where's the gas coming from?" he whispered.

They both examined the attic. It was empty except for the trunk, ladder, and sandbags. Jenna could picture Ingrid coming down here with her broom, sweeping up and collecting the sand in bags, then lugging them up the ladder. She'd consider it her workout for the day.

A laugh slipped from Jenna, startling Cabo.

"What's funny?"

"I just realized why Ingrid always had more sand in her shop than the rest of us." She shook her head. "I wish she'd told me. I could have helped her. Maybe it would have saved her."

"That's for later," Cabo said. "Right now, some-body is getting ready to burn this whole place down."

He pointed at the stairway. Another extension cord went from the end of the light string down the stairs and disappeared.

"Let's go."

§

Cabo went first down the narrow stairway, turn-ing sideways so his shoulders would fit.

Jenna tried to see past him, but even his neck was too wide to see past.

It was irritating.

She caught another whiff of gasoline, stronger now, and tugged on his sleeve.

"I smell it," he whispered. "Careful, now."

They emerged on the second floor of the bank. More work lights hung from wall sconces and framed photographs, casting a yellow glow over everything. They stood at the end of a hallway spanning the width of the building with a single closed door halfway down the left wall.

Across from that another hallway ran toward the front of the bank.

But straight ahead, at the end of this hallway, someone—likely Ingrid—had cut a hole in the wall. There apparently hadn't been an alley between the First Bank of Sanctuary and the Shoreline Gaming House, because Jenna could see the edge of a roulette table through the opening.

Work lights showed sand heaped across that floor, some of it close to knee-deep. The breeze came from there, stronger now, and with it came the sound of someone moving.

A dragging, shuffling sound.

"Stay here," Cabo whispered.

"Yeah right," Jenna whispered back.

They crept along the hallway. Cabo checked the hallway to the right and kept going. Jenna peered that way. Closed office doors with etched glass on the upper halves lined the walls, which widened out at the front of the bank to make a luxurious-looking waiting area.

Plush furniture sat beneath large windows, which must have overlooked the park (or cemetery) and marina at one time, but now showed only a wall of dark sand.

Jenna took a moment to think of the pressure around them, the weight above them. The *building* above them.

If something gives out…

No. It's stood this long, why would it collapse now?

A fire, perhaps?

Yep. Good point.

Somewhere on the other side of the opening, something heavy fell.

A muffled voice cursed.

"We have to hurry," Cabo said.

Jenna moved toward him and glanced at the office door on her left. The etched glass had a single word in black paint and gold foil: KAVANAUGH

"Wow," Jenna breathed. She touched the letters with a fingertip.

The history…

Cabo had his back against the left wall, trying to see into the next room through the narrow opening. He glanced back at Jenna.

"I'm going in."

"Wait for me," Jenna said, and beyond him saw movement.

Bart stepped into view, holding Mr. Wolfie and standing between two piles of sand up to his shins.

"Hey guys," he said. "Jenna, you touched my door. Now I'm gonna have to kill you."

§

Jenna said, "Bart, what are you doing down here? Where is the gas?"

Bart laughed. "It's everywhere. These old buildings are gonna burn like matchsticks. What happens when something burns underground? I guess we'll find out."

Cabo eased toward the opening.

"Okay, come on buddy. I think you're still a little tipsy. Let's head back up and get some fresh air."

"You know who can't get fresh air? My father. Because you let him get killed."

"Bart," Jenna said, "didn't you kill him?"

He shrugged. "Semantics."

"Where is Sherri?"

Mr. Wolfie's ears perked up at the sound of her name.

Bart smirked. "Oh, did you find my nice doll? Fooled you the first time you saw it. You and everybody else."

"Is she okay?" Jenna asked.

Bart looked down at Mr. Wolfie. "What do you think, you little monster? Is Sherri okay?"

Mr. Wolfie's tongue popped out and his rear end wiggled.

Bart lifted a chrome lighter. "Do you think we should burn this all down? Along with a few new bodies? You do? Oh, good boy."

Cabo stepped to the opening.

Jenna was right behind him.

She said, "Put it down, Bart."

"Nope." He flicked the lighter open.

Cabo put a foot through.

"He's coming to get us," Bart told Mr. Wolfie. "Do you want to go get him? You do? Okay, *go get him*."

He set Mr. Wolfie down as Cabo stepped into the opening. The tiny dog scrambled across the sandy floor and skidded to a halt between Cabo's feet. Cabo looked down, pure reflex, and Jenna realized he was about to die.

The crushed skulls, hit from above.

No, not above.

They were all looking down.

She grabbed the back of Cabo's belt with both hands and heaved with all of her strength. Cabo budged—maybe an inch or two—and Jenna hoped it was enough.

He fell back just as the shovel swung from the other side of the opening. The handle smashed into the wall, halting the metal blade just before it caved in the top of Cabo's head.

"Whoa!" he yelled, continuing his backward stumble and taking Jenna with him. They fell in a heap on the hallway floor as Sherri peeked around the corner of the opening with the shovel in her hands.

"Good boy Mr. Wolfie," she crooned. "Now you stay here just a minute. Mommy has to deal with these two."

§

Jenna and Cabo untangled themselves, clunking heads more than once, and got to their feet in the hallway.

Sherri stepped through the opening with the shovel close and ready to swing again.

Cabo moved between her and Jenna, his bodyguard training taking over, but Jenna just stepped around him and opened her arms for a hug.

"Sherri, you're alive!" she said.

Sherri hesitated. "Yeah. Duh."

"We thought Bart murdered you."

"Well, he didn't."

"But you murdered Ingrid. And Harrison Kavanaugh."

Bart emerged from the opening behind her. He

still held the lighter. The stench of gasoline coming from the rooms behind him made Jenna's eyes sting.

"They both had to go," Bart said. "And now so do you two, along with all of this mess down here."

"Why, so you can build the Lost Haven Resort and get even richer?"

Bart looked at Sherri. "I think she's finally getting it."

"I get it just fine. *You* don't get it. Look around. These rooms, these buildings, this furniture—it's all priceless, Bart. It's worth ten times more than some eyesore hotel. A *hundred* times. Hotels are everywhere. There's only one Sanctuary, and you could own it. Look."

Jenna stepped back and pointed to the office door.

"Your name is already here."

Bart glanced at the door. "Nobody cares about a couple abandoned buildings buried in the sand, Jenna."

"Yes they do. But even more, they care about what *else* is buried in the sand. Bart, we haven't even started to explore what's been right under our feet in Lost Haven. People will pay thousands of dollars to come find out. Millions, maybe."

Bart frowned, thinking it through.

Jenna stayed quiet and let him.

Cabo touched the small of her back. She gave him a small *I got this* gesture with the palm of her hand.

"Bart, I want a spa," Sherri said.

Bart's frown deepened.

"The Sanctuary Spa," Jenna said. "It sounds perfect. Healing sands, subterranean vibrations, a peaceful underground retreat away from the rest of the world."

"Nice," Bart said. "What do you think, babe? We can give it a shot, and if it doesn't work, we'll find a way to build our resort the right way. Right on top of everybody else."

"I guess. I get to run the spa, though."

"Of course." He kissed her on the forehead and looked at Jenna and Cabo. "As for you two, what do you want out of this? A cut?"

Classic Kavanaugh, Jenna thought.

Bart pushed on. "I'll make you a deal. Everything that happened down here—and the murders, I guess—will be our little secret. You'll each get... three percent of the profits from Sanctuary."

"I was going to suggest two percent," Jenna said, "so it's a deal."

"Damn," Bart said, then waved the lighter left to right in front of him as if reading a banner. "*Sanctuary: The Town that Time Forgot.*"

"Oo," Sherri said.

"Or no: *Sanctuary: The Lost City of Sin.*"

"Yay!"

"Fantastic," Jenna said. "Oh, can you also pay to rebuild my shop, since you burned it down?"

"No," Bart said. "That's what insurance is for. I hope you have a good policy."

"Why did you do that?"

"Distraction," Bart said. "If we just started a fire down here, they might find it and put it out. If your place is burning like a bonfire, and smoke starts popping up all along Main Street, then the whole thing burns down, well—it all started in your dinky shop."

"Hm," Jenna said. "And my brakes?"

Bart snorted. "I never thought you'd make it as far as you did. We were counting on you going off the road and taking the whole Ingrid investigation with you."

"But she didn't have anything to do with Ingrid's death," Cabo said.

"Exactly! While Olson and dumb Garrett were trying to figure out what happened—was Jenna the next target? Was she crazed by the pressure of the investigation, the guilt of killing Ingrid, and tried to kill herself? By the time it all got sorted out, we'd be locked into our Main Street takeover."

"So I was just a decoy?" Jenna asked.

"A *snoopy* decoy," Sherri said. "But I'm glad you didn't die, I guess. I mean, the whole underground spa thing makes up for it."

Jenna blinked. "Well. What a relief. Okay, my lips are sealed about all of that, you didn't murder anybody, or *try* to, and we're all going to be rich. I say we go back up, give it a day or so to let the fumes clear out down here, then stumble across the hatch. The town celebrates, money starts flowing, and pretty soon nobody even remembers the whole Lost Haven Resort thing."

"I like it," Bart said. "But stop acting like the boss, because you're not."

"Noted."

Jenna turned toward the stairs and gave Cabo a tiny nod. He moved into the other hallway to let her and the rest pass.

Jenna put a foot on the first step. "Sherri, how soon can you have that spa open? I don't know about you, but I could use a massage."

"Oh hon, I don't think you'll be able to afford it."

Bart and Sherri strolled past Cabo. Sherri had Mr. Wolfie cradled in her arms, leaning down so their noses could touch.

"She can't afford it, can she Mr. Wolfie? No she can't. It's going to be too fancy! Just like you."

Bart mused, "Do you think the building back there is big enough to become Barty's Party Sports Bar? I don't think so. But—oh!—is gambling legal underground? Like it is out on the water?"

He never got an answer.

Cabo stepped behind them and wrapped a massive arm around both of their necks, hooking his forearms under their chins and squeezing.

Bart managed to say "Gah!"

Sherri dropped Mr. Wolfie, who scampered

between Cabo's feet and looked up at him, waiting for his turn.

Then Cabo eased Bart and Sherri, both unconscious, to the wooden floor. He scooped Mr. Wolfie and stood up, scratching the little dog's ears.

"Wow," Jenna said.

"That's what the nod meant, right? Take them out?"

"Yeah, but I thought it would be harder than that. I was ready to jump in and help as soon as you started."

"Blood choke," Cabo said. "Turns the lights out pretty quick. They'll have headaches when they wake up in ten or so minutes, but other than that, they're fine."

"Nice. I think I need some bodyguard training."

"Yeah, what were you going to do when you jumped in, exactly?"

"Hey. I was gonna crack you with a full coffee pot when you came to my shop all covered in blood yesterday. I would have figured something out."

"You were gonna crack me?" Cabo said, shocked.

"Just give me the dog." Jenna took a shivering Mr. Wolfie. "Can you get those two up to the ladder? I'll go tell the cops and firefighters we need to hoist a couple murderers out of here."

"Oh, *now* you don't want to help."

"You want me to grab Bart's feet?"

"Nah," Cabo said. He lifted Bart off the floor

and slung him over a shoulder like a sack of laundry. "Honestly, it's easier if I just do it."

"Go team," Jenna said.

CHAPTER THIRTEEN

A month later, Jenna's Welcome Shoppe was still an empty lot with some charred pieces of foundation sticking up from a patch of sand and charcoal.

Jenna sat across the street from it on a bench in Lilac Park, sipping one of the best cups of coffee she'd ever had.

The July morning was already warm, even with the breeze coming off the marina, flowing through the park and ruffling the Fourth of July decorations on Main Street's light poles. The parade was set for later that morning, and Jenna couldn't wait to see what the Holiday Committee put together.

Word of buried Sanctuary spread immediately from the chaotic scene on Main Street. When the sun rose that smoky Sunday morning, the entire town came to hear the Mayor, City Council, and Historical Society give an impromptu speech about what this meant for Lost Haven and its citizens.

The truth was, nobody knew yet.

But it was going to be exciting.

Belma opened her shop's front door and propped it with a stone painted to look like a cupcake, spotted Jenna, and came across the street to sit next to her.

"Hey sweetie."

"Hey," Jenna said. "You want some help in your shop today? It's going to be busy."

"That would be wonderful. And it'll drive Lawrence crazy."

"I already offered to help him too, so I'll be going back and forth."

"Traitor. You'd better wash your hands before you leave his dump. And when you get to my lovely establishment. Oh, look. Mention his name and he emerges from his cave."

Lawrence poked his head out of Elegant Confections, blinked in the sunlight, and saw the two women. Despite Belma trying to wave him back into the shop, he wandered across Main Street without looking for traffic and plopped on Jenna's other side.

"I just can't get used to it," he said, staring at the vacant lot where Jenna's Welcome Shoppe used to be. "I mean, Belma's dog food store *cannot* be the first thing people see when they come up Main Street. What does that say? 'Hey, welcome to Lost Haven and Sanctuary. Here, have some diarrhea.'"

"Nobody invited you over here," Belma said.

"And yet, here I sit."

They all watched the movers bustling in front of Wilford's art gallery for a spell. The men carried odd-shaped pieces wrapped in heavy blankets to the freight truck parked along the curb, the final displays that Wilford hadn't been able to transport in his car to load from home.

The Lost Haven Art Gallery was relocating to Clearwater, Florida, where Wilford vowed to spread the legend of buried Sanctuary and divert tourists away from the beaches and cruises and send them north.

When Jenna asked him why he was leaving now, just when things were getting exciting, he'd smiled and winked: "That's exactly why."

The largest man among the movers stepped away from the rest and looked up at the blank facade, where the art gallery's sign had been for so long. He wasn't dressed like the others, because he wasn't one of them—he was just lending a hand.

"I'm still not sure about that," Belma said.

Jenna sipped her coffee. "The Main Street shop owners voted, lady. It was unanimous."

"I love it," Lawrence said. "Let's bring some energy to this drag."

Jay Cabo turned from the empty gallery and waved.

All three of them waved back.

"What's he calling it?" Belma asked. "Lost Haven Yoga, Pilates, and Self-Defense Studio?"

"That's the old name," Jenna said. "He thought

it was too on-the-nose. He's just calling it Lost Haven Bodyworks."

"I can't believe he does yoga," Lawrence said. He stretched his arms over his head and arched backward against the bench, began to shake from the effort, then belched and patted his belly.

"Huh. It works."

"Heathen," Belma scowled. She leaned into Jenna and sniffed at her coffee. "What's in there?"

"I don't know, but it's fantastic. You should go get one before the place is packed."

They looked toward the end of the block, where patrons filled the tables in front of the Sanctuary Cafe having coffee, juice, and fresh cheese puffs. McTavish came out with a sterling silver carafe to top off any who needed it and make sure no one lacked cheese puffs.

Jenna's stomach tugged her in that direction.

Mr. Wolfie swerved between McTavish's polished shoes as he moved among the tables. The little dog had refused to leave his side since Sherri and Bart were arrested, and McTavish realized there was still one Kavanaugh, more or less, who needed his service.

He glanced up, saw Jenna and the rest on the bench, and gave a slight bow before hustling back inside.

"I don't recognize any of the people at the café," Jenna said. "They're all media or tourists."

"All of the hotels here are full," Lawrence said.

"Even the motels. And not just by the hour—I'm talking weeks."

Jenna couldn't help smiling. "Imagine what's going to happen when we actually open Sanctuary for them to see."

"Honey," Belma said, "we need a Welcome Shoppe."

"I know. The City Council said the new one has to be at least twice as big to fit the crowds. I should have the plans finalized by the end of the week. They say it will be done within a month."

"That fast?" Lawrence said.

Jenna smiled again. "Hey, this Kavanaugh construction crew was about to build a whole resort. One little Welcome Shoppe is a piece of cake."

"Hopefully mine," Belma said. "Not that slop they serve down the street."

Jenna sipped her coffee again and settled in between her two friends.

Some things in Lost Haven would never change.

But everything else in her beloved hometown was about to be completely different.

A new future wrapped around the mysterious past.

She couldn't wait.

THANK YOU FOR READING

THE LAST
RESORT IN
Lost
Haven

BOOK ONE
OF
THE LOST HAVEN COZY MYSTERIES

To learn more about Lost Haven, Sanctuary, and the next book, please join the Penny Plume First Readers Club at:

PENNYPLUME.COM

ABOUT THE AUTHOR

Penny Plume is a lifelong reader, historian, and storyteller. She loves nothing more than getting lost in a great story.

www.ingramcontent.com/pod-product-compliance
Lightning Source LLC
Chambersburg PA
CBHW050915250626
47155CB00001B/242